lily love

lily love

MAGGI MYERS

Published by
LAKE UNION
PUBLISHING

This is a work of fiction. Names, characters, organizations, places, events, and incidents are either products of the author's imagination or are used fictitiously.

Text copyright © 2014 Maggi Myers

All rights reserved.

No part of this book may be reproduced, or stored in a retrieval system, or transmitted in any form or by any means, electronic, mechanical, photocopying, recording, or otherwise, without express written permission of the publisher.

Published by Lake Union Publishing, Seattle

www.apub.com

Amazon, the Amazon logo, and Lake Union Publishing are trademarks of Amazon.com, Inc., or its affiliates.

Cover Design by Anna Curtis

ISBN-13: 9781477822425

ISBN-10: 1477822429

Library of Congress Control Number: 2013921695

Printed in the United States of America

For CJ and Cameron:

Every day you teach me, and everyone
you meet, that different does not mean
less. I love you more than life.
Ugga Mugga, always,
Mama

prologue

"Where's my baby?" I startle awake. My heart starts racing before my mind completely registers where I am. A nurse hovers above me, tending to the frantic beeping of a monitor.

"Welcome back, darlin'," she drawls out in a thick Southern accent. "You gave us quite the scare."

"Where's my baby?" I try to sit up but can't coordinate my movements. The nurse silences the alarm on the machine she's tending to. It's then I realize that all that noise was the rapid increase of my own heart rate on an EKG. As the veil of unconsciousness lifts, I become aware of my surroundings.

No Peter.

No Lily.

I panic. Every instinct in me screams for me to get up and go find my daughter and husband. My body refuses to cooperate with my brain; it takes a herculean effort just to lift my head.

"Shh, now." The nurse speaks with a gentle firmness. "Your baby girl is just fine. She's in the nursery with your husband. You can't get yourself riled like that. You had a stroke, Mama. You've been in and out for two days."

A stroke.

I close my eyes to sift through the pieces I can recall. I remember riding in the back of the ambulance and feeling nauseated from the motion. The paramedic who rode with me did his best to keep my spirits up, chatting about movies and books, anything to keep my mind off of my early labor.

"Caroline?"

The sound of my name brings me back to the present and to a harried Dr. O'Donovan.

"How are you feeling?" she asks. I blink at her, confused, as she uses her pen to scratch the bottoms of my feet, sending an uncomfortable shiver through my body.

"Reflexes are good. You're very lucky." She sits next to me on the bed and shines a penlight into my eyes. "Do you remember what happened?" Her face reflects such kindness and compassion it makes me want to cry.

"Is Peter here?" Dr. O'Donovan smiles brightly. Too brightly. I place a protective hand across my swollen belly and wait for bad news.

"No, he had a meeting he couldn't get out of." I swallow hard. "Why? What's wrong?"

"Well, you have some protein in your urine, and your blood pressure is elevated. Those are indicators of preeclampsia, which is very serious. The good news is, the baby isn't showing any signs of stress. Her heartbeat is nice and strong." The doctor places her hand on my knee, squeezing gently.

"What is the treatment for that? Do I go on bed rest or something?" My mind races through the litany of things I thought I had two more weeks to take care of, none of which seems important now.

"The only way to resolve the preeclampsia is to deliver the baby," she says in a manner so matter-of-fact I'm almost put at ease. "Jackie will start an IV, so we can begin a course of magnesium sulfate immediately—"

"Wait," I say. "I need to go get my overnight bag and call Peter. Can't I meet you at the hospital?" To punctuate my question, Dr. O'Donovan's nurse, Jackie, comes into the exam room with her IV kit.

lily love

"Caroline, I don't want to scare you, but this is very serious. Reception will contact Peter to let him know what's going on." Dr. O'Donovan knows how hard it was for me to get pregnant. She's been my doctor through all of my fertility treatments and three miscarriages. She would never unduly alarm me.

"What exactly is going on? I don't understand." Fear shakes my voice.

"Listen to me very carefully, Caro." Dr. O'Donovan grips my hands in hers and levels her resolute gaze on mine. "Jackie is going to start an IV so we can begin to treat you right away. The sooner we get your blood pressure under control, the better. This means that I need you to stay calm, okay?"

"Her name is Lily," I whisper. I need her to know this isn't "the fetus" or "the baby." This is Lily Hope, the little girl I've dreamed of holding for the last nine months and prayed for all these years.

"Concentrate on Lily, Caroline. Once the IV is in, we're going to ambulance you to Durham as a precaution. Duke is the closest hospital with a NICU. We're being extra cautious; there's no reason to think we will need it, but we want it on-site if we do. Lily is full term at thirty-eight weeks; it's going to be okay," Dr. O'Donovan reassures me. "When we get you all checked in, we'll induce your labor and then Lily will be on her way. You'll be able to hold your little girl by tomorrow, Caroline." As if Lily senses that the conversation is about her, she kicks with a force that shakes my belly. "See? She's ready for her debut."

My little girl. I'll get to hold her in just a matter of hours.

I tell myself to concentrate on that and not to be scared, but I'm terrified.

Dr. O'Donovan is talking again. "We had to induce your labor, and you had a very strong reaction to the Pitocin we used. It sped up the rate and strength of your contractions, also causing your blood pressure to spike. You had a mild stroke, Caroline. Do you understand?"

I nod my head, but I don't really understand. My pregnancy was easy. Sure, I'd had some morning sickness in the first months, but that was it. Everything else had been flawless.

"Neurology will be in shortly to explain the logistics of what happened, but I'll give it to you straight: you're very lucky to be alive, and

3

even luckier that the stroke was as mild as it was. You're going to make a full recovery, Caroline, but this is it. No more pregnancies." She studies my face while she waits for my reaction. Before I get a chance to make sense of what she said, Peter walks into the room.

"Caroline, baby," he whispers as tears fill his eyes. The instant my husband sits on the bed and wraps me in his arms, my anxiety disappears.

"She's so beautiful." He is weeping. "She's absolutely perfect."

A moment later, the nurse with the heavy accent brings Lily to me. My arms shake with the effort of holding my beautiful girl. Hazy details of her delivery begin circulating through my mind.

Lily didn't enter this life with her eyes swollen shut, howling at the injustice of being ripped from her mother's womb. She came into the world with her little eyes blinking in wonder, her lips pursed into a perfect pink rosebud. While the doctors and nurses rushed around my broken body, scrambling to keep me from slipping into the quiet call of darkness, a nurse placed Lily against my chest, encouraging me to focus.

"Look at her, Caroline. Look at your baby girl." The nurse's words had sounded tinny and distant through the thickness of my exhaustion. "Stay with us."

"Caroline, open your eyes."

I recall the furrowed concern on the doctor's face as she cut the umbilical cord, and how Lily's tiny body shuddered as she drew her first breath. It's the last thing I remember before I closed my eyes.

When Peter kisses my temple and brushes a finger down Lily's cheek, my heart melts. I'm the luckiest woman in the world. After so many years of struggling with infertility, we've finally gotten our happy ending.

If I could go back to the moment I bought into that lie, would I change anything? I don't know. To change the past would mean changing the future. If I admit I would change my choices, it makes me an awful person. If I say I wouldn't change a thing, I'd be lying. That's the way of the world, I suppose. We've been conditioned to believe that

lily love

things always have a way of working themselves out and that happily ever after is within our reach, if we just work hard enough. The truth is that none of us are immune to tragedy. No matter how hard you work, no matter how good you are, life isn't obligated to give you a fairy-tale ending.

a sorta fairytale

As I glance out the window of the University Hospital waiting room, the memories of my daughter's birth haunt me. I'd been so incredibly naive back then.

"Mrs. Williams?" I glance up as the nurse pulls me from my memory.

"Yes?" I sigh.

"Lily is asking for you now." The physician's assistant is dressed in cartoonish scrubs that are meant be soothing to the young patients of the pediatric wing. I find them mocking. You'd think after three years I'd have grown accustomed to the fluorescent lights and sickly smell that are unique to hospitals, but they do little to soothe my frayed nerves as I wait, yet again, for Lily's MRI to be done.

God, when did I become so cynical and bitter?

I follow the PA into the belly of the MRI clinic, where I hear Lily's shrill cry.

"Mama, Mama," she wails.

When Lily finally started to use words in a meaningful way, her speech pathologist told me that "mama" was just a word approximation: a meaningless consonant-vowel combination that she was using to test out her voice.

lily love

"She's getting used to how her voice sounds, Mrs. Williams. It could be 'baba,' 'yaya,' 'dada.' Those are sounds most babies make when they're discovering language," she condescended to me.

What the speech therapist didn't understand was what the word meant to me. It resonated with me on a level no one else could ever grasp. It meant that Lily recognized me, and it was a connection I needed just as I needed air to breathe.

Now the most beautiful word in the world sounds like nails on a chalkboard. I feel like the biggest hypocrite for even thinking that.

"Is English her first language?" the PA asks.

If she'd bothered reading Lily's chart, she'd know that Lily has profound speech delays. Her use of language is different from ours; her words sound foreign. Different. Everything about Lily is different; that's why we're here.

"Mama," Lily slurs when she sees me. Without hesitation, I climb into the hospital bed and wrap her in my arms.

"Shh, Lily Pad. Mommy's here," I whisper against her beautiful strawberry-blond hair.

"Mama, Mama, Mama . . ." she murmurs rhythmically into my chest.

"She'll be out of it for a little while longer, Mrs. Williams," the nurse explains.

I know the drill; this isn't the first time Lily's had to be put under general to have an MRI. It's the only way she can be still enough for them to get an accurate reading.

My phone chirps from my purse as I close my eyes and breathe in the scent of Lily's hair. Only one person would be texting me right now, and it makes my heart hurt.

He's just checking on Lily; he doesn't want you anymore.

No, Peter doesn't want me anymore.

Despite my battle scars, the skin of my emotions is thin. The familiar pain of rejection tears open my heart once again. It hasn't gotten

7

any easier. The hurt is as pervasive as Lily's problems—never ending or offering clear answers. Some things are never meant to make sense.

"Carolina on My Mind." Max, the MRI technician, interrupts my downward spiral. He fills the doorway and smiles at me. Max is beautiful, at well over six feet tall; his gorgeous clear-green eyes are set against skin the color of coffee with cream. I blush when I catch myself sizing him up.

"Hey, Max," I whisper. "Still speaking in musical metaphors, I see." I give him a weak smile. His easy manner and the quirky way he speaks in song lyrics only add to his appeal.

"How's our girl?" he asks, brushing a hand across the top of Lily's head.

"She fell back asleep." I watch with interest as he checks her chart notes.

Given the amount of time we spend at the hospital, we've seen quite a bit of Max. It shouldn't surprise me that he cares about Lily—she is so easy to love—but it does.

My phone chirps again.

"Do you need to get that?" Max nods toward my purse, never taking his eyes from Lily's chart.

"It's okay." I swallow hard and try to sound carefree. "I can call him when we're settled into a room."

"Caroline, take a break." He lifts his eyes to mine. "Call Peter back; grab a cup of coffee. I will stay with Lily Love."

"Thank you, Max." I smooth the hair from Lily's face and gently climb down from the bed. "Please page me if she wakes up."

"Of course, Caroline." Max settles into the chair next to Lily's bed. "I won't let anything happen." I know he won't.

The first time I met Max, Lily was barely two years old. We had been ambulanced to the pediatric ER after Lily suffered a febrile seizure. I was a neurotic mess. Peter had been away on business and my sister, Paige, was on her way. I was staring at a pile of paperwork left behind by the admissions clerk when Max rescued me.

"I'm Max Swain from the MRI clinic. I can't take Lily for her scan until they have an IV for anesthesia," he said. "If you give me your insurance card, I can fill out the paperwork for you, and you can sign it when she goes in for her MRI."

"Thank you," I choked out.

"It'll be all right, Mrs. Williams." He placed his hand on my shoulder and gave me a warm smile.

"Caroline, please." I sniffled.

When Lily's IV was finally in place, Max had escorted us to Radiology, chatting with Lily the entire time. It didn't matter to him that she didn't answer; he just kept after her.

"I bet you like *Sesame Street*," he said. "No? How about *Max and Ruby*? *Daniel Tiger's Neighborhood*?"

Even though she couldn't answer him, she fixed her hazel eyes on him and smiled. They clicked, and from that point Max became the bright spot on our trips to the hospital.

I look down at my phone now, at the text message on the screen, and feel sad.

Peter: Hey, checking on Lily. How'd it go?

There's this image I used to have of family coming together in moments of need, holding on to one another, being strong and resilient for each other. No one tells you how divisive crisis really is. How you're forced to take on roles that you never intended, thus becoming someone you never wanted to be. I never wanted to be the mother of a child with special needs. I never wanted to be a failure as a wife.

I am both.

My daughter has an unspecified developmental disability, and I'm alone. It's not Lily's fault and it's not even Peter's fault. It just is. That's the horror of it all. I've had to sit by and watch my life crumble around me, knowing that there is no blame, no reason, just a tragic set of circumstances that no one has any control over.

Peter: Getting on the road in 15. Can I bring you dinner?

9

Me: Grabbing coffee, then heading back to MRI. Lily's still in recovery.

If it weren't so sad, I would laugh at how cordial we've become. I still feel an echo of the love we shared, but pain has long since taken its place. All that's left is a bittersweet memory of the joy we had before Lily.

. . .

I met Peter in the fall of my senior year of college. I was standing in the keg line at the Sig Ep house, hoping to drown my chronic indifference with cheap beer. I was in a rut, feeling stuck in a relationship that had run its course—or at least that's what I was thinking when I found myself at the front of the line. A boyishly handsome frat boy manned the keg and made my heart stutter in my chest.

"Hi," he yelled over the party noise. "I'm Peter." He held out his hand and, when I gave him my cup, laughed at me. Resting my cup on top of the keg, he reached his hand out to me again.

"Hi, Peter." I blushed as I shook his hand. He stared at me expectantly, refusing to release his grip.

"And you are?"

It made me nervous, how he commanded eye contact while he stroked my skin with his thumb. He was bold, unlike most of the boys I'd met so far.

"Taken." I forced a smile and tried to ignore the stab of disappointment I felt.

If you'd just broken up with Trent, you'd be having lukewarm beer with this hottie, Ms. Noncommittal Caroline.

Screw Trent. I cocked my head and flirted anyway. "It was nice to meet you, Peter. Can I please have a beer now?"

"Ouch." Peter laughed and let go of my hand to grip his chest dramatically. "You slay me, beautiful nameless girl." His smile spread

lily love

warmth up my neck, staining my cheeks. "I'll tell you what: I'll refill your beer if you tell me your name."

"Blackmail? Certainly a good-looking guy like you doesn't need to resort to such things to get a date," I teased, not feeling the slightest bit guilty.

"You think I'm good-looking?" Peter's playfulness was adorable, and it was impossible to resist his charm.

"You know you're good-looking," I countered.

"I know you're beautiful."

I laughed. "*Wow.* You just have an answer for everything, don't you?"

"Not everything. I still don't know your name." He handed back my full cup with reluctance.

"Caroline," I finally answered.

"Caroline." He smiled wistfully as he tried it out.

I wasn't one of those girls who giggled and swooned at the sight of a cute boy. Yet here I was, struck dumb by the sound of my name moving across the very delectable mouth of an equally delectable frat boy. I needed to get out of there before I started batting my eyelashes or something else just as horrific.

"Thanks for the brew, Frat Peter." I chuckled when he crinkled his nose at the name.

"Caroline," he called as I turned to leave. Glancing over my shoulder, I found him still smiling at me. "I won't need to blackmail you to get you to go to dinner with me."

"Tell that to my date." I giggled and blew him a kiss as I kept walking. I wasn't ready to give Peter an easy in. Even back then, something in me knew how effortless it would be to get lost in him.

A few weeks later, the boyfriend was a thing of the past. While I stood in the campus breezeway, waiting at the coffee cart, I ran into Peter again. He was right; he didn't need to blackmail me into that date. I fell hard and fast, never taking a backward glance. I was young, in love, and completely idealistic. I finally had a plan, and it was all about me, Peter, and the life we would build together.

building a mystery

The hospital cafeteria is relatively quiet this afternoon and I'm grateful to find my favorite booth vacant. It's in the corner, sheltered from the fluorescent glare from above. I shift across the seat and place my back against the wall. I pull my knees to my chest and rest my cheek against my knee. Just a few minutes of peace, that's all I want. But my mind won't allow it; even in the silence, it churns and spits mercilessly.

"Ma'am?" I jump, startled by the man standing at the end of my table. I must look as strung out as I feel, because his face reflects pity.

Screw your pity, buddy.

"You left your coffee." He raises the latte I just paid for and left at the counter. "Is it okay if I sit?" he asks, but he's already moving to sit across from me. He folds his tall, lanky frame into the booth with care not to bang his knees under the table. I take in this strange man warily. His hair is dark brown with a slight curl to it; it's cropped close to his head, but not short enough to hide the gentle bend of the strands. He runs his hand through it and exhales heavily. I reach for my latte and curse under my breath at the lingering weakness in my hand. I rest it against the table and reach with my steady hand. The stranger pretends he doesn't notice; at least I don't have to suffer more of his pity.

"I won't ask you if you're okay." He chuckles nervously. When he sees that I'm not sharing his humor, he clears his throat. "Sorry, I just . . . I don't know. Can I just sit here and not talk to you for a minute?"

"Why?" I don't know why I care, or why I'm even bothering to engage this man. I should get up and make my way back to the MRI clinic. His inquisitive brown eyes lock with mine. Something in the way he stares, unapologetically assessing me, reminds me of Peter. Pain blooms anew.

"I don't know." He shrugs. "Does it matter?"

"No." I sigh. "I guess not. I'm just not accustomed to chatting up strange men in the hospital cafeteria."

"Is there someplace else you're more comfortable chatting up strange men?" He laughs, and despite myself, I laugh too.

"Are you here a lot?" he asks cautiously.

"More than I want to be. My daughter is a patient right now."

"I'm sorry," he whispers, and I cringe at the tears welling behind my eyelids.

"Don't be." I shrug and look into my coffee.

"Can't help it," he throws back. "Can I ask what's wrong with her?"

"You can ask, but I don't really have an answer." I look up from my coffee and find him watching me intently, waiting for me to explain. "My daughter has a developmental disability and a seizure disorder. Neither of which is specified, so we are here for tests. More tests. Endless tests . . ."

"They don't know what's wrong?" he asks, sounding surprised.

"Nobody knows; she was born healthy but started to miss a few milestones in her first year. By her second birthday, she was at the developmental level of a nine-month-old and started having seizures. After that, she started to regress. She's five now. Developmentally she's a toddler. She doesn't fit into any one diagnosis. She's all over the place and no one knows how to help her." I stammer over the last few words, embarrassed by my candor.

He shakes his head. "That must be incredibly hard." He dips his pinky finger into his coffee, swirling it while he speaks.

"It is what it is." I dip my head and watch him with curiosity as he lifts his finger to lick the froth from his fingertip.

Odd.

As if he can hear my thought, he glances up. Blotches of color stain his cheeks.

"Sorry, I'm really not a Neanderthal." He chuckles. "I nearly burned every taste bud off my tongue earlier. Just testing the temperature. Y-you know," he stammers.

I feel my eyebrow raise involuntarily. "So you're willing to burn your finger and not your tongue? What did your finger do to you?" He smiles, transforming his face. I smile in return.

"I don't have to taste anything with this." He waves his pinky at me.

"I guess not." A wave of self-consciousness envelops me as silence stretches between us. I clear my throat and sip from my own cup.

"What's your daughter's name?" he asks.

"Lily," I whisper. The sadness I'd forgotten for just a moment cloaks me in darkness once again.

"Lily is a beautiful name," he offers. The brown of his eyes reflects the warmth in his tone. Peter has warm, kind eyes, too.

"I should really get back to her. She'll be awake soon," I blurt as I scoot out of the booth.

"It was nice talking to you, Lily's mom." He offers his hand and I shake it without meeting his eyes. I don't think I can look at them again without allowing nostalgia to pull me down further. I notice he doesn't ask for my name. I don't ask for his either. Besides, I'm used to being "Lily's mom." I haven't been just Caroline for many years.

My phone chirps with perfect timing.

Max: Lily Love is starting to wake up. We're good; don't rush. Just wanted you to know.

"That's my cue." I hold up my phone. Unsure of what else to say, I smile tightly and walk away. He doesn't stop me and I'm relieved.

we never change

I can hear singing coming through the door before I open it. Max is crooning an Irish lullaby. Lily's eyes are open, but her body is uncharacteristically still. Her gaze is fixed on Max leaning against the rail of her bed as he sings. My heart can barely contain the tenderness I feel watching her drink in the song that bears her name. As a smile tugs softly at her lips, I find myself wishing she would smile at me that way. I've sung that song to her from the beginning, but it's never garnered this reaction.

"I wouldn't have taken you for a Chieftains fan, Max," I whisper as I enter the room.

Max nods in acknowledgment and continues his serenade. Lily glances my way, but is quickly drawn back in by the song. When the last words are sung, Lily holds her hands up and waves them back and forth.

"Use your words, Lily," I encourage.

"Yay, Maxy," she cheers and claps her hands, beaming up into Max's adoring face.

The nurse comes in to check more vital signs, so I step into the hallway to cry without Lily's audience. Laughter through tears is a familiar combination, reserved for moments just like this one. I'm so happy to see her connecting to people around her. I just wish she'd see me that way, as more than just a fixture in her environment.

Max opens the door, waving enthusiastically at Lily as he goes. His bright smile falters when he sees my tears. Closing the door with a gentle click, he pulls me into a tight hug. I don't have time to steel myself against the onslaught of feelings I'm not ready for. I return his hug, fisting the back of his scrubs in my hands. I weep without restraint into his chest, too tired to care anymore.

"Is my singing that bad?" He chuckles. I half-laugh, half-sob at his attempt to cheer me. Max sighs in defeat.

"Caroline, it's going to be okay," he says as he holds me against his chest. I'd give anything for the bliss of that kind of ignorance right now.

"No, Max," I hiccup. "Nothing will ever be okay. I'm praying for 'manageable,' but it will never be okay."

"You don't mean that." He leans back just enough to see my face, concern etched into his handsome face. "What's going on, Caroline?"

I suck in a shaky breath before I can answer him.

"Peter left me," I whisper.

"*What?* No. Oh, no." Max's voice is rich with sorrow. "Why? How could he leave you and Lily?"

"It's not his fault, Max," I answer.

Max scoffs.

"It's not. Some things love can't withstand." It's the truth. Sometimes love just ends.

"That's crap, Caro." Max's flippant answer surprises me. I let go of him and take a step back. In all the years I've known Max, he's never spoken a harsh word to me. I don't like it. It makes me feel judged.

"It's not crap, Max," I bite back. "It's life. Shitty things happen to fairly good people all the time. Look at you and Nina."

Max flinches at the sound of his ex-wife's name. I feel guilty for bringing her into the mix; Max knows how cruel life can be. His ex-wife made that point when he came home and found her wrapped around their neighbor. I'll never forget the look on Max's face at Lily's

lily love

birthday last year, when I asked him where Nina was. My heart broke to see him in pain like that. I never would've guessed that *I* would be the one in a failed marriage a year later.

"You deserve better than that, Caroline." He dips his head enough to pierce me with his sea-glass eyes.

"I deserve a lot of things, but life isn't fair, is it?" I don't mean to sound glib, but I know I must. Max's jaw tics as he frowns at me. "I'm sorry I brought up Nina; that was below the belt."

"Did he cheat on you?" Max's voice betrays his own pain. It's sobering to witness how easily it surfaces, even after a year.

"What? No." I grab his forearm. "He didn't cheat." Max puts a hand on my shoulder and squeezes, and I want to sink back into another hug.

"Caroline?" Peter walks up the hall with bags of takeout hanging from his hands. His look of irritation sends my eyes rolling into my head.

Here we go.

Peter never got over the fact that Max was there on that first day and he wasn't—which is ridiculous, because Peter was never able to be there. He can't stand Lily's attachment to Max.

"Peter." Max nods.

"Thanks for taking care of my girls, Max." Peter forces a smile, but I can see the muscle in his jaw pulse from clenching his teeth.

I'm not your girl anymore.

"Max stayed with Lily so I could take a quick coffee break," I explain.

"I could've brought you coffee," Peter counters. It's moments like this that are the hardest on me. Sure, he could've brought me coffee. He could've done a lot of little things to show me he cared, but he *left*. These little acts of chivalry feel more like a slap in the face.

"Don't." I hold my hand out in front of Peter. "You. Left. You don't get to act wounded for not being there for me now. It's too late for that." My voice shakes and my eyes fill with tears.

"I'll come by and check on you later." Max shakes his head, and for a moment I think he's going to say something more. Instead he gives me a tight smile and heads toward the nursing station. Once he's out of earshot, Peter leans down, leveling his eyes with mine.

"That is grossly unfair, Caroline." He speaks softly, but anger and hurt are evident in his eyes. "I wanted to be there for you. You never let me. You shut me out."

Before he can continue, the door to Lily's room opens and the nurse looks warily back and forth between Peter and me.

"Mr. and Mrs. Williams," she says, "Lily's room is ready, so we'll be transferring her soon."

"Hunter," I reply.

"What?" Peter and the nurse ask in sync.

"Ms. Hunter," I say with confidence. "I'm not married anymore."

Peter shoots daggers at me and the nurse shifts nervously on her feet.

"Well, Ms. Hunter and Mr. Williams, it should only be a few more minutes." She mutters as she pretends to make a note in her chart and scurries off.

"What the hell, Caroline?" Peter seethes.

"What did you expect, Peter?" I ask. "This is what you said you wanted. I'm trying to move on; maybe you should too."

"None of this is what I wanted," he shouts. "I wanted it *all* to be different, goddammit."

There it is again, the same sordid story. We worked tirelessly, went through counseling, checked every single box on the long list of things successful couples do to stay together. Still, as much as we tried, Lily's challenges became bigger than our love for each other.

"I know." I sniffle. "So did I." Regardless, wanting something to be different cannot make it so. Round and round we circle the same common issue: *I love you, but I need to love myself more.*

"You're so quick to say that I left you." Peter cups my face in his hands, speaking softly. "I may have left our home, but you left me a long time ago." His words slice into my heart.

"Somebody had to take care of her, Peter," I weep. I hate that he's right. I hate that I was forced to choose. I hate myself for having had nothing left to give my husband after taking care of our daughter. I want to scream every time I think about it.

"I know," he whispers. "I get it, Caroline. Understanding doesn't make me miss you less or want you less. It makes me feel like an asshole. I'm so tired of hating myself."

A sob tears free from my soul at Peter's quiet confession. I know exactly how he feels; I'm intimately familiar with self-loathing. I never wanted him to feel this way. I certainly never wanted to be the reason he did.

"Peter," I whimper. I don't know what to say to convey how deeply I hurt, or how badly I miss him. It's not fair that we should love each other so much and still lose everything. Grief is a battle of endurance, and this kind of pain is as inescapable as Lily's disability.

I place my hand on Peter's and lean my forehead against his. Silently, we let our tears splash on the floor. I feel his breath against my cheeks, smell the crispness of his aftershave. Every piece of my heart aches for how empty I am without him. I take a tentative step to fill the space between us and place my hands on his shoulders. His breath shudders as he pulls me against his body. A sorrow-filled moan vibrates in my chest as he kisses my forehead.

"I love you so much, Caroline. I always will," he whispers. "But I had to go. I couldn't spend another day watching you drift further away, and end up hating our daughter for it." With one last kiss to my temple, he lets me go. "I didn't like the man I was becoming—and, if we're being honest, neither did you." Stepping past me, he walks into Lily's room, leaving me behind to marinate in his words and fall apart alone.

The wall is cold against my back as I slide down to the floor. The imprint of Peter's lips linger against my forehead, burning my skin in their wake. I don't know what's worse: this unrelenting pain or the numbness that I know will follow.

How can it be better to feel something when everything I feel hurts so much? I want to smack every person who has told me, "The pain reminds you that you're alive."
Idiots.
The pain only reminds me of everything I have lost.

what do i do now?

About an hour after Peter's arrival, the orderly from Admissions finally comes to take us to Lily's new room. Lily's scheduled for a stay in the Epilepsy Monitoring Unit, where they will monitor by EEG and video for several days in hopes of mapping out the patterns of her seizures. The doctors assure us that the more information they have, the more likely they will be able to determine the cause. I'm not holding my breath.

"Hi, Lily." An overly cheery nurse enters the room with a basket of electrode wires and a plastered fake smile. "I'm Chelsea, and I'm going to put all these rainbow colors in your hair." She condescends to us with her overpracticed spiel. It seems it's amateur hour up in the Epilepsy Monitoring Unit; this whelp is trying to make a game out of supergluing wires onto Lily's scalp. It's insulting. Most of the patients have been coming here their whole lives. They'd rather poke their own eyes out than be sequestered for a stint in the EMU. They're veterans of a war against the misfiring synapses of their brains; they deserve more than Suzy Sunshine and her saccharine brigade.

On cue, Lily shoots Chelsea a wary look and begins her rhythmic anxiety chant: "Mama, Mama, Mama." Lily doesn't do social niceties.

Either she likes you or she doesn't, and it's not looking good for Chelsea right now.

"Since she's asking for you, do you want to hold her while I glue these on?" Chelsea asks, flashing her nauseating, perma-fake smile. I want to shove that basket right up her—

"I will," Peter interrupts my mental violation of Cheesy Chelsea. He gives me a warning glance as he moves to sit next to Lily on the bed. She looks at him, then at me, and starts to cry.

Chelsea's brow furrows nervously and I wonder if she really expects every child to lie still and relax while she hooks them up.

"Feel free to help out, Mama," Chelsea grits through her forced smile. Looking a little less cocky than when she first came in, she gestures toward Peter holding a writhing Lily. I hold my breath and start counting backward in my head, so I don't knock this girl's head right off her shoulders.

"She can't," Peter snaps. Chelsea recoils as Peter's brows meet in the middle of his forehead. I let the air out of my lungs slowly, afraid to disturb the charged atmosphere. When did we flip roles in this relationship? Peter's the calm one; I'm the volatile one. Oh, that's right: we don't have a relationship.

"I have weakness in my right side from a stroke I had during her birth," I explain gently. "I can't hold on to her very well." My hope was for Chelsea to take a hint and help me de-escalate the situation, but she looks at me incredulously. Her loud, irritated sigh saps the last of my patience.

"If you'd read Lily's chart, her entire life history, including her birth, is in there," I respond sharply. Chelsea pales against the harshness of my words.

"Caroline." My name comes out of Peter's mouth on a defeated sigh. "Why don't you go home. You've been here all day. It's my night to stay with Lily anyway." I try not to take it personally, but I can't help but feel vilified by the tone of Peter's words.

lily love

"Mama, Mama, Mama," Lily continues. Ignoring Chelsea, I sit opposite Peter on Lily's bed.

"Are you sure?" I whisper, "I can stay and help get her settled." Panic coils like a snake in my belly. Shared hospital nights are a part of our custody agreement, but this is the first time that I won't be with Lily while she's here. Surely Peter understands that.

"Go, Caroline. We'll see you tomorrow afternoon." His final dismissal stings. There's no sympathy for my anxiety over leaving her—just impatience. He's pretty damned clear: *Go home, Caroline.*

Reluctantly, I rise from Lily's bed and gather my bag. It's not easy to walk away; I've taken care of all the hospital stays. I'm the one who does all the caregiving. I've spent the last five years running myself into the ground to be everything Lily needs. It's a role I despise, but it's the one I'm accustomed to. I don't know what to do when I'm not taking care of her.

"I love you, Lily Pad," I murmur as I run my hand down the back of her head.

"Bye, Mama, Mama, Mama," Lily answers.

Before I can change my mind, before the voice in my head tells me that I'm a rotten mother for going, I leave.

When I reach the safety of my car, I lean against the steering wheel and try to process the day. Lily's tests, Max, the stranger, and Peter all swirl around my brain in a toxic brew.

Mick Jagger wails from my phone, "Dance little sister, dance," saving me from further self-deprecation. I can always count on my sister to make me laugh. She has a propensity for changing my ringtones. Last week she programmed my phone to play a dirty little ditty when she called. I'm positive she waited until I was in a public place to light up my phone with "I'm your pole and all you're wearing is your shoes." That's my Paige, ever the comedienne.

"Hi, Paigey." I force a chipper tone and try to hide my mood.

"Sweet Caroline . . . ba ba ba . . . ," she sings off-key. My sister is crazy and I love her for it, but I'm just not in the mood right now.

"What's up, sis?" I cut into her song.

"I'm checking on my little sister and my beautiful niece," she answers. "How are you, honey?"

I'm so grateful for my sister. She's five years older than I am, but at least ten years younger in spirit. She's wild and carefree in a way that I admire but could never be myself. Even if my personality were similar to my bohemian sister's, my responsibilities could never allow for that kind of life.

"Lily is with Peter," I begin. "I'm headed home." I hold my breath, trying not to cry. I don't want Paige to worry.

"What do you mean, you're headed home?" Her tone is laced with suspicion.

"I'm headed home, Paige," I repeat. "I just need a break; I've been at the hospital since seven a.m." My voice cracks, and fresh tears pool in my eyes. Paige's silence on the other end makes me nervous.

"I'm coming over," she says.

"What?" I sniffle.

"I said, 'I'm coming over,'" she repeats with irritation. "I'm not going to let you wallow in misery the first night you leave Lily and Peter in the EMU without you."

"I'll be fine, Paige," I promise. "I just want to be alone." The last thing I want is for Paige to be wasting her time on my train wreck of a life.

"Right," she smarts back. "That's exactly why I'm coming over. You don't need to be alone, Caroline. I'm your big sister, and I love you. Let me be there for you."

"What if I can't do it, Paigey?" I cry. "What if I can't handle being away from her?"

"You can handle it, Caroline. You're the strongest person I know. First thing you need is to get the hell out of that house for a while. Go get your ass in the shower, and I'll pick you up in an hour," Paige demands.

"Paige, I'm tired." I'm mentally exhausted; I don't want to go out.

lily love

"You need to eat, Caro," she scolds. "I know you, and I know you don't have shit to eat at home. Let me take you to dinner and then we'll hole up and watch *Mallrats*."

She knows how to play dirty. *Mallrats* is my favorite movie.

"Can't we order in?" I beg.

"Caro, it will do you good to see something other than the inside of that house and the hospital," she says softly. "You've got to get out, babe."

I know she's right, but the thought gets caught in my throat. I can't breathe.

"Are you still there?" she asks.

"Yep. Here," I sputter.

"See you in an hour, okay?"

"Okay." I force myself to answer. It's a small step, but something's got to change.

when a heart breaks

It'll do you good to see something besides the inside of that house.
Paige's words cling like static as I step into the foyer.

I toss my keys into the bowl on the hall table, avoiding the framed picture of my wedding day, and head straight for my bedroom.

Paige is right: I need to get out of this house. In the stillness there is a quiet melancholy that hangs in the air, and I can't remember the last time I was happy here.

Along the hallway wall there are photographs of Peter and me over the years, and of course Lily. Peter and me at our graduation. The trip we took to Asheville where he proposed. Peter in hospital scrubs, holding Lily the day she was born. The three of us covered in cake from Lily's first birthday. Each moment preserved in its frame from the wear of time. I can't bear to look long enough to put them away.

We were so happy.

My eyes fix on the photo of Peter, Lily, and me from her first birthday. My head is thrown back in laughter at Lily's cake-covered hands holding Peter's face. We were blissfully ignorant.

There isn't a day that goes by that I don't wish to go back to that place of ignorance: the morning before Lily's evaluation at the Early

lily love

Intervention Clinic. She was just eighteen months old at the time and it's the last time I remember really being happy.

It hits me like the shockwave from a bomb, sending me stumbling into my bedroom. Collapsing on my bed, I let grief filter through the memory of that day.

I start singing her favorite lullaby for the third time as I pull Lily from her car seat. It's the only thing that has kept her happy since we left the house. She sucks furiously at her pacifier and crinkles her eyebrows at me. I laugh at the seriousness of her gaze. Her hazel eyes are focused on me, but they don't see me. I can't put my finger on it. I don't know what it is; I just feel a disconnect. I have high hopes that the team of doctors and therapists will be able to help. Maybe some speech or occupational therapy. Peter and I convince ourselves it's nothing major. In our naive confidence, we decide it's not worth Peter taking time off for the appointment.

Our visit is set up in two parts: a team of early-childhood specialists observing Lily playing, while a developmental pediatrician asks me hundreds upon hundreds of questions.

"Mrs. Williams, I'm Dr. Miles." The gentle voice of the doctor sends fear skittering across my spine. I hold my hand out for him to shake and allow him to escort me from the room to an adjoining conference room.

"I need to ask you a few more questions about Lily's behavior." His sympathetic eyes meet mine and my heart sinks.

"What do you mean?" I ask.

"Does she make eye contact with you?" His gaze is serious, and I fear what my answer will mean. I want to say that she looks me in the eye and smiles, like I want her to, but I can't. I can't lie, either, so I give the most ambiguous answer I can get away with.

"Sometimes."

"Does she smile at you?"

Shit.

"Not really."

"Does she have any rituals? Does she tantrum if you deviate from her routine?" He continues without hesitation, taking copious notes in the margins of Lily's paperwork.

"I thought I was supposed to keep her on a steady routine. Has that changed? Is that bad?" I panic.

"No, of course not. It's just that some children react more strongly than others. Some children will head-bang or rock rhythmically, detaching emotionally or overreacting emotionally. I just want to understand Lily better," he reassures me.

I want to cry. I want to scream. I want to grab Lily and run. All of a sudden I don't want to know. I just want a few more moments of blind ignorance. I'm not ready for the look that is crossing Dr. Miles's face.

"There are no wrong answers, Mrs. Williams," he says. "The more we know, the more targeted we can be with helping Lily. That's all any of us wants, right?"

I want Lily to get better. She needs to get the right help so she can grow up and out of this hiccup in her development. Putting on my bravest face, I start from the moment I first noticed something was "different."

"Not long after she started walking, she started to pace the length of the fence at the playground, staring through the chain links," I whisper. "She wouldn't play on the equipment or with the other toddlers. Trying to leave the playground caused really awful temper tantrums, so we stopped going."

"How old was she when she started to walk?" His question takes me off guard.

"Oh . . . um . . ." I stammer, reaching into my internal Rolodex of Lily milestones. "Ten months. She got up and started running to keep herself from falling forward. She just kind of took off." I smile at the memory of her little legs working frantically against face-planting in the living room.

"Did she crawl first?"

"No." My heart races when he takes several minutes to scribble more notes.

"Did she ever willingly bear weight on her hands and knees?" He won't look me in the eye. It terrifies me.

"No, she didn't." I swallow the fear clawing up my throat. "What does that mean?"

"It means she's tactile defensive; she's hypersensitive to sensory input," he starts. "Lily definitely suffers from Sensory Processing Disorder. She is sensory-seeking in some areas and tactile-defensive in others."

I try to process what he's saying, but my own senses start to waver. Block out. Shut down. "I don't understand." My voice is thick with fear.

"We see Sensory Processing Disorder in many children with disabilities."

I can't breathe. This is not happening. This can't be happening. I can't speak, so Dr. Miles continues.

"Children with SPD live under constant stress, because their brains interpret even the most harmless touch as threatening. They can also be underresponsive to pain, heat, and cold. All of these factors make their environment a war zone."

He keeps talking, but I quit hearing him. I'm still hung up on "We see this a lot in children with disabilities."

Disabilities. Everything I thought I knew has suddenly become a mocking nightmare. Dr. Miles stops talking and looks at me quizzically.

"Do you understand what I'm saying, Mrs. Williams?"

"No," I snap. "No, I don't understand at all. I brought my daughter in to be evaluated for speech therapy, possibly occupational therapy, and now you're telling me she has some sensory thing that 'many children with disabilities have' and I'm just supposed to 'understand'? What are you trying to tell me? Please just quit walking on eggshells and tell me what's wrong with Lily."

"Mrs. Williams," Dr. Miles begins, with a nervous shift in his seat. "Lily doesn't fall into a singular category. She has global developmental delays, which means she is profoundly behind in every area of development. This doesn't always come with a clear diagnosis; the best I can say for Lily right now is that we need to watch her development for the next year or so. In the meantime, we want her in therapies to get her caught up and see how it goes from there."

"So with therapy, she will outgrow this. She'll be fine, right?"

"Mrs. Williams." The doctor reaches across the table and places his hand over mine. I squeeze my eyes shut, trying desperately to block out Dr. Miles's next words.

"There are five areas that we look at: language, social-emotional, gross and fine motor, physical, and cognitive. While Lily's development has been slow, she has progressed. Her cognition is lagging further behind the other areas."

I yank my hand away. "She's eighteen months old!" I cry out in shock. I don't know what else to say or how to fight, to argue.

"Lily is still struggling with concepts like object permanence and recognition, among other things. Her deficit places her at a developmental age of around nine months old."

I remember that I stared at Dr. Miles for a long time, unsure of proper protocol. I vaguely remember thinking that it would be rude to curl up in a ball on the floor and weep. Instead I signed more paperwork and nodded my head when Dr. Miles told me he would call to make an appointment to go over the official findings.

I don't remember many other details about that day. I don't remember pulling into our driveway, taking Lily out of her car seat, or walking into the house. I hardly recall our neighbor, Mrs. Brown, coming to the door to tell me that my car was still running. I remember only the way it felt as the kickback from Dr. Miles's words struck me. They say when a bomb strikes the earth, your senses shut down.

No sound.

No sight.

The only thing you feel is the force of the blast rattling your body. All that is left is a crater where something stood before and a shockwave that flattens the surrounding area for miles. Every dream I had for my daughter, every plan, every single thing was flattened to the ground, and at the center was the crater where I had been.

comes and goes in waves

Paige: Up off your ass. 10 min out.
Great.
I grab the first clean shirt I can find and throw on a pair of jeans. Honestly, as long as my clothes are clean, I'll consider it a win. It would be nice to appear to have it together when she arrives, though, even if it's just an act. For good measure, I put on some mascara, blush, lip gloss and call it good.
You're not a hot mess. You are fine.
After a minute of self-talk, I hear Paige knock. When I open the door she takes me in with a genuine smile and an approving nod.
"Not bad, Caro. I'm glad to see your sense of humor is still intact." She chuckles as she points to my shirt. "'My Patronus is a Bookworm.' Nice."
I roll my eyes. It figures I would grab my Harry Potter T-shirt. I haven't worn this in years. I haven't read a book for enjoyment for longer than that.
"It was the first clean shirt I could find." I shrug. "Go figure."
"I like it. I miss snarky Caroline." She wraps an arm around me and squeezes me against her. "She was a lot of fun."
"Yeah, I miss her, too." I sigh.

I really do miss her, and I will never be that person again. *Harry Potter* and *The Little Prince* have been replaced on the nightstand by *Breakthrough Parenting for Children with Special Needs* and *Reconstructing Motherhood and Disability*. The piano is an expensive surface for picture frames and knickknacks. These things that nourished my soul are just fossilized trinkets sitting on a shelf collecting dust, waiting for me to pick one up and say, "Remember when . . ."

"You ready?" Paige pulls me back to the present.

I'm ready.

"All set." I smile. One foot in front of the next, one baby step at a time. "Let's go to the Ale House," I suggest. "I could really go for a Magners Draught."

I try not to smirk as Paige's eyebrows disappear under her bangs. I feel lighter. For the first time in a long time, I feel good.

"The Ale House it is," says Paige. "I'll drive; you ride. God knows how long it has been since you've had a few ciders in you."

I look at my sister—I mean *really* look at her. The pain and worry on her face breaks my heart. My focus has been so tied up in my own failures that I've completely lost sight of how this is affecting her. Grabbing onto the one true anchor I have, I squeeze her against me.

"Thank you," I whisper.

"It's dinner, Chicken Lips. No big whoop." She chuckles, but I hear her words grow thick with emotion.

"You know what I mean, brat." I close my eyes and squeeze tighter. "I couldn't survive this without you."

"You never have to worry about it. I'm here. Always." She rubs my back in reassurance, just as she has since we were children.

On the day Peter left, it was Paige who cried. All of the emotions I should've been feeling reflected back at me through her. Her heartbreak and frustration should have been mine. I should have been able to feel it, feel something. Instead, I lived it in a vicarious parallel through Paige. Part of me wonders if that was what she wanted, to feel the pain for me so I didn't have to.

"I'm proud of you, Caroline." She pushes me back by the shoulders and levels her eyes on mine. "That's the first time I've heard you say that you'll survive this. You will. I promise."

"I know." I'll just keep telling myself that until I start to believe it.

"Good, now let's get out of here." She yanks my ponytail and shoves me out the door.

• • •

Me: Did Lily do ok after I left?

Peter: We managed. It's all good. Asleep now.

Me: K. Goodnight.

Peter: Night.

They're surviving without me. The world didn't come to an end. I don't know if I should weep or jump up and click my heels. I wait for the guilt, the fear, *something* to start slapping me around, but it doesn't. I hold my breath, anticipating the residual guilt for not feeling guilty. Still nothing.

Get a grip.

"So are you going to tell me about what happened today?" Paige asks as we settle at the bar.

"Nothing to tell yet." I shrug. "You know how that goes. We have an appointment in two weeks to go over all of the test results."

"I know that. I want to know about Max. Did you see Mr. Swain today?" Paige wiggles her eyebrows.

"For God's sake, Paige. Get your mind out of the gutter." I laugh nervously. "Max is a good friend, and no, he wasn't happy to hear that Peter and I split."

"I'll bet." She winks. "That man has been circling you for years, biding his time."

"Bullshit!" My reply carries across the bar. The bartender and several patrons stop and stare. "The ink isn't even dry on my divorce papers, Paige," I warn. "Can you hold off on setting up the next victim?"

"Victim? Hardly," she chides. "You're a catch, babe."

My hysterical laughter fuels the continuing glances from the rest of the patrons.

"Take a look around, Caroline," Paige whispers. "There's a legion of men who would be happy to buy you a drink."

"Uh, no." I shake my head. "If they're looking, it's to catch a glimpse of Calamity Caroline's breakdown. I'm thirty-seven years old, newly single, and I have a daughter with very complex needs. Who is going to want me?" I grab a cocktail napkin and angrily swipe fresh tears from my eyes. "No one. *I* don't even want my fucking life, most days. I don't have a choice," I whisper. "If I had a choice, I would not choose to be the mother of a special needs child. If I wouldn't choose this, then how can I ask someone else to?"

When I hear the words spoken outside the sanctuary of my own mind, it sounds so pathetic. Still, I could never ask anyone to sign up for this ride. Even if I found myself on the precipice of attraction with someone else, I just couldn't. The thought of that kind of rejection inspires my anxiety. I'd rather be alone than subject myself to that.

"Caroline," Paige murmurs, placing her hand over mine. "You can't think so little of yourself—or of men, for that matter. You are allowed to be frustrated and angry. But don't you think for a second that your worth is tied up in Lily's needs. Her disability doesn't negate what a beautiful person you are, inside and out."

"You're obligated to say nice things to me; I'm your sister." I sniffle. The bartender snickers, not even trying to hide his eavesdropping. Paige cocks an eyebrow and nods in his direction. I giggle despite myself, and hide my creeping blush in my pint glass.

"Whatever." Paige shakes her head. "Quit fishing; you're gorgeous, smart, funny as hell . . . you're a total catch. Don't get wrapped up in feeling sorry for yourself."

That is my cue to drop it. I'm all for a change of subject, but my mind is still hung up on all of the uncertainty. My deepest fear is that the best is behind me.

lily love

"If you don't mind me saying, you're a total babe." The bartender winks and gives me a wide, dimpled smile. He's adorable.

Oh, for chrissakes.

"How old are you?" Paige asks him.

I kick her stool. "Paige," I warn.

"What? It's an innocent question." Her shit-eating grin suggests something entirely different.

"I'm twenty-five." He leans against the bar top, showcasing intricately corded forearms and biceps. I look up into a set of twinkling hazel eyes.

Busted, Caroline.

"You're just a baby." I blush.

"You're thirty-seven." He shrugs. "So what. MILFs are hot."

I can feel the blood drain from my face. He was listening to everything. I want to die.

"My advice," he continues. "Don't overthink things. Start with having fun. It sounds like you could use some."

"No shit," Paige mutters. I kick her stool harder this time.

"How do you manage so much wisdom at twenty-five?" I ask.

"I'm a bartender. It's a job requirement."

"Well, thank you," I concede. "I will take your sage words under advisement."

"Witty." His mouth tips in a sexy smirk. I gulp the rest of my cider and bring the pint glass down with a solid *thump.*

"What?" Paige asks, as she signals for another draft for me.

"Gorgeous, smart, funny as hell, and witty," he answers. "Witty is very sexy."

I bury my face in my hands. *Let the floor open up and swallow me whole, please.*

"I'll stop." He laughs. "You've got to learn to take a compliment, girl."

"Wait!" I call as he starts to walk away. "What is a MILF?"

"Christ, Caroline!" Paige howls, tipping her head back in laughter. The bartender turns a deep shade of purple and laughs nervously.

"What did I say?" I throw my hands in the air.

"I'm not touching that one." He chuckles. "Flag me down when you're ready to order." He shakes his head as he walks away, and I look to Paige for an explanation.

"Honey, you need to get out more," Paige says with a snicker.

For the rest of the evening, Paige and I talk about anything but Peter and Lily. We have so much fun at the bar, we decide to forgo tonight's showing of *Mallrats*. She catches me up on the progress of her graphic design business, telling me all about the book covers she's designing. Rather reluctantly, she tells me what a MILF is, and we laugh until tears roll down our faces. I don't know what I would do without her. Paige has always been able to grab life by the horns and just go for it. I was happy to be complacent. Or was I? Who knows. The more time passes, the more certain I am that I don't know anything at all.

and so it goes

The light filtering in through the curtains shoots waves of panic through me, jackknifing me from the bed.

Lily.

The fog of sleep lifts slowly, reminding me that Lily is with Peter in the Epilepsy Monitoring Unit. I lie back against my pillow and try to level my breathing. I can't remember the last time the sun woke me up. Lily doesn't have the ability to regulate her own sleep cycle. When most people wake up in the middle of the night they roll over and go back to sleep; Lily wakes up and starts wandering the house. It's not unusual for me to find her half-asleep, eating Cheerios out of the box at three in the morning.

When she does sleep all the way through the night, her feet hit the ground running at five in the morning. She wakes up full of fire and stays that way until I can muscle in her first round of Focalin. It's a vicious cycle. The Focalin enables her to calm down and be less combative, but trying to get medicine into a wild and irrational child is like trying to herd cats. Once the Focalin kicks in, then I fight to get her antiseizure meds in her. She can't swallow pills, so I have to pierce the capsules and squeeze the medicine into a few tablespoons of applesauce. There can't be too much applesauce or she won't eat it all; there can't be too little or she can taste the medicine. It's not uncommon for me to be covered in medicated applesauce before my first sip of coffee. Hell, it's not uncommon for me to brew a pot of coffee and never get to it at all. Lily's occupational therapist tells me it will get better, and that she can learn to tolerate swallowing a pill. I have my reservations; she barely tolerates the textures of most foods. Pills? Give me a break.

I listen to the silence and am at a complete loss. There's no one here to hide behind. There are none of Peter's shirtsleeves to press into sharp creases; there's no wrestling match to get Lily to eat a few bites of breakfast before her daily occupational, speech, and behavioral therapy sessions. Lying in the cocoon of my bed, I feel utterly exposed. For years I would've killed to have a moment just like this. Just one second to breathe. And now that I have it, I've forgotten how.

Get up.

The voice in my head pierces the quiet. There are no answers hiding in the wrinkles of my sheets. My only companions are the excuses I've been marinating in for the last five years. Life didn't come to an end when Lily started having problems. No, the world didn't cease to be, but I did. Every time I said, "Lily needs to keep to her routine," instead of, "Yes, Peter, let's go out to dinner tonight," I made a choice to give up another piece of myself. If I'd been better about that, if I'd just tried harder, maybe I could've been strong enough to save us both.

Maybe?

Hindsight is a coldhearted bitch. We can never go back and change those moments that take us off course; we just have to learn to live with our choices. Peter and I wanted children. If I could change one thing, it would be that. I would choose to walk away from that dream— but I'll never admit that to anyone. I love Lily with a capacity I never knew possible, but if I had known what was ahead, I wouldn't have had her. I don't know how anyone comes to terms with that. I know I haven't—I've only allowed for it to fuel my guilt and self-loathing. Admitting it to myself doesn't change how much I love Lily; it only showcases how much I hate myself.

lily love

Having met my daily quota of self-hatred, I fix a cup of coffee and head toward the living room. One night away from the fray and I'm ready to take something back, something mine alone. My fingertips barely graze the surface of the ivory keys, sending goose bumps up my arm. I rest my cup next to the trinkets on the top of the piano and sit on the stool.

Fear of this moment has held me captive since the day we came home with Lily. Not because of motherhood, but because watching my right hand shake with hemiparesis is something I don't allow myself to wallow in. Ever. I was never a gifted pianist to begin with; I only learned to play so I could accompany myself singing. It shouldn't matter if I'm rusty, but that's the thing about fear. So often, it's irrational and misplaced.

C—F—Am—C

The first chords flow through my hands and onto the keys as I play the first line of the first song I ever taught myself.

C—G—Am—C

My pace is sluggish, but the notes are clear and sure. The chords spill from my memory as I close my eyes and let the words bubble up into my throat.

"But if my silence made you leave . . ."

The echo of my voice hangs in the air, followed by the sob that tears free from my heart. It was my silence—and Peter's—that laid waste to our life, the first time I came home from Lily's early-intervention evaluation and answered "Good" when Peter asked how it went. I told myself that I didn't want to scare him like the doctor had scared me. I didn't want to be the one to tell him that his daughter was developmentally disabled. Deep inside I think I just wanted to pretend that everything *was* good a little while longer. I waited and let Dr. Miles tell him, two weeks later when we met to go over Lily's report.

Peter was furious; he didn't understand why I would keep that from him, and I let him be angry, because it made him feel better to have someone to blame. We were so stupid with grief; we walked right over a land mine and then acted surprised when it blew up in our faces.

I don't go back to playing my song but mess around with a few scales, just so I can feel that rush again. I'm not as bad as I thought I'd be. I'm so self-conscious about the hemiparesis in my hand that I usually hide it at all costs. That means I've also limited myself unnecessarily. There's no way to know what I'm really capable of if I'm too afraid to try. But it's so frustrating and awkward, I'd rather ignore it altogether. Hemiparesis—it even *sounds* embarrassing, like "hemorrhoid." These are the ailments of the elderly, not of a woman in her mid-thirties.

Ironically, my singing needs more work than anything. On days like today, when Peter has Lily and I'll have time alone, I need to remember to sit down and do this for myself. It feels good and it's mine. Just mine.

When my right hand starts to fatigue, I take my cup back to the kitchen. I'm washing the remains of cold coffee down the drain when I fix my gaze on the counter where my phone is charging. A brazen idea flashes in my mind, and before I have the chance to change my mind I type my text and hit send.

Me: Hey, do you want to grab some coffee before I head to Lily's room?

Shit. Shit. Shit.

I rest my forehead on the counter and run through the many reasons why that was a really bad idea. Maybe he just won't reply and I can pretend that it never happened.

Max: Carolina on My Mind! I was hoping I'd see you today. What time are you headed to the hospital?

Oh crap! What have I done?

I stand, stuck to the kitchen floor with my phone in my hand. Max's text stares back at me, and I feel flames creep up my chest and neck, into my cheeks. I haven't done something this rash and impulsive since . . .

For the love of God, it's coffee. Get over yourself.

Something between a snort and a giggle erupts from my mouth and nose. For a moment I wonder if I have finally lost my mind and am swan-diving off the cliff of my sanity.

Me: I'll be there in 45 and will have an hour before I relieve Peter. Does that work for you?

I smile down at my phone, waiting for his response.

Who cares? He's cute. He's your friend. Enjoy.

What does Paige always say? "You're married, not buried."

Well, I'm not married anymore, so that's a moot point anyway. Coffee with a friend is well within reason and something I haven't done in a really long time.

Max: Sounds great :D Looking forward to catching up. I don't like where we left it yesterday.

My eyelids flutter to a close as I tip my head toward the ceiling and release an exasperated breath. I was hoping to practice talking about things that didn't involve my life falling apart. Still, I don't want Max to think anything he did made things worse than they already are.

Me: You bet. See you in a bit?

Max: Sounds good. See you soon.

Breathing deeply, I rest my phone back on the countertop and head for the shower. So coffee is not going to be the casual conversation I'd been hoping for. It doesn't negate my need for company, and I could do a whole lot worse than Max. He's already versed on the history, so maybe talking to him won't be so hard. Who knows?

caroline i see you

The line at the coffee cart in the cafeteria gives me time to still my nerves. I pretend to be carefully considering what mocha-frappa-yadda-chino to order, when I'm really standing here wondering how not to make an ass of myself in front of Max. The line moves faster than I want it to, and before I know it the barista is looking at me expectantly.

Shit.

My mind is utterly blank. Too much time practicing conversations in my head so I don't act a fool and here I am, wordless and foolish as ever.

"Uh . . ." I stammer and look at the menu again.

"Grande skinny vanilla latte," calls a voice behind me. I spin on my heel and come face-to-face with the stranger from yesterday.

"Hey, stranger." I smile. "You remembered?"

Stranger? Jesus, Caroline.

"Hi, Lily's mom." He taps his temple. "I've got a memory like an elephant."

"Three-fifty, ma'am," the barista interrupts. I hand him my money and turn back to my mystery man.

lily love

"Are you sitting in here somewhere?" I ask. His warm eyes are drawn today, and days' worth of scruff covers his face. He looks tired, and my heart reaches out to his in empathy.

"No, not today." He sighs. The lines around his eyes deepen as he pinches his eyes closed. His face turns pained, and I want to kick myself for not asking why he was here yesterday.

"Caroline," Max calls out as he crosses the cafeteria. He waves when I turn my head, and my stomach starts to flutter.

The stranger tips his head to the side while the smile returns to his lips. "Caroline," he repeats, exploring the syllables with his upturned mouth. "It was good to see you again."

"You, too," I return. There is a vacancy in his eyes, where his smile can't touch. I know that feeling all too well and my heart breaks a little for him. I can only imagine what news he's been left to digest. Considering where we are, the possibilities are endless. "You sure you don't want to sit with me and my friend for a minute?" I touch his arm to keep him from walking away.

"Thank you, but I've got to get back." He sighs heavily and places his hand over mine. His eyes roam over my shoulder and then back to me. "Bye, Caroline."

"Bye," I murmur as he walks away.

"Carolina on My Mind." I turn to find Max smiling down at me. "Who was that?"

"I don't know his name," I answer. "He sat with me yesterday when you were with Lily. He listened to me drone on about her. I wish I'd returned the favor; he looks rough today."

"Ah." Max nods. "The Comfort of Strangers."

"Another song?" I ask.

"Beth Orton, from the album *Comfort of Strangers*," he replies. I shake my head at his inner catalog of music knowledge.

"Learn something new every day," I shoot back with sarcasm. Max gives me an inquisitive look.

43

"Back at you," he chuckles. "I never knew you were such a smart-ass."

"Yeah, well, a girl's got to have some secrets."

Max orders his coffee and we grab a table by the window. My mind drifts back to my stranger and how I wish I knew his name—something.

"Thinking about Lily?" Max's voice brings me back to the present.

No.

"Just wondering how she and Peter did last night," I lie.

"I'm sure they were fine," Max reassures me. "You can't be there all the time."

"I'm learning that." I sigh.

"Good." He sounds surprised. "You're the most dedicated mother I've seen, Carolina, but you're also the loneliest." Of all the things that Max could've chosen to call me, that shocks me.

"Lonely?"

"You don't let anyone in," he says. "Strength is something you've got in spades, but you've got to let others be strong for *you*, too." He regards his coffee for a moment and then lifts his piercing eyes to mine. "I'm worried about you."

My response lodges in my throat and tears fill my eyes.

"Jesus, Max." I sigh. "All I do around you lately is cry." I laugh and try to make light of my waterworks, but Max is not amused.

"Did you know that in all the years I've known you, yesterday was the first time I've seen you cry since we met?" he asks. I shake my head and wait for him to continue. "I've watched you shoulder Lily's care without so much as a heavy sigh. That doesn't tell me that you have superhuman strength; it tells me that you are tuned out. That's not living."

"Max," I whisper, as the tears streak down my face. He ignores me and continues talking.

"And I know that I'm supposed to be impartial with the patient's family, but I'm so mad at Peter." He shoots me a warning look when I try to interject. "Don't. I get that you aren't pissed, but I am. I've

lily love

watched as you've given up everything for Lily, never taking anything for yourself. It's not right."

"Max, sometimes it isn't anyone's fault," I plead. "Sometimes things just end. You just told me that I need to let others be there for me. Don't you think Peter felt that way, too? I stopped seeing him; I was only focused on Lily. It's not fair to just blame him."

"You're *my* friend, Carolina," he says. "My loyalty belongs to *you*. Don't expect me to sympathize with him. I can't do it."

I let his words take root in my heart. As misguided as his anger may be, it feels good to have someone on my side.

"I'm sorry about the scene in the hallway," he goes on. "Peter didn't seem too happy to see me there, and the last thing I wanted was to make things harder." He shakes his head. "I just don't understand how he could walk out on you and Lily."

"You're a good friend, Max." I sniffle as I wipe my eyes. "I appreciate your standing by me, but blaming Peter isn't the answer. It's a hard enough adjustment for Lily without people mapping battle strategies." I look down for a minute and consider carefully what I'm about to say. "I don't know how to do this," I whisper.

"Do what?" His concern is clear.

"Be a friend," I start. "I mean a *real* friend, or a . . . Never mind, I don't know what I'm saying." I slink down in my seat as Max starts to chuckle.

"Caroline, you *are* a real friend, always have been." He smiles and reaches across the table for my hand. "You were there for me when Nina left, bringing me casseroles to make sure I ate. Now it's my turn."

"You're going to bring me casseroles?" I snort.

"Smart-ass," he mutters, and shakes his head. "Let me be there for you. You need a sitter to go out with Paige? I'll hang with Lily Love. You need to talk? I'm here for you. Okay?" He squeezes my hand and then leans back in his seat.

"Thanks, Max." I smile and sip my coffee, unsure of what to say.

45

As if he can sense my thoughts, Max leans his arms on the table. "Look at me," he urges, so I lift my eyes to his. "You've been in that bubble too long. This isn't weird; it's what friends do. So quit squirming."

I stare in shock for a minute before I regain my composure. I haven't had friends in so long it feels foreign to me. The friends I had before Lily fell into two categories: those who didn't have children and couldn't relate to what I was going through, and those who did and still couldn't relate. I tried to make those friendships work, but it hurt to watch other parents and see their children breezing through the developmental milestones that Lily couldn't quite reach.

I even joined a support group for moms of children with special needs, thinking that would be a better fit. It only made me more insecure about not having all the answers where Lily was concerned. They spent the bulk of our meetings talking about the newest therapies, diets, research studies—you name it. All I wanted to do was commiserate about how hard it was to still be changing diapers at Lily's age, or how frustrating it was just to go to the grocery store with her. God forbid you disagreed with one of their methodologies. One mother had the audacity to chastise me for my choice in behavioral therapy for Lily, just because it wasn't her choice.

"Applied Behavioral Analysis? Isn't that monkey training?" she sneered. I was so shocked by her gall I was surprised I had the ability to answer her.

"Actually, ABA is the only behavioral therapy that's based in actual science. It's driven by individualized data, which is proven to be the most effective way of predicting and correcting behavior." Monkey training. What a bitch.

After that meeting, I determined that I didn't need support like that. It left me with the feeling that I was being judged as a parent, and that's hard to shake when you feel like everyone's eyes are on you and your child who's different from everyone else. It became easier and easier to just shut everyone out.

"Jeez, you've got me all figured out, huh?" I laugh nervously. It's uncanny how well Max knows me. He's absolutely right, I've been in a bubble for far too long.

"Caroline I See You." He smiles.

"James Taylor, from the album *October Road*." I smirk when his eyes go wide.

"Well how 'bout that." He beams. "There's something else underneath the facade after all."

"Ha, ha." I roll my eyes and try to ignore the knot forming in my stomach.

The last person I felt really knew me decided not to stay. It's equal parts scary and sad: Scary that letting someone know you means letting them near enough to hurt you. Sad that Peter was the last person I let get close at all.

fall apart today

The elevator in the Neurology wing feels like a tin of sardines and smells slightly worse. I'm sandwiched between a very tired-looking nurse and a man with a big bouquet of flowers. On each floor I step out and let a few more people off before stepping back inside. The Epilepsy Monitoring Unit is on the top floor, of course.

By the seventh floor the car has emptied enough that I don't have to jump off and on. When the doors open, I don't know what makes me look up, but I do. Standing in the hallway is my stranger and what appears to be a doctor. My stranger is facing me, but his eyes are shut tight, his fingers furiously working the bridge of his nose. My heart stops, the doors close, and I am whisked to the next floor—Pediatric Neurology: Epilepsy Monitoring Unit.

My stranger.

I see myself in him and his pain feels like my own. Kindred spirits moving on a parallel through the same myriad of emotions. It's totally presumptuous. Ridiculous. Still, it feels like my heart senses his hurt, and all I want to do is hold his hand.

I wander down the hallway, replaying the scene in my head. The pain was etched on his face. Even though I only saw it for a few seconds, the look is seared into my memory. Probably because it's familiar.

I can't remember which department is on the seventh floor, but someone my stranger belongs to is there.

"Hi, Mrs. Williams," the charge nurse calls as I approach the nurses' station.

"Hunter, Audrey. My last name is Hunter now." I smile sympathetically when she blanches.

"I'm so sorry," she stammers. "I didn't know."

"It's okay. Hey, what's on the seventh floor?"

"Seventh?" Audrey repeats. "That's Neurosurgery. Why do you ask?"

The image of my stranger standing alone in the halls of Neurosurgery has me swallowing a knot in my throat.

God, I don't even know his name.

Once upon a time, that was Peter. He stood in the hallway while a surgeon explained how he would seal off a bleeding blood vessel in my brain with a tiny coil inserted through my groin. I was blissfully unconscious, but poor Peter was alert and present for the entire thing.

I wish I could jump back on the elevator and see if my stranger is still there. Instead I plaster on a happy face and answer the nurse.

"Oh, I thought I saw someone I knew getting off on that floor." I quickly change gears. "How was Lily's night?"

"We got some really great readings from her EEG." Audrey smiles encouragingly. What she is really saying is that Lily had several seizures during the night. I've gotten good at deciphering medical speech. *Idiopathic absence seizure*: We're not sure why Lily's eyes roll into her head, while her head lists forward, multiple times a day. *Encephalopathy Unspecified*: There is something indefinitely wrong with Lily's brain, but we have no idea what. *Pervasive Developmental Disorder Not Otherwise Specified*: We have no effing clue what's causing Lily's disability, but we have to call it something.

"Enough data to shorten our stay?" I ask hopefully.

"Dr. Baker should be by soon, and I'll be sure she's aware of what we have so far and ask how much more we need." Her tone is as gentle

49

as her manner, and I find myself so grateful. Her compassion and patience make the time here manageable.

"Thanks, Audrey, you're the best," I call over my shoulder as I head down the hall to Lily's room.

The door is cracked open and I can hear the cartoons playing on TV. When I push the door open, Lily is watching *Daniel Tiger's Neighborhood* through half-mast eyes and Peter is passed out on the bed next to her. They look like two peas in a pod, with their matching strawberry-blond hair and fair skin. My beautiful and broken family.

"Mama, Mama, Mama," Lily chants, waking Peter.

"Hi, Lily Pad," I whisper, and lean in to kiss her forehead.

"Hey." Peter rubs his eyes and gives me his sleepy smile. It's the first time I've seen it since he left two months ago. It still makes my heart flutter, but only for a second. Those automated responses I've grown accustomed to are slowly fading. A heart flutter when he smiles, a kiss on the lips to greet him, an "I love you" when he leaves. The knee-jerk reaction has stilled, but I feel its absence like a phantom limb.

"Hey," I whisper. "Did you sleep at all last night?"

"Not really." He yawns. "I was in and out. You know how it goes."

Do I ever. The hospital provides a "sleep chair" that reclines into something resembling a cot. It's a hard and uneven torture device. Barely passable as a chair, let alone a bed.

"Why don't you go home . . . uh," I stammer, "to your apartment, I mean . . . that's home for you now . . ."

Shut up, Caroline.

"I knew what you meant," he interrupts my rambling. "I want to wait for Dr. Baker." I nod and focus my attention on Lily. She's smiling and singing along with her favorite show.

"Grown-ups come back." She sings the same line over and over again. I know somewhere in the recesses of her mind, she's processing my return. She likes to piece together dialogue and songs from her favorite shows to communicate with me. She finds the words she can't articulate herself by quoting the things she knows.

lily love

One day, after she used my mascara as lip gloss, I said, "Lily, what am I going to do with you?" Her response was from something we'd just heard Cookie Monster call himself. "Me-nima." An enigma. My little echo has her mama's sense of snark.

I unplug Lily's EEG monitor from the wall and plug it into a portable battery pack, careful not to tug on any of the wires glued to Lily's scalp. The two of us take a walk to the playroom and give Peter a little time to clean up. Immediately upon clearing the threshold, Lily makes a beeline for the Sesame Street play set she adores. She plops down on her bottom, with her legs bent away from her body in a position her occupational therapist calls the "W" sit. He'd be having a coronary right now, insisting that I encourage Lily to sit "crisscross-applesauce" to help strengthen her core muscles. Once upon a time, I would've engaged in that battle with Lily. She would end up crying, and I would end up a sweaty heap on the floor beside her. She'd still be sitting in her "W" and I'd be seething with frustration. I'm learning to choose my battles very carefully. I'd much rather be sitting next to my girl, going over our cast of characters.

"Who is this, Lily Pad?" I hold up an unfamiliar pink fairy. "Is this Zoe?"

"No, Mama." Lily giggles. "Zoe orange, not pink!" She snorts, and it sends me into my own fit of giggles. My baby girl is so much like me. Poor thing.

"Is it Rosita?" I tease.

"Mama," Lily scolds, wagging her finger at me. "That's Abby Dabby."

"Of course! How could I miss Abby Cadabby?" I gently articulate *Ca*-dabby, to encourage Lily to copy me.

"Abby Dabby," she repeats. I smile and let it go. She's focused on the figurine in her hand and has blissfully tuned me out. When I lean forward to check out who she's got, I narrowly miss getting pelted with Kermit the Frog. He whistles through the air and hits the far wall with a loud crack.

"*No Kermie,*" Lily bellows; she doesn't understand that Kermit is a double agent. He doesn't exist in her vision of what Sesame Street is. He is an interloper on The Street; there will be no rational conversations about how a Muppet can be on two shows.

"Lily." I speak with the soft but firm voice the behaviorist taught me to use to de-escalate Lily's tantrums. Her fits were appropriate when she was two, but they're scary at five. Some of Peter's and my biggest arguments were over how to handle them. He wanted to draw a line in the sand, show Lily who was boss. I knew that engaging in a power struggle with her would end with no victors, just more wild behavior. You can't just tell Lily not to do something and expect her to listen. She has to be walked through everything piece by piece. It's very hard not to throw your hands in the air and scream, "I give up!" So often that's what it felt like Peter was doing when it came to parenting Lily.

"We don't throw toys. You can hurt someone that way." I hold out my hand and meet her frustrated gaze. Her eyes are swimming with unshed tears of betrayal over a misplaced frog.

Fucking Kermit.

I take Lily's hand and guide her across the room to where Kermit's corpse lies facedown on the worn carpet. In Lily's world, she likes things predictable and safe. It brings her comfort to have a certain amount of monotony to rely on. Anything that deviates from her personal ideology is a threat to her balance; something like a Muppet out of place can send an entire day off its axis.

"Where does Kermit go?" I ask her, hoping that giving her freedom of choice will make her feel empowered over her loss of control.

"In-a twash." She sniffs. Poor Kermit.

"What if another little boy or girl wants to play with him? They'll be sad that he got thrown away," I reason. Lily huffs as she grabs the toy off the floor and stomps over to the bin marked "Misc."

"You shame, Kermie," she screeches while casting him to the box of mismatched toys.

No mercy for you, frog. That'll teach you to ruin my kid's day.

lily love

"No, play more," Lily whines.

Getting Lily to clean up the mess is a battle. I have to walk her through—placing my hand over hers, picking up each thing she played with. In moments like these it's hard not to resent other parents who can simply say, "Go pick up your toys, Johnny," and be done. I'm exhausted and it's not even noon.

By the time we get back to the room, Dr. Baker is there. She's a short woman with a big heart and an even bigger personality. She is the antithesis of every neurologist we've ever met. She has a gentle bedside manner and limitless patience when it comes to getting Lily on board and compliant during our visits. She never makes me feel stupid for asking questions, and she takes extra time to make sure that I understand everything well. She is a treasure and I absolutely adore her.

"Hi, Lily." She greets my daughter with a warm smile and ushers us into Lily's room. She shakes hands with Peter and me, and then gets straight to the point.

"We aren't seeing a lot of difference with the pattern or the location of Lily's seizures on the EEG. The MRI report isn't ready yet, but preliminary findings are negative for abnormalities." She sighs heavily. "While I'm happy that there is nothing overtly wrong with Lily's brain, it doesn't help us solve the puzzle of why all this is happening. I know how frustrated you must be."

She has no idea, but I appreciate her acknowledging the effect it has on us as a family, and not just Lily as her patient.

"We will know more in a couple of weeks, when you come back in for the follow-up. For now, I'd like to keep Lily here for another twenty-four hours, so we have a basis of comparison between yesterday's EEG and today's." With that final comment, any hope I had for progress is dashed. She takes a few minutes to play with Lily, making her giggle with delight, and then moves on to her next patient.

Once again we are left with more questions than answers. I'm really starting to doubt that there will ever be answers. Peter packs his things into his overnight bag and kisses Lily on the cheek as he heads out.

"I have to work tomorrow, so I won't be able to see her until after six," he reminds me.

"It's okay. Paige is going to swing by tomorrow, and I'll call you when they discharge us so you know whether to head here or back to the house." I've got it covered. I always do.

"Bye-bye, Daddy." Lily smiles and then turns her attention to me. "Mama, snakes," she says, pointing to the electrodes on her head. When I look up, Peter is gone. That's how it happened in our marriage: one minute my eyes were on Lily, and the next he was gone.

gotta figure this out

One thing about being the mom of a child with special needs: you get to see the world in a way few others do. I've watched other parents take for granted the way their children catch a ball or swing from the jungle gym. I watch their children and see the things that Lily has to go to occupational therapy to learn how to do. Some of those things will never be options for Lily: the jungle gym, a bicycle, even a swing without a harness. Until we can get her regulated, the risk of Lily having a seizure and falling off is too high.

For now we work on things in small steps, fun games with hidden value. Today Lily and I are curled up in her hospital bed, working on motor planning with the iPad. *Fruit Ninja* is my weapon of choice. In clinical terms, we're working on bilateral and eye-hand coordination. In layman's terms, she's learning to hold the iPad with one hand while she slaughters fruit using the pointed index finger of the other. I've learned to appreciate the little things. Most people would see a kid playing a video game; I see the triumph of Lily enjoying a game that other kids her age also like. We're just conquering a frenzy level when there is a knock on the door.

"Ms. Hunter? Lily?" A wisp of a woman enters, pushing reading glasses up the bridge of her nose as she reads Lily's chart. I've never seen her before; it sets my nerves on edge that a stranger is scouring through the doctor's notes.

"Hello," I reply warily. "Can I ask why you have my daughter's chart?"

"I'm Patricia Nix." She grins, unaffected. "I'm a social worker here at University Hospital." She reaches out to shake my hand. "I'm here to make sure that your family is connected with all available resources in our area. I'm just checking to see if anything has changed since Lily was admitted."

"You could've asked me if something has changed. It's a little unsettling to have a complete stranger poring over Lily's chart notes." I attempt to sound reasonable, but I know I'm failing miserably. I sound defensive and, frankly, rude. I just don't want some social worker coming in here, trying to label Lily when we don't really know what's going on.

"Actually, what I'd like to do is get you in contact with someone from Exceptional Education for Exceptional Children; they are a parent-advocacy group that can help you find the best placement for kindergarten this fall." She pauses to pull a business card from her purse. "This is Cameron James's number. He's a really wonderful parent advocate, full of lots of great information about the Gaston County School District."

"Thanks, Ms. Nix, but isn't this is all a little premature until we can figure out what's wrong?" My voice shakes, betraying my fear. I thought Lily would've developed more before she started school. Our goal was to have her ready by kindergarten, but Lily barely knows her colors, the alphabet, how to count to ten. She's nowhere near ready.

"Of course," she concedes. "The last thing we want is to jump the gun, but Lily will need to start school in the fall, regardless of whether she has a diagnosis. The school district will do some assessments to see what class will best suit her."

I stare at her blankly. I have successfully avoided kindergarten registration. I can't fathom what next week will look like, let alone the coming school year. I can't register Lily, because I can't let go of the dream I have of her attending our neighborhood school. The best one in the district, the one we chose when we were buying our home. PTA bake sales and book fairs; I was going to be the soccer mom cliché. In light of everything else going on, it seems silly to be holding out for that. Still, something about letting it go feels like a finality that I'm not ready for yet, and I will be damned if this pint-sized pixie forces me into it.

"I understand what you're going through," she says.

I feel my body flinch, like the words have physically struck my face. *Like hell you do! You don't know an effing thing about it.*

"Right." I watch her face fall as the sarcastic bite of my word penetrates.

She shakes her head and sighs heavily. I *almost* feel bad. Almost. She ignores my attitude and continues explaining. "My daughter, Jenny, is nine years old and has Rett syndrome. I *do* understand and I have been where you are."

Okay. Now I feel bad. "I'm sorry," I mutter, ashamed.

Why can't she just be a bitch? Being angry is so much easier than being hurt. It makes me feel like a warrior, and I thought that's what I needed to be. I only ended up fighting the truth and the people who could've helped me accept it.

"Don't be," she says. "I just want you to understand that I am not your enemy. I'm here to help."

I think back to what Max said about letting people in and allowing them to help shoulder the burden. Pushing everyone away can't change Lily's prognosis, and yet that's what I've been hoping for. I doubt I would've pushed away anyone willing to tell me that all the doctors were wrong, that Lily would be fine.

"Will you leave me your card, too?" I want to ask a million questions, but not in front of Lily. I want to know how this woman can mention her daughter's disability and not burst into tears or throw something across the room. I want to know how to stop hating other

57

people for their perfect children. I want to know how to move on. I want to know how to live, when the life I was supposed to have was ripped away from me.

"Of course," she chirps, clearly happy at my change of heart. "We can set up a time to talk in the next few weeks, if you'd like."

"I would." I take the card from her and pretend to study it. Not looking at her is keeping me from crying. "It would be great to have some guidance on all of this." Maybe she can teach me, like a wise shaman, to find my inner Zen mama. To tackle the anxiety of the unknown and weave flawlessly through the maze of social services for Lily.

"Anytime, Caroline." She smiles. "I mean that. You can call me anytime."

I nod. If I say anything, I won't be able to stop the tears stinging the back of my eyes. She gives a small wave to Lily, who is oblivious and focused on the iPad. Once Ms. Nix is gone, I let the tears fall. Careful not to let Lily see me, I hide in the bathroom and weep. No matter how hard I try to deny the limits of Lily's capabilities, the vast reality of her condition is barreling toward me like a speeding train. One that's going to come off the rails the second it hits the station, wiping out everything in its path.

"Caroline?" My head snaps up at the sound of Audrey's voice. The tissue in my hand is long past its usefulness, so I wipe my face on my sleeve.

Great. Just effing great.

"Come on, now," Audrey clucks at me like a mother hen, gently gripping my upper arm and tugging me to my feet. "I gotcha." I watch silently as she takes a washcloth from the shelf and wets it in the sink. With gentle hands, she wipes my face; it's been a long time since anyone has taken care of me like this, and her tenderness only makes me cry harder.

"Sweetheart," Audrey coos, "why don't you take a break and let me play with Lily?"

"Thanks, Audrey." I sniffle. "But I'm all right." I lie, because I'm ashamed. I should be able to handle myself without falling apart. Audrey puts the washcloth down and takes my face in her hands, forcing my chin up and my eyes level with hers.

"I insist," she says firmly. "Besides, Lily needs to catch me up on this iPad thing."

This isn't a battle I'm going to win, so I let Audrey straighten me up, hand me my purse, and point me toward the elevators. While I'm waiting, I can't help but think about what's happening on the seventh floor. Still, scary-splotchy Caroline isn't the friendly face I want to present the next time I see my stranger. I want to be someone he can talk to, not someone he wants to run from. Until I can figure myself out, I'm not much use to anyone else. Whether I want to be or not.

talk

The hum of lunchtime activity in the cafeteria keeps my feet moving away from the noise and toward the doors to the patio. Sunlight shines between the towers of the hospital, casting a single pocket of warmth on a lone picnic table. A beacon for my refuge. I take a seat and pull Cameron James's business card from my purse.

>Cameron James
>Parent Advocate / District Liaison
>Exceptional Education for Exceptional Children

The thought of finding placement for Lily without assistance is far more frightening than calling this person—and yet, I find myself terrified.

Why? What are you afraid of?

I flick the card against my fingertips while I go through a mental rundown. I knew the day would come when Lily would have to start school and we would have to make a decision. I just never thought we'd have so little choice. The reality is, Lily isn't suited for a general-education setting. I know this, and yet I have avoided discussing it at all costs. In fact, it's not something I have ever talked about with anyone.

Not Peter.

Not Paige.

No one.

Talking about it makes it real.

Therein lies the problem: I've separated my head from my heart, to rationalize what I've done. In my head, pretending nothing is happening is just stupid. It's not like I'm keeping some big secret; everyone who knows us knows that Lily has special needs. But in my heart, formulating the words and expressing my fears makes everything all too real. Instead of addressing the conflict, I just keep hiding from it.

Who do you think you're kidding?

No one.

I dial the number at the bottom of the card and wait anxiously while it rings. I run through a hundred different things I could say and am about to hang up when someone picks up.

"James," says the voice on the other end.

"Uh . . . um . . ."

"Hello?" he says.

"Sorry, wrong number," I mumble, and hang up.

Idiot.

I throw my phone back in my purse and tap my forehead against the cool metal of the tabletop. Next time I should practice what I'm going to say. At least I didn't give my name.

"That bad, huh?"

I yelp, startled by the voice. I snap my head up and find my stranger standing on the other side of the table. I pray for the floor to open up and swallow me whole.

Oh, God. This isn't happening.

"Hey, there, stranger." I want to crawl under the table and hide. My knack for the ridiculous is a curse. If something's embarrassing or laughable, more than likely I'll be front and center.

He tilts his head and eyes me carefully. It makes me laugh nervously.

"Hi, Caroline. You all right?" He furrows his brow in confusion. It's so adorable and I am so flustered, I can't stop the maniacal gigglesnort from escaping.

Oh, for the love of Pete. Just kill me now.

"Peachy," I mumble, burying my head in my hands. There are no limits to my ability to mortify myself. Here I was thinking I'd take some time to collect myself before offering him a friendly ear, and in he walks, into the middle of *another* meltdown.

"Did you just snort?" he asks, incredulous. Smart-ass.

"Don't mock me." I bury my face in my hands again. "I'm dying over here." I lift my face and circle it with my index finger. "See the tomato face? Proof of my discomfiture." There's no point in pretending I'm demure or sophisticated. I can only hope that he's not repulsed by my lack of refinement. His warm eyes twinkle when he smiles, flashing me a set of heart-stopping dimples.

Oh, my swoony stranger. I am an utter and hopeless mess. Please take pity on me.

"No mockery here," he promises. "Wait . . . have we actually met?" His smile is sweet and distracting.

"Actually, no." I crinkle my nose. "I don't even know your name."

He sits down across from me and holds his hand out. "Hi, I'm Tate Michaels."

I place my hand in his and our eyes lock. "I'm Caroline Hunter," I say with as much confidence as I can muster. "Nice to meet you, Tate."

"Likewise, Caroline." His hand is warm and strong where it grips mine. It feels nice, and I wonder if that's because of Tate or because I'm that starved for human contact.

"Sorry about that; you caught me in a moment." I clear my throat and look away.

"I came out here to just breathe for a minute." He sighs and lets go of my hand. "I stepped outside and there you were, banging your head on the table." His smile returns and I feel my cheeks warm.

"You got me." I shrug. "Head banging is the shtick I employ to charm unassuming strangers."

His laughter reverberates throughout the concrete confines, giving me a keen sense of accomplishment. It's nice to know that I made him smile, after seeing him so pained earlier.

"You've got an interesting way of saying things." He studies my face like he's trying to read my thoughts. It makes me squirm. "You must be a writer or something."

I can feel my eyebrows jump to meet my hairline. It's been a long time since I've been anything other than Lily's mom.

"Or something," I say. "I'm a dabbler."

"A what?" He cocks an eyebrow at me.

"A dabbler. I dabble." I try to explain. "I dabble with writing and with music. I'm proficient in both, but not gifted enough to make anything of it." I feel silly as soon as the words come out of my mouth.

Why are you telling him this?

It took a long time for me to accept that I was never going to find that *something* I'm really good at. I spent a lot of time wandering in college for that reason. When I finally did find my passion, it was for other people's writing, not my own.

During my senior year, the editor of the literary magazine recommended me for an internship with a small publisher. I spent the summer reading thousands of query letters from aspiring writers. If they pitched something that sounded interesting, I passed it up the chain, where it would be graded again before even making it to an editor's desk. It fascinated me how one person's opinion could make or break someone else's life's work.

Lo and behold, I was finally good at something: I had a knack for weeding out the potential from the crap, and in the fall I was hired as an assistant to the acquisitions editor. When the company expanded a few years later, I was promoted to acquisitions editor myself. Not bad for a girl who had so much trouble making up her mind.

I had a husband I adored and a career that I loved. My job was my solace when Peter and I started to have trouble conceiving. It was a place where I could get lost in someone else's story and not be sad while

I was there. That's what I missed the most about it, when I had to quit to focus full-time on Lily's needs. There were no more stories to hide in when I could've used them the most.

"I can't imagine you're not gifted." He penetrates me with those warm eyes. "With that sharp wit of yours, I'm sure anything you write is brilliant."

"Wow." It's all I can come up with. He takes my monosyllabic response in stride and gives me that dimpled smile. I haven't thought about writing in years, and I'm surprised to find that his compliment strikes such a chord within. Just the thought of putting pen to paper again awakens an old yearning I'd given up on long ago.

"Are you hungry?" he asks, unfazed by my slack-jawed expression. He pats his stomach and says, "I'm starved."

"Sorry?" I urge my brain to catch up, but it's still stuck back there at "I'm sure anything you write is brilliant."

"Food." He pantomimes spooning food to his mouth. "Eat. Tate hungry."

No mockery, my ass.

"Are you trying to tell me that you're a Neanderthal after all?" I smirk. "Because I'm pretty sure they were pre-utensils." I copy his gesture of spooning food.

He beams at me. "I like you, Caroline. You've accomplished an impossible feat by making me laugh on a perfectly crappy day." And just like that, the playful banter ceases. He tries to keep smiling, but the warmth fades from his eyes as he wavers.

Helplessly, I watch as his face falls and he reaches to pinch the bridge of his nose the same way he did earlier, and it breaks my heart. I grasp his hand before it makes contact with his worry spot. His sad eyes search mine in confusion.

"Do you want to talk about it?" I ask, as evenly and matter-of-factly as I can. I want to be careful to keep my personal feelings in check. If he wants to share, I want him to feel comfortable. Nothing was worse for me than having to deal with someone else's emotions when I could

lily love

hardly deal with my own. When I told my mom that Lily had been diagnosed with a developmental disability, she was devastated. She didn't go to my father, my sister, or even my brother to be consoled; she brought all of her emotions to me. I could've used my mother's support; I desperately wanted someone to listen. Instead, I ended up comforting her.

He's hesitating, and I don't blame him. He may like me, but he hardly knows me. Then again, maybe that makes it easier. Who knows.

"Listen," I suggest. "You said you were hungry, so I'm going to go grab us a couple of sandwiches from inside. You sit here and think about it. When I get back, I'm not going to say anything. You decide what we talk about. No harm, no foul." He nods slowly, still contemplating. I give his hand a good squeeze before I let go. "I'll be right back."

From the line inside, I can see Tate's back through the window. He's slumped forward, elbows to table and hands in his hair. I think about all the times I've been exactly where he is, digesting whatever crap news the doctors have doled out that day. How nice it would've been to have had someone to talk to after that first appointment, before I made a habit of keeping it all to myself.

As if he can hear my thoughts, he glances over his shoulder and meets my eyes. I smile and give him a small wave.

I'm here, Tate. You're not alone.

comfort of strangers

We sit in silence as we eat our sandwiches. I miss the playfulness of our earlier conversation. I nibble at my sandwich and watch Tate study his food. I know this trick, the "pretend to be focused on anything else" tactic; hell, I practically invented it. The longer he ponders his corned beef on rye, the more excuses he'll find not to talk. The way his shoulders are slumped forward and his head dropped, I know he's already close to folding in on himself, shoving everyone else out.

"Did I do okay?" I interrupt his retreat. "If you don't like corned beef, I'll trade you. I've got turkey and Swiss on wheat." I smile innocently as he glances up from his plate. So it's slightly gnawed on. Whatever. It's small talk.

"Corned beef is great, thank you." He gives me a tight smile. I miss the dimples. "How is Lily?" he asks nonchalantly.

I chew slowly, buying time to consider my answer. I could answer him honestly, and head down a rabbit hole that has nothing to do with him, or I could be a complete hypocrite and avoid talking about her at all. I'm weighing my options carefully when he cuts in, "It's not easy, is it?"

"What's not easy?" I ask.

"Talking about *it*." He even uses air quotes to mark the point.

Well, crap. Touché.

"*It's* tricky. It doesn't mean that *it* isn't worth talking about." I sigh, shaking my head at my total lack of eloquence. "I don't know if that makes any sense . . ." I let my words trail off. This is exactly what I mean; walking naked through the hospital atrium sounds easier than talking about Lily.

"Yeah." He nods his agreement and picks at a chip on his plate. "It makes perfect sense."

"I'll make you a deal," I offer. "You tell me something about you and I'll tell you something about me. If *it* comes up, all the better." I shrug like it doesn't matter, but my heart is boxing with my rib cage. I just want him to keep talking.

"Okay." He clears his throat and licks his lips. I blush. I blush? *Get a grip, Caroline.*

"Deal." He extends his hand across the table. I take his hand in mine and we shake on it.

"Deal," I say, "but you have to start; you already know that I have a daughter and drink skinny vanilla lattes."

I wait for him to say something. He sits across from me, stoic, pensive, and silent.

"Tate, you don't have to say anything." I backpedal. "I'm sorry if I was pushy, I—"

He interrupts my apology. "I have a twin sister," he blurts out.

Well, that's a start.

"Who's older?" I ask. I'm so keenly focused on Tate, I reach for my chips with my right arm. Tate's gaze follows the movement of my quavering hand. I concentrate on holding on to the chip and getting it to my mouth without dropping it. My heart and my rib cage are in a full-out MMA battle at this point. I know I'm red-faced with embarrassment; I can feel the heat pulsing under my cheeks. Tate's eyes lift from my hand, locking with mine. There's no pity, just curiosity. I wait for him to say something. Anything.

"Tarryn," he says. His eyes never leave mine, holding me captive with their caramel warmth.

"Huh?"

"Huh"? Caroline speak pretty.

"Tarryn." He smiles, flashing his dimples. "My sister—she's three minutes older than me. Tell me something random about yourself."

I start to squirm under his penetrating stare. When he finally looks away, my words find me.

"Random?" My life has become so singularly driven, I don't know what to say that doesn't involve Lily. I search the coffers of my memory for some interest that's somewhat current. There's nothing.

"What's your favorite TV show?" he offers. "This is important, because if you say *The Bachelorette* or *Real Housewives of Scranton*, I don't know if we can be friends." He chuckles and leans back in his chair, waiting for me to—what? Proclaim my undying devotion to reality TV?

"Scranton, Ohio? Seriously?" I tease. Lucky for Tate, I'm vehemently opposed to the exploitation of women so desperate for a date, they duke it out over one dickless moron on national television.

"Don't deflect; you know what I mean," he says, eyeing me suspiciously. "Wait! You don't really watch that, do you?" The look of mock horror that crosses his face cracks me up.

"No way." I laugh. *"Sons of Anarchy."*

"Sons of Anarchy," he repeats.

"SAMCRO, baby."

"Sons of Anarchy Motorcycle Club, Redwood Original." He nods his head and looks at me in wonder. "Marry me?" A playful smile stretches across his face. Of course he's kidding, but I still blush scarlet. "You're too good to be true."

"Oh, please, I'm a calamity." I wave off his bewilderment and force myself to sit still.

"Your first concert?" Tate leans his arms on the table, waiting with rapt interest.

"Stevie Ray Vaughan and Double Trouble." The words shoot out of me like rapid gunfire.

Charming, Calamity Caroline.

Tate laughs at my awkward display even as his forehead crinkles with surprise. I give an impish grin and shrug my shoulders. What can I say? It was a strange "first" for a twelve-year-old, but I was always a peculiar girl. I used to bask in my nonconformity, but now I just feel . . . well . . . odd.

"Aren't you too young to have seen him in concert?" he asks. There is an ease to his demeanor that I envy. He's relaxed and completely chill, while I'm strung higher than a kite. I can't help it; I want him to think that I'm a cool chick, good friend material. Yet all I seem to do is emphasize my lack of finesse.

Sophisticated and demure I'm not. Comical and graceless I am. Yoda, my subconscious is, hmm?

I glance across the table, and it's my turn to watch in wonder as Tate continues to eat his lunch, entirely unaffected by my spectacle.

All worried for nothing, I am. Gah! Enough, Caroline. Focus. Focus. Focus.

"I was twelve. Charles, my big brother, got saddled with babysitting me that night, so he brought me along. SRV's copter crashed later that summer. Such a waste." I shake my head and make a mental note to call my brother tomorrow. I miss him. Our relationship has been tough since Peter and I separated. They were good friends; I know it's hard for him not to feel like he has to take sides. The irony is, there are no sides. There are no bad guys, only a crappy set of circumstances.

"You're one cool chick, Caroline." Tate's words raise goose bumps all the way up through my scalp. I feel my mouth drop as I stare in disbelief.

"What?" He looks at me, confused.

"Nothing, it's just I was mentally berating myself for my inelegance," I admit. "My gift, grace is not."

Unable to contain himself a minute more, Tate throws his head back and bursts open with laughter. His guffaws draw attention from across the courtyard. People are staring at us like we're on display at the zoo. This only serves to make me laugh too, when typically I'd be under the table by now. However, this is a stellar moment in the growth of Caroline Hunter. My satisfaction in making Tate laugh trumps my fear of being ridiculous. Perhaps there is hope for me after all.

"Patience you must have, my young Padawan." I'll give him credit; he tries to say it with a straight face, but he's laughing so hard, tears pool in his eyes. The sound rumbles from deep in his chest; it's pure delight, unapologetic mirth, and is absolutely infectious.

"You're mocking me!" I feign distress, clutching my hand to my heart. In truth, I'm rather pleased with myself. There's more than one way to skin this cat, and Tate doesn't want to talk about who's on the seventh floor. That's fine by me; I'm willing to bide my time and wait him out.

He takes a couple of deep breaths to calm himself before he answers. "Never." He places his hand over his own heart, and grabs my hand with the other. "You don't know how badly I needed to laugh like that. Thank you."

"My work here is done," I proclaim to our courtyard audience, with a dramatic wave of my hand. "Now, it's your turn to share some randomness."

He lets go of my hand and rubs it over his head. "Okay, I'll try to stick with the theme here. Favorite TV show? *Sons of Anarchy*. No kidding. First concert? Toad the Wet Sprocket. Inner dialogue narrator? Dirty Harry."

"You're not pulling my leg about SOA?"

"True story. Scout's honor," he promises. "I have a little crush on Maggie Siff."

I wasn't expecting that at all. She plays the pediatric surgeon / old lady of the motorcycle club, and she is *badass*. Not your typical Hollywood cookie-cutter beauty, either. I adore her. I'm also a big fan of Toad the Wet Sprocket. I think I need to revisit the theory that Tate is a mind reader.

"Well, I have to say you're a bit of an anomaly, Tate." I begin to clean up our table. He tips his head and studies me. "What?" I ask.

"Seriously, what's with the vocabulary?"

Tate's question catches me off guard. I'm stupefied. How's that for vocabulary?

"Inelegance, anomaly, discomfiture . . . That's more than dabbling. People get lazy with words these days. I like that you're not." He shrugs.

"Thanks." I beam. He may not know it, but he's just paid me the best compliment in the world. I love words. I miss them.

"Once upon a time, I was an acquisitions editor." I sigh wistfully. "Now I'm a full-time mommy." I try not to let the disappointment show. "Speaking of, it's time I get back to Lily."

The look on Tate's face halts my reverie midsentence. His eyebrows are all askew: one's arched high, the other dipped low across a squinty eye. I find my own eyebrow rising, wondering what he's thinking.

"Are you married?" he asks nonchalantly.

"No." I shake my head. "I'm separated." It doesn't get easier to say. Even as charming as my stranger may be, I still feel like a failure saying it.

"You said you were a stay-at-home mom." He shrugs his shoulders. "I was curious . . ." His words stumble to a halt as he struggles with what to say next.

I want to reassure him, and it shocks me. I haven't needed to explain my custody arrangement, or lack of it, to anyone, and yet I find myself caring very much what Tate thinks. "I haven't worked out the logistics with my ex yet, but when Lily starts school in the fall, I'll try freelance editing part-time. Maybe twenty or so hours a week. We'll see." I try not to think about all of the change ahead, or the fact that I haven't worked in five years. Tate watches me, concern etched in his expression.

"I'm sorry; I assumed," Tate apologizes. The eyebrows are back, meeting in the middle, tipping up toward his hairline. His look is slightly pained and sheepish; I can't help but grin. I bet he could hold an entire conversation solely with the position of his eyebrows.

"Don't be sorry," I say. "It's all good; it's just a lot of change, you know?"

"I imagine it is," he agrees.

"Has anyone ever mentioned you have astonishingly expressive eyebrows?" I ask.

"Nice segue." He grins. "I've got to get back, too. Can I walk you to the elevator?"

I rock back and forth on my heels as we stand in the lobby waiting for the elevator to whisk us back up to the Neurology wing. I don't want to dive back into reality yet; I like the way I feel when I'm talking with Tate. He thinks I'm funny and interesting. Maybe I'm being selfish, but it's nice to be the center of attention.

Tate pulls his phone out of his pocket to check the time, and I find myself grabbing it out of his hands. He tilts his head and looks at me. I smile and bring up his contact list, tilting the screen for his approval. I'm not sure where this capricious Caroline came from, but I like her. She dances along the fringe of my subconscious, urging me to be bold.

"Can I?" I ask.

"Yeah, I'd like that," he says with a grin. The look gives him a boyish playfulness. I bump my shoulder into his and smile back.

I busy myself with typing my information into Tate's phone and hand it back to him just as the elevator chimes. The car is empty this time; it's just the two of us marinating in silence as it ascends. We are both casting sideways glances, but neither of us says a word. All of our playful banter fades as we're swept farther away from the courtyard and closer to the lives that await us above.

"Tate?" I wait for him to lift his gaze to mine. "If you ever want to talk, about anything, you can call me anytime." I let out a shaky breath, wondering if he will.

"Thank you, Caroline." He sighs. "It's been a long time since I've had someone to talk to."

lily love

The elevator jerks to a stop on the seventh floor. The doors open in a mechanical yawn, beckoning Tate to the sterile surgical floor outside. There's a pregnant pause where neither of us moves, our eyes locked on the open doors and the goodbye it signifies. In a swift and unexpected movement, Tate sweeps me into a gentle hug. I press my cheek into his chest and wrap my arms around his waist. Tears prick the backs of my eyelids. I want so badly to help him. Focusing, I minister every ounce of compassion I can, willing it to seep into him where our bodies touch.

"Anytime," I whisper. "I meant it." Reluctantly, I let him go when the elevator doors threaten to close again. Tate steps off, offering me a weak smile that breaks something in me. Perhaps it's the familiarity of his bravery in the face of his grief, or maybe it's the vulnerability he shared with me. Empathy flows through my blood, pushing my own pain to the surface. I force the tips of my lips to turn up, even as my heart drops. I hold the plastered grin on my face until the doors close, and only then allow the tears to flow freely.

my little girl

The moment I step off the elevator into the EMU, I can feel that something is wrong. There's an unnatural stillness on the floor, a void where sound and movement should be mingling. By the time the phenomenon registers in my brain, the silence is pierced by Lily's scream. The sound of her fear echoes in my own voice as I sprint down the hallway, yelling, *"Lily!"*

When I round the corner I find Lily thrashing madly in her bed. Audrey is at her side, trying desperately to console her. Chelsea's presence in the room sends my heart beating in erratic frenzy. Call it a mother's intuition, but there was something about her I didn't trust the first time we met. I wish my instincts had been wrong. I watch in terror when Chelsea's eyes meet mine as she tries to hide the soft restraints in her hand.

"What the hell do you think you're doing, Chelsea?" I keep my voice even, letting only my eyes reflect my murderous intent. Lily's face is sweaty and red with rage. I get it. I feel exactly the same way. Audrey moves to sweep away a strand of hair that's stuck to Lily's forehead, but she shrieks and swats at Audrey's hand.

lily love

"Clearly you can see that Lily is out of control," Chelsea says. She motions toward Audrey and Lily with her free hand and tucks her contraband behind her back with the other.

"What did you do?" I cry out. There's no way Lily got this way on her own. She's not self-injurious, and she's been doing so well in behavioral therapy.

The hurried steps of soft-soled shoes turn my attention to the door. Dr. Baker hustles into the room, evaluating the scene unfolding. She looks at me sympathetically, but then quickly shifts her focus to Lily. She tentatively approaches the bedside while she assesses the tantrum with a keen eye.

"How long has she been like this?" Dr. Baker addresses the room, never taking her eyes off of Lily.

Audrey checks her watch. "Fifteen minutes," she murmurs softly. Both doctor and nurse understand the need to read Lily's level of tolerance and are careful not to upset her further by making sudden movements or raising their voices. Everyone understands this but Chelsea, who sees fit to start defending herself in loud, irritated bursts.

"Dr. Baker, I called the code green because the patient struck me and I couldn't get her to comply with the soft restraints." She punctuates her statement by revealing the Velcro cuffs she intends to use on my girl. Over my dead body.

"You called a code green?" My heart stops beating. Code greens are for violent patients who are a threat to the staff and themselves. They aren't for five-year-old little girls.

"That was a gross abuse of authority," Dr. Baker scolds. "You're trained to use nonviolent crisis intervention to de-escalate these situations, not default to using restraints."

I want to kiss Dr. Baker. Tears of gratitude mix with my frustration. They silently fall while I listen to her belittle Chelsea.

"Doctor, all I did was come to check on a loose lead," Chelsea says. She shifts nervously, crossing her arms.

"Did you read her chart first?" The calm of my tone doesn't betray the seething fury inside. I grab the metal clipboard from the foot of Lily's bed and start to recite her diagnosis. "Sensory Processing Disorder. Noted tactile defensiveness."

"Excuse me?" Chelsea sneers.

"It's a patient's chart," I say. "When you read them beforehand, you learn things like, 'is fearful of strangers. Doesn't like to be touched.'" I point out each bullet in the patient orders.

Dr. Baker's attempts to soothe Lily are met with more maniacal thrashing. I watch in horror as Lily starts to beat her head against the bedrail. Dr. Baker grabs a pillow to place in front of Lily to soften her blows, and addresses Audrey in a whispered flurry. What I can make out threatens to buckle my knees: *point zero five milligrams of haloperidol.* Haldol. They want to give Lily an antipsychotic. Before I can protest, Audrey nods at Dr. Baker and runs from the room, shoving Chelsea along with her.

"Wait," I plead. *"No!"* I rush to replace Audrey at Lily's bedside, wanting to sweep her into my arms and whisk her away from this nightmare.

"Caroline, I need you listen to me very carefully." Dr. Baker's voice is stern but gentle. She waits for me to look at her, locking my eyes with hers. "Lily is hurting herself. None of us wants her to do real damage. Haloperidol is the quickest and safest way for me to protect her right now. Do you understand?"

"No, I don't understand how any of this is happening," I cry. "She was fine when I left." I must sound like an idiot. I never should've left.

While I mentally berate myself, Lily grabs the protective pillow and launches it across the room. She grips the bedrail and throws her head backward, keening like a wild animal. She's crazed, unrecognizable to me. My heart has no time to break as her intent becomes clear. Reacting on pure instinct, I lunge forward and block her face as it comes careening toward the rail.

Sharp pain radiates up my wrist when the force of her head slams my hand against the bed rail. My only thought is, *Thank God it wasn't her forehead.* A moment later, Audrey is there to shuttle me out of the way so Dr. Baker has room to hold Lily still. With the smooth and precise movements of a seasoned nurse, she prepares the syringe and gives Lily the drug with a quick stab to the thigh.

Dr. Baker takes Lily's arms, crosses them over her chest, and slides onto the bed behind her. Gentle but firm, she places Lily in a therapeutic hold, the one the hospital staff is supposed to use before restraints are introduced. Nonviolent crisis intervention—NCI—is meant to keep the patient and staff safe until the situation de-escalates. In this case, until the meds kick in.

I can feel my heartbeat in my hand, each beat bringing another wave of pain. Everything else is numb, but the pain helps to keep me anchored in the moment. Dr. Baker whispers softly to Lily, reassuring her that she's safe. I'm mesmerized by her soothing bedside manner; I startle when Audrey reaches for the hand I have clasped to my chest.

"Caroline, let me see," she demands. I wince as she probes, yelping when she gets to my wrist. "You need to have this X-rayed." She sighs. Her tone betrays what she knows. What I know—it's broken. I can only imagine what the ER doctor is going to say when I tell him that my daughter crushed my hand between her skull and the TV remote built into the hospital's bed rail.

"I need to call Peter first. I'm not leaving her alone again," I say. In truth, calling Peter is the last thing I want to do. I don't know where I'd even begin to tell him what's happened. Thinking about it sends a new wave of tears falling, because I can almost hear his frustration. I already feel like I've failed Lily. I don't need or want him to remind me.

I hold my breath as his line rings, dreading the moment he answers. How am I ever going to explain this to him without him freaking out? If Peter called me with this news, I would be completely out of my mind.

Voice mail. Voice mail. Voice mail. I will it to be, but Peter answers on the fourth ring.

"Caroline, I can't talk now. I'll have to call you back."

"Peter, wait," I urge, "it's an emergency. Lily and I had a little accident."

"*What?*" he yells into the phone. I pull the receiver away from my ear. "I thought you were at the hospital. How did you get into a car accident?"

"No, no," I stammer. If he would just shut up for a second I could explain. "It's a long story, but we're still here at the EMU. Lily had a really bad tantrum, Peter. I've never seen her like that. She was thrashing around violently, trying to hurt herself. I threw my hand out to keep her from banging her head on the bed rail, and smashed it. I need to have it X-rayed and I don't want to leave Lily alone."

"Jesus, Caroline," Peter breathes into the phone. "Has she calmed down? I can be there in thirty minutes."

"They had to sedate her," I say.

"Come again?" Peter sounds incredulous.

"They sedated her," I repeat. "She was trying to hurt herself. We didn't have a choice." Peter stays silent on the other line. I can only imagine what he's thinking, how angry he must be with me right now. It hurts my heart so badly. I have failed so miserably. "Say something, please," I beg.

"I'm so sorry."

His softly spoken words floor me. I was ready to face his anger, not his compassion. A sob tears free from my chest. All of the anguish I've been keeping at bay runs in steady streams down my face.

"I can't imagine seeing Lily like that. It breaks my heart to think about it," he continues.

"Peter," I sob. My breath comes in staccato gasps, making it impossible to say more.

lily love

"I'm on my way," he promises. "Hang in there." Then he's gone. A warm hand rubs steady circles across my back. I look up to find Audrey holding out a box of tissues and an ice pack.

"Thank you," I whisper.

"Stay strong, Caroline." She continues to rub my back as she speaks. "This too shall pass."

I believe her, but I'm scared to death at what awaits me in X-ray. Deep down I know my wrist is broken. Even if I tried to explain, would anyone believe that I was protecting Lily? My hope that people will accept Lily slowly circles the drain. People are rarely accepting of things they don't understand, and no parent would let their child play with a girl who broke her mom's hand.

reason why

"The Haldol will last a few hours," Dr. Baker says.

"I want to take her home when she wakes up," I respond. Dr. Baker's silence meets me, and I worry she'll disagree. "You've already said that the EEG hasn't shown us anything new. You have almost thirty-six hours of data. I want her home."

"I wasn't going to disagree, Caroline," she assures me. "I'm just at a loss for the words to say how sorry I am. I'll go write up the orders so they're ready when you are."

"Is this going to keep happening?" My voice is a breathy whisper of my fear. "Will her tantrums be violent like that now?" The walls of the room bend inward, hemming me in. Trapping me inside the prospect of the doctor's words and a fate I can't handle.

"Do I believe Lily is inherently aggressive? No. I do feel like she would benefit from the aid of a behaviorist. Someone who can teach you as a family how to cope with Lily's deficits. Lily can learn to self-regulate before she gets that upset, and you and Peter can learn how to help her do that." She gives me a reassuring smile, but I'm too overwhelmed to return it. "I'll come check on her later," she promises before she leaves to continue her rounds.

lily love

Dr. Baker's words swim through my mind as I brush silky strands of hair off Lily's forehead. Every time I think things can't possibly get harder, something happens to prove me wrong. Someone sent me a card once that said, "If God doesn't give us more than we can handle, then He must think you are a real badass." I didn't think it was funny. I didn't chuckle at the sly wit of the friend who'd sent it. It pissed me off. It made me irate at God. Furious that He would do this to me—and for what? What purpose does it serve, to make my child suffer? Why should *she* go through any of this? So some fucking whacked-out crack whore can give birth to a healthy child she neglects? Don't get me started on God. He is a sadistic thief who took everything away from me without a glance backward. Where is He now? Nowhere around here, that's for damn sure.

Lily breathes in a shuddering sigh, like she can hear my hostile thoughts. Thick, acrid shame spreads like venom through my veins. Unfazed, Lily snuggles closer against my body. All she needs is my acceptance, and all I'm doing is cursing God for who she is. I don't deserve her.

"Uh-oh. I know that face." My head snaps up at the sound of Peter's voice. He levels his kind eyes on me, bathing me in sympathy. "Stop blaming yourself, Caroline. It won't help."

I recoil from Peter's words. What right does he have to assume what I'm feeling? It's easy to oversimplify what someone else should or shouldn't be doing. It's a lot harder when you're the one living it day-to-day.

"Thanks, Peter." I let my words drip with sarcasm. "That's insightful of you." I shimmy my body out from under Lily, and fuss with the sling Audrey wrapped my arm in. I try tugging it into place, but it keeps digging into my neck. What I'd really like to do is wad it up and throw it at Peter.

"Caroline, you can't keep condemning yourself," he presses. "You can't—"

"No, *you* can't, Peter," I snap, cutting him off. "You can't tell me how I'm supposed to feel. In fact, you don't get an opinion on how I feel at all." I deserve to be condemned; look what I let happen. If I'd just come back a little sooner I could've stopped it.

I grab my purse and head toward the hall; Peter's footsteps follow, so I keep talking. "She should be out for another hour or so. Dr. Baker is coming back in a few minutes to remove the electrodes, so you'll need to get the hair conditioner out of Lily's bag and comb out whatever glue the acetone doesn't get to. I will wash it out when we get home."

"Caroline," Peter starts.

"Someone from Administration is meeting me in Radiology to take my statement for the accident report." I ignore Peter and continue. "I shouldn't be more than a couple hours."

"Caroline, stop." Peter grabs my shoulders, swinging me around to face him. "It's not your fault. You can't be there all the time, no matter what you've been spinning in that stubborn head of yours. You can be pissed at me for saying so. Whatever. Just stop, please." He rubs my shoulders, placing his forehead against mine. Instead of comfort, it feels like acid where he touches me. He winces as I push him away. Where was this comfort when we were together? Why didn't it occur to him to treat me with this kind of care when it mattered? Why now?

"*What do you mean, you don't know what happened?*" Peter bellowed. "*What else do you have to do but supervise her, Caroline?*" His outburst hung like a poisonous cloud in the Urgent Care waiting room. The woman in the seat next to me got up and moved a few rows away. I hung my head in humiliation.

"Will you please keep your voice down, Peter. People are staring at us," I whispered as I looked around at the curious stares. "I was in the bathroom. It's not like I left her to fend for herself."

"Yeah, well, you left her long enough for her to crack her head open on the coffee table."

My heart shattered on the impact of his words. I knew that Peter was angry; I was, too. I was exasperated that the moment I took to use the toilet was also the moment Lily had a seizure and hit her head. I felt more guilt than Peter could've fathomed.

"You don't think I know that? I'm the one who has to live with that on my conscience. For what, Peter? What would you have me do, wet my pants?" I cried. "I know you're frustrated, Peter. I am too, but you can't blame me. It's not fair. I don't deserve your poison."

"You should know better than anyone, Caroline," Peter scoffed. "Life doesn't give a shit what any of us deserves."

"Is that what you tell yourself, Peter?" My gentle tone did nothing to soften the sting of the words that followed. "That it's not your fault you were never there? Screw you."

Hindsight is always more clear than the present. If I had to pinpoint the moment that our marriage started to fall apart, that day would be it. The memory of those words, and what they did to my heart, fuel the fury building inside me. Peter's never had to worry about feeling the way I did that day, because Lily's care has never been his responsibility. It's *always* been mine. It's easy to criticize someone else's efficiency when you're never around to experience it yourself.

"Caroline, I'm sorry," Peter pleaded. "Talk to me. Yell at me. Something!"

I couldn't. My voice was crushed under the weight of the guilt I carried. There was nothing I could say that could erase his outburst anyway. I didn't want to absolve myself or him. I wanted to hoard the pain, cloak myself in it and use it to validate my misery.

"I should've been there. I don't blame you for your anger." My words were as flat and colorless as I felt. Neither of us could cope with the hand we'd been dealt; we just kept repeating the same toxic pattern. Peter would explode with painful words and I would lose all ability to use mine.

"Goddammit, Caroline, you can't believe that." Peter gripped his blond hair in frustration. He waited, but I was adamant in my silence. "I don't know what else you want me to say," he mumbled as he stalked out of the kitchen.

"I love you" might've worked, though at that point I don't know if I would have believed him, anyway.

As I walk down the hallway, I fight the urge to turn around and apologize for being so combative; Peter was only trying to help. Grief makes people say the most awful things. I know that Peter is not a cruel man. I would never have married him, let alone had a child with him, if he were. That day was a nightmare. It took seven stitches to close the gash above Lily's eyebrow; the faint scar it left was a constant reminder.

I understood the desperation Peter was feeling, back then; I was feeling it, too. I was grieving, too. I forgave Peter for saying what he did, but he can never take those words back. Clearly they've remained a trigger for my own cruelty. I can't decide which is the lesser of two evils: Caroline the silent martyr, or Caroline the sharp-tongued bitch. Honestly, I'm not very fond of either one of them. I don't like who I am when I'm around Peter anymore. I don't want the anger or resentment. I just want to move on. I choke back a sob as it occurs to me: that's exactly the reason Peter left. Somewhere along the way, the magnitude of caring for Lily eclipsed that of our love. Unwilling to reach out to the rest of the world, we lashed out at each other, ripping lethal wounds in our marriage.

Hindsight might be clear, but it burns all the same.

fault line

The elevator is excruciatingly slow on the way down to Radiology. I have too much space to think, and remembering my exchange with Peter makes my head throb in time with my wrist. In his defense, he has no idea where I'm coming from. He didn't when we were married, and he certainly doesn't now. Attacking him was a stupid move on my part; I can't exactly move on to a brighter future without finding a way to be civil to Peter. Poor guy. I'm sure my attitude was a shock; that's the most verbose I've been about my feelings in years.

There was a time when I was happy to conform myself to exist in Peter's likeness. He never asked me to; it was my own doing. I floundered in college, never really finding my niche. I was at the peak of my wandering when I met him. I'd spent three years trying to discover what I wanted to do for the rest of my life. Three major changes later, I was still drifting without vision.

The only thing I cared about was writing, but my dad had put the kibosh on that dream: "I'm not paying for a bachelor's degree in creative writing that you will never use."

I tried to major in education; I really did. That lasted one semester. Then I thought I'd try journalism but soon discovered that making up news stories was frowned upon. I was a writer of fiction, not a columnist or news writer.

The one good thing that came out of the journalism department was my involvement with the literary magazine. At least there I didn't feel so lost. I had purpose. In addition to writing my own submissions, I got to help choose the work that went into publication. That was the only reason I lasted three semesters—I loved that magazine.

I was too far into my schooling to reasonably change my mind again. My advisor was fed up with my apathy; my father had made it clear that he would not be paying for a fifth year of school. So I did the only thing I could at that point: I changed my major again. With a quick trip to the advising office, I was now *Caroline Hunter, liberal-arts major*.

Adding to my self-doubt was my "boyfriend," Trent. We'd been dating for a few months, and I knew it was going nowhere. Still, I couldn't even make the decision to break up with him. I was pathetic. A loser. All the things that Peter wasn't. I was amazed at his confidence. He knew exactly what he wanted and where he was headed. In his third year of studying to be an electrical engineer, he already knew he wanted to work alongside the military as a defense contractor. I was fascinated and intimidated. I adored Peter, so it was easy for me to like the things he did. I let go of trying to figure out what I wanted out of life, and hitched my star to his. I felt safe tethered to his plans, but I never made any of my own. In fact, it was Peter's suggestion that I turn my love of the written word into a career. I'm so grateful to him for that. Still, as bright as Peter's star shone, it wasn't meant to illuminate us both.

The fluorescent lights flicker as I meander down the hallway, lost in my depressing reverie. Not paying attention, I bypass X-ray altogether and end up in the reception area of the MRI clinic. It figures my feet would automatically carry me here. My thoughts turn to Max, and my mood instantly brightens. I could really use a friend right now.

"Need to sign in?" The triage nurse taps her pen against the clipboard in her hand. She looks at me expectantly. "Hello?"

lily love

"Oh. Um. No," I stutter. "Is Max Swain here, by chance?"

"No, he's taking a late lunch," she says. I watch as her sharp eyes home in on my left hand and the absence of a wedding ring. She arches a judgmental eyebrow at me and adds, "Can I tell him who stopped by?"

Nosy cow.

"No, that's all right." I sigh. "Can you tell me how to get to X-ray, though?"

"Down the hall and to the left." She smiles sweetly, but her eyes are still picking me apart like a turkey vulture on roadkill. I fight the urge to fidget under her scrutiny, and I nod my thanks as I retreat. It's not that I blame her; Max is totally hot, and single to boot. I have a feeling that's the kind of reaction all women have around him.

I fight to regain my composure as I check myself in at the X-ray clinic. The receptionist waves me toward the waiting room, where I'm shocked to stillness in my tracks.

"How'd you know I'd be here?" There's no hiding the surprise in my voice or the smile on my face. I debate whether to tell Max that he's supposed to be having a late lunch, but I'm sure the triage nurse back in MRI will fill him in soon enough. Let her gossip all she wants. I'm so relieved to see a friendly face, I don't care.

"Word travels fast when there's a fight on hospital grounds." Max chuckles and pulls me in for a quick hug. "Though I hear the bed won." He gently places his hand over the front of the sling.

I breathe in slow and steady, willing myself not to cry.

Max wraps his arm around my shoulders and guides me toward the seats. "You don't have to talk about it. I just didn't want you to be down here alone."

Together, we sit in silence on worn blue vinyl seats, waiting to hear my name. Despite a herculean effort on my part, the tears fall en masse. Ever my hero, Max passes me tissues and pretends that there isn't a hysterical woman sniveling all over his shoulder. He just holds me tighter and rests his cheek on the top of my head.

"Ms. Hunter?" I turn my head toward my name, to find a tall man in a business suit scanning the room for me. Clearly this isn't the X-ray tech. My stomach hits the floor. When his eyes finally meet mine, I give him a small wave and he walks my way.

"Ms. Hunter, my name is Alex Drake; I work for the hospital." He shakes my good hand and sits in the chair across from Max and me.

"You're a lawyer," I say. It's not a question; I want his confirmation so I can steel myself for the coming conversation.

"Yes, I am. I didn't want to lead with that, though." He smiles genuinely, regardless of my chilly reception. He leans back and crosses his ankle over his knee, not bothered by my wariness at all.

"Before you have your wrist looked at, I wanted to go over a few things with you." He pauses to look back and forth between Max and me.

"This is my friend Max," I explain. "I'd like him to stay." There's no way I'm letting this guy dismiss my lifeline. Max stays. Period.

"That's fine," Alex assures me. My face must reflect my surprise, because he grins as he continues. "First, all of your care will be covered by the hospital. At no time will you incur any expense related to the accident. Second, I want to assure you that nothing discussed in the accident report will be included in your daughter's medical file. Honestly, the only thing I need from you is an account of what happened from the moment you entered the room until you struck your hand."

I try not to tense at his careful choice of words. His face reflects sympathy, not the calloused legal eagle I was expecting.

"The other staff that were present will be interviewed as well, and you will be notified of any disciplinary action that may be taken as a result." He heaves a heavy sigh and reaches into his breast pocket for his card. "Ms. Hunter, I have a twelve-year-old son with high-functioning autism. I know that isn't what you're dealing with, but I hope you believe me when I say that I understand. We want to get to the bottom of what happened today, but that in no way means we're looking to blame Lily. I promise you that."

"Thank you, Alex," Max speaks up for me, as I've been rendered speechless by the compassion of this lawyer. Aren't they supposed to look for a way to absolve the hospital of blame? I thought for sure he'd be going over all the ways that Lily was an aggressive and out-of-control child who beat the crap out of her mother. Nothing ceases to surprise me today.

"Now, let's get you looked at, so you can get back to your daughter." Alex shakes my hand again, and encourages me to call with any questions that might come up. I smile and nod, unable to articulate anything else right now. All I can do is stare as Alex Drake walks away; I'm completely and utterly overwhelmed.

"Carolina." Max's hushed voice breaks through my anxiety. I look up at him, and he tips his chin toward the door. "They just called your name." My brain and my body continue to misfire. I hear Max; I just can't seem to get up. He stands, pulling me along with him. "I'll be here when you get back," he promises.

My first reaction is to say, "I'll be fine." It's what I've been saying for years. Three words with multiple passive-aggressive meanings. There's the "I'll be fine" I gave to well-meaning family who asked if they could help with Lily, understanding they were asking because they felt it was the right thing to do. In reality, the whole thing made them uncomfortable. My mom and dad mean well, but they've got no idea how to relate to Lily—or to me, for that matter.

Then there were the ones I gave Peter. "I'll be fine" could've meant exactly the opposite, and that I was irate that he didn't know why I wasn't fine. It could also have been my response to a half-assed attempt on his part to help me.

Regardless of who you are, an "I'll be fine" from Caroline is the ultimate blowoff. It's the verbal shove I give to get people to back off. I don't want to be that way anymore. I'm so tired of being a martyr—but it's hard to break free from a habit so deeply ingrained.

"Thanks, Max," I manage, without bursting into flames. *Baby steps*, I tell myself. "I'm really glad you're here." With a sheepish smile, I head toward the waiting technician.

After a quick stint in X-ray, Max and I are escorted to a room in the Emergency Department, where we wait for a doctor. Alex Drake stops by with a copy of the incident report for me to read. If I am comfortable with it, I'm supposed to sign. If I'm not, then we go back to the drawing board until it's right. I feel much more empowered than I thought I would.

"Mr. Drake, can I ask you a personal question?" I ask softly.

He looks at me, suspicious and curious at the same time. "I suppose it depends on the question."

"Was it harder when your son was younger?" I cringe at the boldness of my question.

He gives me a reassuring smile before he answers. "I wouldn't say a certain period of time has been harder than another. I used to tell myself that if we could just get through this one rough patch, then everything would be better. I learned quickly that that was the fast lane to frustration, because there is no finish line. There will never be a point in CJ's life that he won't be dependent on my wife and me in some way."

Alex's candid words seep through my skin, into the center of my chest, and take root. He doesn't regale me with a story of hope and wonderment. His honesty is breathtakingly beautiful, in all of its sadness. His acceptance of his son's condition isn't decorated with rainbows or unicorns. It is what it is, and that's okay.

"I've never heard anyone say it quite like that," I admit. Most of what I hear comes from the "helpful" articles my mother-in-law sends me. My favorite was about a father who quit his job, sold all his belongings, and flew all the way around the world for a vial of Australian shark piss, thinking it would cure his son.

"Days like today will strip you raw. They happen regardless of what we do, not because of it." Alex starts to gather his papers as he talks. "Sometimes, it just is what it is," he says with solemn resignation.

It is what it is.

"Geri, it didn't work. His son still has diabetes," I huff into the phone. Peter buries his nose further into the newspaper, pretending he doesn't know his mother's driving me insane. Ever since Lily's visit to the urgent-care clinic, Geri's been flooding my in-box with these "miracle cure" articles.

"Honestly, Caroline, sometimes I think you don't read the things I send you," she sniffs. Oh, I read the crap she sends; just because I don't agree doesn't mean I didn't read it.

"I read every word, down to the part where the shark piss didn't work and the kid is still sick," I bark. A rogue snicker floats over the top of Peter's paper. I'm getting reamed by his mom, and he's laughing. Ass.

"It's urine from a rare white shark species that can only be found off the Great Barrier Reef. Don't belittle this man's journey. He gave up everything for his son."

"He gave up gainful employment, and thus the health insurance his child was covered by. Do you know what happens when you have a chronic illness and have a lapse in health coverage?" I don't wait for her to answer. "You become uninsurable. How's he going to pay for his kid's insulin with no job and no health insurance? The guy is an idiot, not a hero!"

"He gave it all up to do what he thought was best for his son. I think that's heroic. I thought you'd be inspired by his story." She sighs.

"Inspired to do what? Go trek through the Amazon for the rare insect excrement that will cure Lily of a condition they can't even diagnose?" Peter shoots me a dirty look across the top of the headlines. Nice—he'll get upset over his mother's honor but not mine. She started this ridiculous exchange when she e-mailed me the article's link.

"Oh, for the love of Pete, Caroline, quit being so dramatic," she snaps. I want to scream, but that would interrupt me as I bite through my tongue. *"I thought this father was a good example to aspire to, that's all."*

My lungs contract painfully, leaving me breathless. Silence crackles across the phone line as I absorb Geri's barbed words.

"What are you saying, Geri?" I ask. I look over to Peter for a sign of support. He's back to hiding behind the sports page. "You don't think we're doing enough for Lily?" The paper doesn't move. I know he can hear my end of the conversation and still, he acknowledges nothing.

"I think there is never enough you can do for your children," she says. "As parents, we have to be willing to make sacrifices in the best interest of our children."

"What is that supposed to mean?" I throw my free hand into the air.

"Nothing, just that there's always something more we can do as parents. If you're doing everything you can, don't you think Lily would've shown more progress by now?" She can't possibly expect me to answer her. I've given up every single aspect of my life to care for my daughter: my job, my friends, my family, my sanity. All of it.

I can't listen to another word. I place the phone on the table next to Peter, with Geri still chattering away on the other line. Her sour words pitch violently in my stomach. I barely make it to the bathroom in time before nausea overtakes me. On a mighty heave, the contents of my belly empty into the porcelain bowl.

I wish I could purge the conversation as easily, but all I can hear are my mother-in-law's thoughtless words. From her perch in Sarasota, she castigated me with no consideration of the damage she'd inflict. She barely sees Lily twice a year on holidays, but apparently that's enough to know that I'm not sacrificing enough for my child. Giving up my career and dedicating every waking moment to therapies and doctors isn't sacrifice enough? It feels like I've given up everything in Lily's best interest. Maybe I'm kidding myself, and there's more that I could be doing. If Geri is right, then trying to accept Lily's prognosis is as good as giving up on her.

My body hurts from the violence of my retching. Even after I'm empty, I dry heave until I can no longer hold myself up. I press my face against the cool tiles of the bathroom floor and cry.

There will never be enough I can do, and it will always be my fault.

After Alex Drake leaves, I tell Max the story of my mother-in-law and the shark piss. He laughs through some of it, and groans through most of it.

"Only you could make that story seem remotely funny." Max chuckles.

"It's a gift." I wink. "What can you do if you can't laugh?"

"Seriously, I want to know where that woman hides her horns and her tail." He shakes his head. "Damn! That was just evil."

"She just wants there to be an answer," I defend. Why? I have no idea.

Max moves from his chair to squat in front of the exam table. "It's not your fault there's no answer." His eyes plead with mine for acceptance of his words. I can't.

"She just wants what's best for Lily." I drop my gaze to the speckled floor tiles.

"So do you," Max returns. I know what he's waiting for me to say, so he can vehemently disagree. He wants to set me straight, free me from the confines of my guilt. After listening to Alex talk about his son, I want to be. Free.

"She needs someone to blame," I whisper. There it is. She needs someone to blame, and no one has stopped her from aiming at me. When I came out of the bathroom that day, Peter was outside with Lily. He never acknowledged the pain his mother caused me. Geri never mentioned our conversation again. She didn't have to; I knew how she felt. How they both did.

Max's hands lift my face, bringing us eye to eye. "It's not your fault." His gaze ensnares me with its stormy, sea-glass insistence. In the depths of my soul, I know that Lily's disability is not my fault. It wasn't the stroke, but part of me will always be angry that my body betrayed me. As a woman, I'm built to grow life in my womb. When I was finally able to conceive without miscarrying, I almost died in childbirth. For the longest time I felt no greater failure than that of my pregnancy. I didn't know if I'd ever get over it; I'm still learning.

That self-loathing used to make sense to me, but now I think it just makes me sound like a delusional moron. Clinging to this false sense of censure didn't make it any clearer. It only made me a martyr.

A martyr complex? Jesus, Caroline, you're so much smarter than this. Get over yourself.

Then who am I, if I'm not a scapegoat? I have no idea, and I will never know if I don't let myself move on. I've cleaved to my pain for too long, insisting it was a buoy keeping me afloat. Really, I've been drowning the whole time. Swimming with the fishes. Me, Jimmy Hoffa, and every other poor soul anchored to the sea floor by their concrete shoes. The only difference is, nobody's going to come looking for a person who's spent the last five years shutting everyone out. It's up to me to save myself. To do that, I have to be willing to let go.

It's not your fault.

A culmination of words from Alex and Max churn a funnel cloud in my mind. It swirls and spins wildly across the archives of my shame, lifting it from its confines to scatter like ashes.

The paper sheet shifts underneath me as I lean into the refuge of Max's chest. He wraps me in a bear hug, sighing heavily.

"I wish you'd believe me," he laments.

"I do," I answer. The steady rise and fall of his breath ceases beneath my cheek.

"For real?" His voice jumps an octave with his surprise. My heart joins the ascent, growing lighter with each beat of acceptance.

"It's not my fault." There's no hallelujah choir, the sky didn't open and shine forth the light of heaven, but for the first time, I believe it. It's not my fault.

bend and break

I used to be an optimist. I could look at any situation and find a silver lining, regardless of how dire the situation. The first year Peter and I were married, a nasty storm split the Bradford pear tree in our front yard. Unfortunately, my Jeep was parked in the line of fire. I loved that car; she was my baby. Instead of lamenting my tremendous misfortune, I focused on the branches of the tree pressed against the front window. Just another foot and those branches would've been parked on the living room couch with me.

It can always be worse—or at least I used to think so. Maybe that's what has my attention right now: the presence of my long-absent optimism, or perhaps its cautiously optimistic cousin. Regardless, the gentle pull of hope is as foreign feeling as the air cast on my right wrist. Both are exceptionally cumbersome, but oddly comforting.

"You have a hairline fracture of the distal radius, Caroline," the orthopedic surgeon explains. "It's a clean break and should heal nicely, as long as you take care of it in the next four to six weeks."

The last few years have desensitized me to news like this. Between developmental disabilities and seizure disorders, a broken arm is easy. Listening and absorbing the details of how to care for my broken wrist, I am consumed with only one thought: *Thank God it's already my bum hand.* Not that I would ever wish to break anything else, but if I had to break something, at least it's not my dominant hand.

Don't call it a comeback. LL Cool J raps a loop in my brain as Dr. Haren goes over my discharge papers and a prescription for pain. I smile and nod, thinking I'll never fill that script. There's no way I would ever take something that could limit my ability to get up with Lily in the night. She barely sleeps for six hours, if she stays asleep. Most nights I'm up at least once to guide a sleepwalking Lily back to bed.

Once the good doctor has gone through his spiel, Max and I gather my papers and head out. He holds the door open for me, and as I walk by he plucks the prescription out of my hand.

"Hey!" I reflexively grasp at the paper.

"I'm taking this to the pharmacy to make sure it gets filled," Max says. "You've got that look like you're considering Motrin and an ice pack for that break." The steep arch of his eyebrow dares me to argue.

"You got me." I shrug. "I'm not being stubborn, I promise. I just can't take those and care for Lily. She's not a sound sleeper, and those will knock me out cold."

"Then maybe Peter should keep Lily," Max casually suggests. It wouldn't be an issue if it were that simple.

"It's not that easy, Max," I defend myself. "Lily has her routine, and after what happened today, she deserves to reap the comfort it brings her. Changing things up will likely cause another tantrum—and we need that like we need a hole in the head."

"So Peter is just going to go back to his apartment and let you wing it?" I hear the irritation in Max's tone.

"I don't know what Peter's going to do. You've been here with me this whole time; when have I had the chance to fill him in? What I do know is Lily's looking forward to seeing her aunt Paige tonight, because that's what I've prepared her for. She will be thrilled to be going home, because she's comforted by what she knows. Peter's place is too new for her to know. Her going there would be a disaster." I explain the best I can, but no one really understands until they've seen Lily go off the deep end.

"Can Paige spend the night with you?" Max asks.

"No, she flies out to meet a client early tomorrow."

"Can Peter stay at the house on the couch or something?" Poor Max; sometimes there's no easy answer. Besides, this isn't my first rodeo.

"*No*, he can't," I say with more force than I mean. "I'm sorry. I know you're trying to help, but it's complicated, okay? Peter can't stay at the house. It won't be fair to Lily when he leaves again." It won't be fair to me, either, but I don't say that. I've just started to grow accustomed to my life without him; I don't want to fall back into bad habits. I don't want to be lulled back into complacency because it's familiar and comfortable. So are old shoes, but that doesn't mean they don't stink.

We round the corner into the elevator bay, where Max presses the call button. "Then I'll stay with you," he offers, leaning against the wall and folding his arms.

"Max, you're not staying with me," I argue. I cross my good arm over my sling, and we stare each other down. Pride coils tightly, like a diamondback ready to strike.

"Why is it so hard for you to accept help?" He sighs in frustration.

His exasperation deflates me. Why am I being such a hard-ass? It's not like I *can* do it on my own. I do need someone with me; Lily's needs are physically taxing.

"I'm sorry. I'm just used to going it alone. I don't mean to sound ungrateful," I say.

"Then don't be, and accept my help," Max replies.

"Ouch." I laugh nervously. "I guess I deserve that. Thank you for helping." Saved by the bell—the elevator doors open and I step inside.

Max holds the door open and gives me a Cheshire Cat grin. "Have some faith, Carolina." He shakes his head. "The three of us will have fun, I promise." He takes a step back and waves as the doors close between us. "Text me when you're leaving the EMU!"

There's no way I'm texting him when we leave the EMU.

mercy

The doorbell rings in perfect unison with Lily's bolt for freedom. My butt hits the floor with a resounding *umph* as I lose my one-armed grip on my wet and squirmy child.

"Lily, wait!" I plead, as I watch her bare bottom disappear around the corner. The only thing covering her is the hooded end of her towel. Terry-cloth pig ears perch proudly on top of her freshly scrubbed head, while the rest flows behind her like a giant pink cape.

"Ah ah ah!" she shrieks as her footfalls trail off down the stairs. The telltale jingle of the chain on our front door sends me scrambling to my feet, cursing myself for not having engaged the deadbolt. I fly down three steps at a time, racing to make it before she takes off outside.

"Lily, no!" I yell. "No nakey outside."

Whoever's at the door, they're getting the brunt of Lily's full frontal right about now. Turning the corner, I'm grateful to find that Lily has attempted to drape herself in her towel. She's giggling up at Max, who's smiling at her from the doorway. She flaps her hands and turns her mischievous smile on me. I've come to accept the hand flapping and toe walking as a part of Lily's personality, not her disability. An occupational therapist gave me several sensory explanations, but learning to see it as a part of Lily and not just a therapy goal brought me closer to my daughter. She hand-flaps when she's really excited, not just when she's looking for sensory input. She toe-walks when she's agitated, not just when she's being tactile defensive. Don't get me wrong; therapists have helped Lily tremendously. However, they're appointments that we work into our life, not a life lived inside of them.

"Maxy bring pizza, Mama." Lily beams. Max gives one of the pig ears a gentle tug as he greets my girl, but shoots me the hairy eyeball through his periphery.

Ruh-roh.

"Hey, Max," I say with canned excitement. He ignores me to close and bolt the front door. I watch in fascination and envy as he shifts his duffel bag on his shoulder, grabs Lily's hand, and balances two steaming boxes of Joey's Pizza in the other. Grace like his is the seventh world wonder to those of us lacking it.

"Sweet Caroline," he drawls out with sarcasm. I shift nervously on balls of my feet. He regards me with a mixture of amusement and annoyance. I swallow hard and aim for a convincing smile.

"Neil Diamond?" I force a laugh. Clearly I didn't think my plan through very well, and now the consequence is walking toward me, scowling.

"Don't you Neil Diamond me." He shakes his head, exasperated. "You're fired." He brushes past me on his way to the kitchen with Lily in tow.

I trail behind them, caught in the aromatic wake of garlic and oregano. My stomach starts to sing the hallelujah chorus.

"Max," I start.

"Uh-uh," he cuts me off. "You were going to call when you were released. Why didn't you call me?" He slides the pizza boxes onto the counter and drops his bag on the floor. I open my mouth to reply, but nothing comes out. I'm struck dumb. Max doesn't wait for me to formulate my excuse.

"Lily Love, why don't you show me where your jammies are?" He squats in front of her, swaddling her where the towel's come loose. "You're going to catch a cold, Ms. Thang."

"Ah! Ah! Ah!" she bellows and is off again, running through the house like a bat out of hell. I prefer Lily's hand flaps to her loud chanting. It's just another way she expresses her excitement, but I miss her broken sentences. After all, Lily didn't speak clearly until she was four and a half. I waited a long time to hear her thoughts out loud.

Max follows the pink blur up the stairs without looking back. It makes my heart sink to know he's upset with me.

"Max," I call after him, and when he stops to look over his shoulder, I'm met with wariness. "I'm sorry. It was thoughtless and inconsiderate. I'm a jerk." With a small smile, he nods and continues after Lily. His lack of response hurts just as much as if he'd called me a jerk himself. I'm blessed every day to have a friend like Max, and I'm a fool for being callous with his feelings.

Way to go, Caroline.

I take Max's bag to the guest room and grab paper plates from the pantry. It's not enough to calm my nerves. I wipe invisible spots off the refrigerator door, wash my hands, pace around the island, anything to keep my mind occupied and off my stupidity.

Push. Push. Push. I'm a pusher. Well, not really a pusher, more like an enabler of emotional warfare. I test people, poking and nudging them until they're at a comfortable distance, and then lament my own loneliness. Who would actually subject themselves to that kind of mind-fuckery? Oh, that's right. Me.

"Mama! Mama!" Lily chants, as her feet pound mercilessly down the stairs. "Pizza!"

I busy myself with trying to cut Lily's slice in half with my good hand. Max follows Lily into the kitchen, but I continue my hack job on the helpless pie. I can't look at him. I'm terrified that I've ruined his lovely gesture. No one has ever been so generous with their time except Paige, but she's biologically obligated to.

lily love

"Can I help?" I jump at the sound of Max's voice. My knife hits the countertop, spraying red sauce across the backsplash. "Chill your antics, Lizzie Borden." He chuckles and takes the knife and the massacred pizza from me. "In half or in pieces?" My mouth opens and closes, but I remain soundless. "Lily, half or pieces?" he asks her, as he shakes his head at me.

"I'ma eat it all." She nods confidently. "I like pizza. Mama messy." That shakes me out of my trance. Eat it all and then throw it all up, maybe. Baby girl doesn't have the gift of self-regulation.

Apparently Mama doesn't have the gift of neatness. I look like a crime scene. Sauce has splattered like blood across the front of my shirt, all the way into my hair.

"Half, please," I manage. "Otherwise, she shovels too much, too fast and makes herself sick." I lift the lid on the second box, and my eyes fill with tears immediately. "You must not be unforgivably pissed; you brought me taco pizza."

I sniff. I love taco pizza, but Peter and Lily hate it, so I never get it. For all the random things Max and I have talked about, I never would've guessed he'd remember my favorite pizza. My heart swells against my ribs, filling me with something I haven't felt in a long time. I feel known.

"Not unforgivably pissed," he murmurs, as he carefully arranges Lily's plate. When he deems his masterpiece acceptable, he brushes his hands across the front of his jeans and shoots me a warm smile that sets my heart at ease.

"Wow, if get Joey's taco pizza when I'm difficult, I wonder what you would've brought me if I'd been more acquiescent." I force a laugh and take Lily's plate from Max and set it in front of her. I feel woefully undeserving of the care Max has taken. It falls so far outside my comfort zone, I don't know how to react. I would've thought by now he'd have grown tired of my defiance.

"Joey's taco pizza," he replies.

"What?" Surprise raises my voice to a pitchy squeak.

"Ever the Same—sung by Rob Thomas," he sighs. "Good, bad, ornery, or acquiescent. You'll get your favorite—taco pizza. It's not contingent on anything."

"Why?" I ask. "Why bother? I'm such a pain in the ass."

"Yes, you are." I meet Max's barks of laughter with my evil eye. "You are a challenging woman, Caroline, but you're worth it."

If it were a physical possibility, my heart would burst free from my chest, roll across the kitchen floor, and pause at Max's feet. The air in my lungs catches on the swell of emotion building in my throat, leaving me speechless. Max lifts his head from the pizza box when I don't answer. How do I explain? What can I possibly say that won't make me sound as pathetic as I feel? All I can think is how different things might be if Peter hadn't stopped feeling that way about me.

"Caroline." Max's warm hands cradle my face before I can blink the first wave of tears back. "Why don't you see what I see? How can you doubt yourself so much?" He rubs the pads of his thumbs through the wet tracks of my tears. My body shudders as I sob. Gently, Max cradles me against his chest, tucking me beneath his chin. In the sanctity of his embrace, I weep for the place in my soul that wanted to be enough for Peter to fight for.

"I wasn't worth it to Peter," I cry. "Why wasn't I worth it to him?"

"He's a fool," Max says. "He lost sight of what was important." My shoulders shake against his chest as his words pour over me. "You are a gift, Caroline, and Peter is an idiot for forgetting that."

"We both did," I whimper. "I lost sight of everything. I only saw Lily, and ended up chasing him away."

"We all bear fault at the end of a relationship. Everyone makes mistakes, but you only want to look at what *you* did wrong."

I roll my eyes at Max's declaration. His body stills, like he can sense my rejection. I peel my face from the warmth of his chest and peek at him through my wet lashes. Sea-glass eyes bore into my soul, permeating the walls of my defenses, stripping my pain bare. I shiver from being naked and vulnerable in his relentless stare.

lily love

"It's what you are, Carolina. You're a gift to all the people around you. When you walk into a room, you bring warmth right along with you. When you smile, it lights people up from the inside out. You're sunshine. Absolutely magnificent, and it breaks my heart that you can't see that in yourself."

Pain is such a personal thing. I wear mine like a cloak of protection, keeping people at bay. Max just casually removes it from my shoulders and drops it to the ground. If that weren't intimidating enough, he lays it out like a picnic blanket, waiting for me to have a seat and join him.

"I haven't been very sunny lately." I laugh weakly. Resting my head against his chest, I save myself from his gaze. "I'm scared, Max. If I start to believe that I'm all you say I am, it will destroy me when I end up with no one to share myself with. No one's going to want to take on a divorcée with a disabled child. Who would ever love me?"

My cheek bounces softly against Max's chest as his laughter reverberates through me. I push off him, freeing myself from his orbital pull. I shoot him the stink-eye.

"Sweet Caroline." He chuckles. "You say 'love' like it's a choice. You just need to decide whether there's someone out there worth loving back."

"How do you have so much faith in me, Max?" I stare at him in awe.

"I told you, 'Caroline I See You.'" In one fluid movement, Max closes the distance between us and pecks me on the forehead. He takes the plate I've been clutching and fills it with pizza like it's the most natural thing in the world.

We sit on either side of Lily, listening to her endless chatter. Every once in a while I meet Max's eyes across the top of Lily's head. I have no idea what I did to deserve such a beautiful soul as this friend.

We eat every slice of taco pizza, and I listen while Max regales me with his latest musical finds. His eyes light up with a kind of passion I envy. I used to get that feeling when a great manuscript would come across my desk. I miss it; I miss that fire. When we're done, Lily escorts Max to the couch to snuggle in for *The Good Night Show*.

"Hey." I turn my head toward the whispered hush of Max's voice. He's cradling a sleeping Lily in his arms. "I'm going to go put her down. Is there anything I should do first?" I shake my head no and lead him up the stairs to Lily's room. I watch him tenderly place my baby girl in her bed and tuck the covers in around her.

"Thank you for being here, Max." I sigh. The weight of the day pulls heavily on my eyelids, and I try my best to stifle a yawn as we head back downstairs.

"You're welcome." He smiles at me. "Come sit with me for a bit," he encourages as he guides us to the living room. I let him direct me to the couch, too tired to argue. "When was the last time you plopped on this couch and just vegged out?"

"Hmm . . . Too long to remember." He grabs the remote and turns on *Talk Soup*. My eyes begin to drift during the reality TV clips, and my mind wanders to Tate. I'm consumed by the giddy warmth of his dimpled smile when I feel the world fall out from underneath me. My eyes shoot open to find Max lowering me onto my bed.

"Oh good, you woke up," he quips. "I thought you were out cold there for a minute. You might want to change your shirt. You're still covered in sauce." He chuckles.

I rub my eyes, fighting to get my bearings. I tuck a loose strand of hair behind my ear and feel the crusty remains of rogue pizza guts.

"Oh, gross," I mutter. Just my luck, a hot guy carries me à la Scarlett O'Hara to my bedroom and I'm caked with food splatter. Max tips his chin at me at walks backward toward the door.

"I'll let you get to it." He pats the doorframe on his way out. "Good night, Caroline."

"Good night, Max." He pauses in the doorway and turns his head my way one last time.

"Tomorrow maybe you'll tell me who Tate is." He laughs as my face flames with embarrassment. "You sounded pretty fond of him in your sleep." With that last little jab, he closes the door behind him.

Crap.

I peel my clothes off and run a steaming bath. I throw some lavender bath salts in for good measure. If I have to bathe like this to keep my cast dry, I might as well make it worth my while. Besides, what do I care if Max asks about Tate? It's not a big deal, even if I was hoping to keep him to myself for a while.

My stranger, I sigh. *I wonder how you are tonight.*

friend like you

Morning light dances across my face, making me blink in confusion. I haven't risen after the sun since before Lily's birth. She is a dawn chaser; no matter how early or late she falls asleep, she wakes between five thirty and six o'clock in the morning. When her muffled laughter drifts through the closed door, I bolt upright, wincing when I put pressure on my broken wrist. Ignoring the throb, I scramble out of bed and into the living room. The TV is playing *Sesame Street*, and wouldn't you know it, Kermit the Frog is interviewing Big Bird. The couch is empty, so I continue to follow the sound of her giggles to the kitchen.

Max is leaning over the back of Lily's chair, helping her cut up pancakes. Lily bounces in her seat, giddy with anticipation, and Max is smiling down at her like she's hung the moon.

"Good morning." I yawn. Max and Lily look up in unison. Max stands up straight, revealing the apron he's tied on. The snort that erupts from me is far from ladylike, but I can't help it. Staring back at me is the Dirty Santa gift that Paige gave me last Christmas. In fancy scroll lettering, "I Kiss Better Than I Cook" is displayed proudly across his chest.

"Nice apron." I giggle.

lily love

Max levels his green eyes at me, and points an accusing finger. "Hey, it's yours." He shakes his head and looks down to assess his attire. He brushes his hands across the front as his deep, throaty laugh meets my ears.

I ignore the goose bumps insisting their way up my arms at the sight and sound of this beautiful man in my kitchen. I've been numb for so long, my attraction to him is surprising and scary. Max would never hurt me; I know this. I trust him implicitly, but I don't trust myself. I'm fairly keen on screwing things up. The last thing I want to do is screw up our friendship.

"Paige gave that to me last year for Christmas." I laugh. "She's a brat."

In these moments, I could kill Paige. Wrap my hands around her cute little neck and wring it. Damn her! I'm already awkward and flushed with long-dormant hormones. I'll combust if I have to discuss kisses with Max.

"I don't buy it." Max shrugs his shoulders and continues to cut Lily's pancakes into perfect bite-size pieces. I flatten my hand across the butterflies in my stomach. I can't help it; watching him fuss over my daughter melts my heart.

"No, really, she did," I try to say nonchalantly. "She's always doing stuff like that to get a rise out of me." With his hands still on Lily's plate, Max's eyes lift to mine. They're dancing with mischief, sending the fluttering butterflies into a fury. A smile spreads across his face at my nonchalance fail.

"You are so adorable." Max laughs as he hands Lily her fork and walks the knife to the sink. He turns back to face me, leaning against the countertop and crossing his feet at the ankles. It's not fair; he's the picture of relaxation, while my anxiety is about to levitate me off the ground.

"Don't mock me." I pout. I feel like stomping my foot on the floor and marching out of the kitchen. It's vastly apparent that I can't regulate myself around Max, and it's way too early in the morning for this kind of tête-à-tête. I'm comfortable with the friendship boundaries.

Max makes me feel safe and known and lovable. Yet, out of nowhere, he can give me a look or say something swoonworthy that has me questioning his feelings and mine. I haven't even had a cup of coffee yet. That needs to be remedied immediately, so I march across the kitchen and grab a coffee cup from the cabinet. Max says nothing, but I can feel him watching me from his perch at the sink.

"Mama, Mama, Mama," Lily calls as she shakes her head and drops a syrupy fork on the table. On a sigh, I abandon my mug and squat in front of her. She looks at me intently, like she hasn't seen me for days. Wrapping a lock of my hair around her finger, she leans in and places her forehead against mine. "Mama." She sighs.

"You need your sprinkles, Lily Love," I croon to her as I kiss her nose and stand. Her morning meds will ease some of the anxiety she's kicking off. If only I had some grown-up sprinkles of my own.

"I gave them to her right before you came in." Max's voice comes from behind me. When I turn around, he hands me my filled mug.

"Thank you," I mutter, and smile sheepishly over the steam rising from my cup. Max nods and gives me a bashful smile. He takes a breath in to say something, but hesitates and rubs his hand across the back of his neck.

"I'm not used to seeing you this way," he finally says. My cheeks heat, as it occurs to me that I bypassed my robe in my hurry to find Lily. I look down at my camisole and boxer shorts and shake my head. Why can't I be one of those girls who sleeps in flirty little pajama sets and wakes up effortlessly beautiful? No, not me. I wake up with sheet marks and crazy hair.

"What, you don't like my Life is Good boxers?"

He drops his head and chuckles softly. Alarms scream inside my head, warning me that I'm teetering on a line I don't want to cross. As tempting as Max is, he's not rebound material. I love him; he's turned out to be a wonderful friend. If I lost him, I'd never forgive my carelessness.

Like he can hear the siren wailing in my head, his eyes lock with mine. There's a palpable mix of tension and hesitation in the air. I swallow audibly, and scramble to find the words to tell Max what he means to me.

"I love your boxers," he whispers, "and I love being here with you and Lily."

My heart catches in my throat at his confession. I can't imagine anyone enjoying the predawn madness of our morning routine, but Max's wistful tone makes it seem like a beautiful daydream. I catch a hint of sadness in his eyes before he veils the emotion from me.

"It's a nice thought, isn't it?" He shrugs, like it's any other passing thought, but the faint smile playing at the corner of his mouth suggests it's more than that.

"Max," I start, "I don't know what to say." I'm uncharacteristically still. My feet are cemented to their spot on the kitchen floor, as I stare dumbstruck. "You're so special to me," I struggle to find the right words.

"Don't, Caroline," Max interrupts. "I'm not on a fishing expedition. I'm not asking you for anything. I just need you to know how wonderful you are. Any man would be lucky to have you and Lily. I want you to understand your worth; you sell yourself so short." He steps toward me, taking my coffee and placing it on the table. Tentatively, he runs a hand from my shoulder to my good hand, holding it gently in the warmth of his own. A tear rolls down my cheek, splashing onto our linked hands. "You're a prize. I wish you'd see yourself that way." He cups my face with his free hand, preventing me from turning away.

I see awe, longing, and resignation reflected back, and it floors me. It's been a long time since anyone's looked at me that way.

"You can't say things like that to me," I say. "I adore you, and it confuses me. You're my friend, and when you talk about me like that, it's so hard not to fall for you." I recoil at my candor, embarrassed that I would profess my heart to the first man to call me "wonderful."

"Your friendship is a bright spot in my life. I don't want to jeopardize that, either," Max promises, as he sweeps a teardrop from my cheek. "What kind of friend would I be if I didn't try to show you how I see you?" Careful of my sling, he hugs me to his chest, and breathes heavily against the top of my head. "Sweet Caroline, someday you'll get how great you are. Until then, get used to me reminding you. Got it?"

"Got it." I've got it all right. What I did to deserve it is beyond my understanding. I squeeze Max one final time before I let him go.

"Now," he says. "Who's Tate?" He smiles, but it isn't very convincing.

"I don't know what you're talking about," I tease, trying to lighten his mood.

"It's okay, Caroline, you don't have to tell me." He sidles up next to me at the sink, taking the plate I've been rinsing and loading it into the dishwasher. "But I want you to feel like you can. I'm still your friend."

"I know you are," I say, as I bump my hip against his. We stand side by side, washing and rinsing while I think. "It's just, I don't know how to explain who Tate is. I'm not really sure of that myself." I don't want things to be weird between us, and the last thing I want is for Max to think I'm hesitant to talk to him about anything.

"Well, why don't you start with how you met?" Max suggests.

Once I tell Max about how Tate brought my coffee to me, the rest of the story practically tells itself. It's easy to recall the details of our encounters, since it's been hard not to think about them all the time. Still, for as simple as it is to remember, it's more difficult to figure my feelings out.

"The guy from the coffee cart? Huh," Max says as he dries his hands.

"Huh, what?" I ask. Max spins in his spot, leaning back against the sink.

"Nothing." He shrugs. "It's just that any guy who remembers your coffee order the next day is interested in more than how you take your latte."

I blush. I can't help it; part of me is really excited that Tate's interested. The other part is still coming to terms with losing Peter.

"You think? I don't know," I reply. "I mean, I'm attracted to him, but I'm just not there yet, you know? My plate is so full, but I find myself thinking about him a lot."

"Well, what do you know about him? Is he married?"

"He didn't have a ring on," I answer. That's just another bullet point on the list of things I don't know about Tate. Maybe that's why I dreamed about him, just a way for my brain to fill in the numerous blanks.

"Fair enough." Max nods. "Why don't you take it a day at a time? Get to know him; be his friend. Don't beat yourself up for being curious; just be careful."

"Well, when you put it like that, it sounds easy." I sigh. My phone chirps from where it's being charged on the countertop. Instinctively, I assume it's Peter. I do a double take when I look at the screen.

Tate: Good Morning, Sunshine. Watching reruns of SOA . . . couldn't help but think of you. Coffee? :)

I can't stop the blush or the accompanying smile from spreading across my face. *It's barely eight in the morning; I wonder if he woke up thinking about me.* It's thoughts like these that make me hesitant to reply. I don't need to be thinking about anyone that way right now.

"Is everything okay?" Max asks.

"Everything's fine," I say, but I'm not very confident it is. "Tate was just wondering if I wanted to grab a cup of coffee. He probably assumes I'm still at the hospital."

"Coffee in the hospital cafeteria is pretty benign, Caroline," he says. "Why don't I take Lily to occupational therapy, and you go see your friend."

He says it like it's no big deal. I suppose it only is if I make it that way. Max is right: coffee is friendly. Just a cup of joe between buddies.

Oh, good Lord, who am I kidding?

"Wait, how do you know what Lily's schedule is this morning?" I ask, because I don't remember telling him. Did I?

"It's on the fridge." He points to the calendar on the freezer door, color-coded with all of Lily's appointments. "Quit trying to think of an excuse and just go. It's coffee, not a commitment, right?" He's right. I'm overthinking things.

"You're right," I concede. "Are you sure you're okay with taking Lily?" It's completely foreign, albeit nice, to trust someone's help with Lily.

"It's no problem, I promise," he says, as he crosses his heart. "We can meet up in the pediatric therapy clinic afterward." He lets out a heavy sigh as the corners of his lips turn up. "Sunshine, huh? I'm already liking this guy."

Me: Good Morning to you, too! Meet you in 45?

"I know, Max, me too," I reply. "That's what scares me."

distance

It's a short drive to the hospital, not enough time for me to talk myself out of going, and definitely not enough time for me to relax. My stomach is in knots and my shoulders brush the tips of my earlobes. I'm a total basket case. All I can think about is how quickly Tate is going to politely excuse himself and make a run for it. How could I blame him? The events of the last twenty-four hours are a lot for me to digest, and I'm a seasoned pro. Tate is in the middle of his own drama; the last thing he needs is me with mine. Despite the perfect package that Max makes us out to be, Lily and I are a complicated pair, and one does not exist without the other. Good, bad, or ugly, we're a team.

Air stutters into my lungs as I park my car. A foreboding sadness crashes over me, surprising me. I really like Tate, and the thought of missing out on the chance to know him better fills me with melancholy.

Nothing ventured, nothing gained, I tell myself one more time as I adjust my sling and wipe my clammy hand on the front of my dress. Through the fog of my lamenting, I can't quiet the part of me that is elated at the prospect of seeing him again.

Lord have mercy, you're a masochist, Caroline!

That's the last thought to cross the plain of my troubled mind before the hospital doors swing open. Without conscious effort, my feet carry me down the hall to the cafeteria.

There is a group of chattering nurses blocking my view into the seating area. When they pause to stand in line at the coffee cart, there he is. The sight makes me smile; he's waiting in the booth where we first met, with two cups of coffee arranged across the table from each other. His back is to me, so I take an uninterrupted moment to memorize him. His broad shoulders stretch his T-shirt across his sinewy form. His dark hair is disheveled in a way that tells me he's been running his fingers through it a lot this morning. My stranger is stressed. Guilt washes over me as I wish for a way to conceal my injury. I'd like nothing more than to offer my comfort without the complications of my life interfering.

I watch as he removes the lid from the cup in front of him. He leans in, blowing at the steam rising from inside. After a moment, he dips his pinky finger and yanks it back out, muttering a curse under his breath. I stifle a laugh at his familiar and endearing trait.

God, I hope he doesn't bolt.

I fight the urge to brush my hand along his shoulder. The simplicity of that gesture would be a paradox to the intimacy it would convey. The last thing I need is to foster any kind of tenderness with someone who's likely to flee.

"Is it okay if I sit here and not talk to you for a while?" I ask.

Tate glances over his shoulder and smiles when he sees me. His face is covered with scruff, but his dimples still greet me with their boyish charm. Before I can take my place across from him, he stands and wraps me in a tender hug. I tuck my sling carefully between us, and hold him with my other.

"Caroline," he whispers on a sigh, "you're a sight for sore eyes."

His breath ruffles the hair on the top of my head. Even with my arm between us, I fit perfectly in his embrace. He holds me against

lily love

him, and I absorb the feel and smell of him. Committing each one to my memory, I tuck them away for safekeeping after he's gone.

He tips his head back, letting his arms encircle me at the waist. "What in the world happened to you?"

Tentatively, I step back and slide into the booth, nodding for him to join me. Now that I can see his face clearly, there are shadows beneath his eyes, and it pulls at my heart.

"Never mind me," I say. "What's going on? You look like you've been up all night."

"I have been," he confirms. "It's my mom. She's who I'm here for. She has glioblastoma, brain cancer. She had surgery last week to remove the tumor, but they couldn't get it all." His explanation comes in staccato-burst phrases.

My chest constricts against his words, filling me with sorrow. I scoot out of my seat and join him on his side. My hand automatically seeks to stroke his shoulder. His head falls forward on a heavy sigh, and we fall into companionable silence while Tate collects his thoughts.

"What happened last night?" I ask.

"When the doctors told me and Tarryn that Mom's cancer was terminal, her oncologist said it could be anywhere from six months to a year. In the meantime they told us she was a good candidate for the rehabilitation center on the fourth floor. We were going to move her there today." He shakes his head, trying to process everything, and failing. "In the middle of the night, she had a grand mal seizure."

My hand stills its soothing. "Oh no."

"She stopped breathing. I've never been so damn scared in my life." His voice quavers as he fights to control his emotions. "Once she was stabilized, they ran some more scans and the fucking tumor is already growing again. It's spreading like a spiderweb in her brain. There's no way for them to treat it."

"Tate, I'm so sorry." My heart is broken for him, and I'm helpless to hide the tears pooling in my eyes. My poor stranger.

"We were supposed to be moving her to rehab." He sniffs. "Instead, I'm trying to find her a bed in hospice . . . I thought I had more time." He lifts his red-rimmed eyes to mine, pulling at my heart. There is nothing I can do to fix this for him. I can't take away his pain. I know how it feels to be helpless inside a situation you have no control over, but nothing like this.

"I'm sorry," he murmurs. "I was planning on buying you a cup of coffee and charming you with my wit, not crying on your shoulder."

"I'm glad I'm here. You have nothing to be sorry for." I blink back the tears and try giving him my best reassuring smile.

Tate sits up and grabs a napkin to wipe his face. He stops for a moment, then reaches for the cup across the table from us. "Skinny vanilla latte." He grins sheepishly.

I take the cup from him and turn it in my hands. My stomach is in knots, and the last thing I want is coffee sloshing around in there.

"Is there something I can do?" I ask. "Make some calls for you? Anything?" Let there be something I can do to ease his burden. I can't sit back and do nothing.

"Nah." He shakes his head. "Calls are all made. Now I just have to wait to see who calls back with an available bed." He heaves a heavy sigh before turning his attention to my sling. "You gonna tell me what happened?"

"It's a hairline fracture," I say. "It's not a big deal; I'll be fine." I pray he sees fit to drop it. My run-in with Lily's fabulously hard head seems so minor in comparison to what he's dealing with.

"Humor me," he pleads. "I could really use the distraction."

I'm practically vibrating with nerves. I don't want to tell him about Lily's episode in the EMU. His day has been crappy enough without me adding my drama to it. I don't even know if I trust him with me, let alone whether he'll ever get close enough for me to trust him with Lily. Talking to him about Lily wouldn't be on my radar at all if it weren't for my wrist. It shouldn't matter to me yet—it's just coffee—but I can't stand the thought of him thinking ill of Lily.

Seeming to sense my stress, Tate flips my hand over, palm up, and places his in mine. "Is it all right if I hold your hand?" It's a rhetorical question. He doesn't wait before he threads his fingers through mine.

I wait for panic to set in, but the warmth radiating from his palm calms my nerves. It's beginning to dawn on me that, regardless of the chaos in our lives, we're drawn to each other. Who knows why. I'd like to think that people are placed in our lives to shake things up, to remind us that we're still living beings inside the bedlam of this world. I don't want think about whether Tate will embrace or reject my daughter; I just want to trust that it will all work out. It would be nice to have faith instead of fear. Maybe that is what Tate and I are meant to be to one another: hope.

I start from the beginning, explaining to Tate the necessity and the ordeal of gluing electrodes to Lily's head. When I get to the part where Chelsea bypassed every conceivable de-escalation technique, Tate squeezes my hand tight. Until now I've avoided looking him in the eye, too afraid of seeing fear—or, worse yet, pity. When I lift my eyes to his, they're burning with frustration and concern.

"By the time I got back to the room, Lily was inconsolable," I say. Tate and I are in our own little bubble as I retell the story with his gaze fixed on mine. With every word I speak, I see the story projected back to me through his eyes. It's breathtaking and humbling. "She started to bang her head against the bed. I couldn't stand it. I couldn't bear to watch her hurt herself like that, so I moved my hand to block her." I pinch my eyes closed as I relive that moment in my mind.

I startle when Tate lets go of my hand. The pain of that separation hurts worse than I imagined it could. I curse myself for allowing flowery philosophy to lead me to think we were connected. He's leaving, just as I feared he would, and I don't blame him one bit.

Gentle pressure on my cast breaks me free of my self-deprecation. Tate carefully lifts my arm to his chest and cradles it there.

In this moment, any hope I could keep Tate at a comfortable distance is vanquished. Emotion pulls deep from my belly, swelling my throat and choking me with tears. I tilt my head up, fighting to keep them contained, absolutely refusing to allow them to spill.

"Caroline." My whispered name across his lips is my undoing. The current of my emotion streams down my face, and I want to hide my weakness from the tenderness he's showing me. "Don't cry. You're so brave, so fearless. Lily is so lucky to have you."

Tate's words only make me cry harder. I was so convinced he would bail, and I couldn't have been more wrong. In my current state of blubbering, I'm confused but thrilled that I was.

"We're a pair, aren't we?" I sniffle. "'Laughter through tears is my favorite emotion.'"

"*Steel Magnolias,*" he responds without hesitation.

"Just when I thought I couldn't possibly like you more," I joke. I'm rewarded with a flash of dimple that spreads a smile across my face.

"I like you, too, Caroline." A blush spreads beneath his stubble.

"We're a mess, you know." My warning is a tease, but there is a seriousness that belies my meaning.

"A beautiful mess, though," he returns. "And all because you let me sit down and not talk to you for a while."

I turn my head to keep him from catching me smile. I'm teetering on a very perilous ledge here. There's nothing casual or friendly about the way I'm feeling right now, but I have far more at stake than just a broken heart. I have a daughter whose needs come first, and I need to protect her more than I need to indulge in my chemistry with Tate.

Still, the last time I was so singularly focused on Lily, I lost Peter. If I learned anything from that, I learned the necessity of balance, but I don't know how to get that.

a beautiful mess

Tate and I sit holding hands for a long time. In the quiet, I begin to sort through the finer details of what "just coffee" has meant this morning. Tate's mother is dying, and I'm at a complete loss for words. My brain just can't fathom what it must feel like to get news like that. For reasons I may never know, he's holding *my* hand. If he feels just a fraction of the peace I feel when I'm with him, then he can hold on as long as he wants. One part of me wills him to tell me everything; another just craves the quiet.

"She raised Tarryn and me on her own," Tate finally says. "Twins with no help from our father. She never complained, and she never made it seem like too much." He stares absently across the cafeteria as he talks. While the current of his memory carries him along, he stays tethered to the present by holding on to me. "I was a rotten teenager. Somewhere around fifteen, I decided *she* was the reason my father was gone. It hurt her; I know it did. I wish I could go back and slap that ornery kid."

"It's 'cause you got all 'em teeth and no toothbrush." I smirk. I'm not going to let him beat himself up, not when there are *Waterboy* movie references to distract him with. There is enough pain without all of the self-hate. We can't go back and change what's done. We can only move ahead with the lessons we learn from our mistakes.

"Medulla oblongata," Tate deadpans. "You're good." He nods his head.

"I don't know your mom, but I'm just starting to know you, and what I've seen would make any mom proud." I nudge Tate with my shoulder until he looks at me. "You're good people. I have a sense about these things."

"Got me figured out, huh?"

"I just recognize a lot of myself in you. When Lily got her first diagnosis, I wasted precious time beating myself up over things I couldn't change. It was pointless and did nothing but rob me of the energy I needed to face what was happening. I don't want to see you do that to yourself."

Before he can respond, Tate's phone rings from his pocket. When he answers, a flood of relief washes over his features. Someone must have a bed available for his mom. I fish around in my purse for a pen and something to write on. I come up with one of Lily's crayons and an old receipt. I place them in front of Tate, and he mouths his gratitude in earnest. I wait while he jots down his notes in Purple Mountains' Majesty crayon. If the subject matter weren't so dire, it would be absolutely adorable. Perhaps this is a prelude to what's ahead—finding the sweetness in our collective dysfunction.

He hangs up the phone and runs his hand through his hair. "St. Joseph's Hospice Center can take her tomorrow morning." He sighs in relief. "I need to go let her doctor know what's going on."

"I need to go meet Lily at her occupational therapy appointment. My friend Max is bringing her for me." I'm sad that we can't avoid reality for a little longer. Secretly, I'm afraid that leaving the sanctity of our little bubble will render it obsolete, like a wonderful dream you can't quite remember but know is there. I don't want this to be a onetime thing that gets relegated to the periphery of my mind. I don't want to let go.

"You know, Peter has Lily tonight," I start hesitantly. "Why don't I bring you some dinner later?" I hold my breath, waiting for Tate to decline my offer.

"I have a better idea. Why don't you let me buy you a burger at Giff's?" he suggests, taking me by surprise. "Tarryn is coming in for a while tonight, and I could use the break." A break being relative. Giff's is the greasy spoon across the street from the hospital. It's far enough to get a change of scenery, but not so far that you couldn't get back in a hurry.

"Mmm . . . Giff's burgers," I practically moan. "You've got a deal. Does six o'clock work for you?" I stand and fix my sling while I wait for an answer. I feel guilty for not feeling guilty about having dinner with a handsome man whose life has just been knocked off its axis.

Oh, get over it, Caroline. You can be a supportive friend without being a fucking succubus.

A set of warm hands rests on my shoulders, interrupting me from arguing with myself. I turn to find Tate standing behind me, regarding me with an affectionate smile.

"Quit overthinking." He arches a knowing eyebrow at me. He's good; I'll give him that.

"You've got me figured out, huh?" I grin.

He flashes his dimpled smile as he uses my words to make his point: "I just see a lot of myself in you. I'm going to focus on the good fortune I have for getting to share a meal with a beautiful girl, and forget about the rest of life for an hour or so." He tentatively places his hand on my back and leads us both to the exit.

"Touché," I say. I can't overthink anything with him touching me. I can't think at all, and it's wonderful and scary and oddly natural, considering. I want to lean into his chest, but I don't. Call me nuts, but I think it's a good idea to slow down this crazy train.

"Quit it," he whispers.

"What?" I feign ignorance. A quick peek through my peripheral vision tells me he's not biting. His brow is arched to his hairline. Damn. "I can't help it! This warrants just a bit of thought."

"True. It's a big decision." He considers for a moment. "How can anyone choose, really?"

I stare at him blankly. "Huh?"

"Fries or rings . . . the question to end all questions." He chuckles.

"Nice dodge," I mumble through my own laughter. All too soon, we're at the elevator bay that will take Tate back to the seventh floor and to his new reality.

"I will see you at six, right?" He dips his head down to meet my gaze. I know he's wondering whether I'll talk myself out of showing up.

"Absolutely," I promise. "I'll look forward to it all day." The smile that spreads across his face almost hides the dark circles under his eyes, or maybe I'm just too dazzled by the dimples to notice. Whatever the case, I can't deny the satisfaction I take in knowing I put that smile there.

He wraps me in the warmth of his embrace, careful not to squish my sling. I step close to his body and tuck the top of my head beneath his chin. This is quickly becoming my new favorite place, and it scares the crap out of me. I give him a good squeeze before letting him go, hoping he doesn't notice how I bury my nose in his shirt. I take a deep breath, taking in the scent of him. It's a mixture of coffee and crisp linen. I step back, but his scent clings to my senses.

"I'll look forward to it, too." He tips his head to the side, trying to hide the blush creeping into his cheeks. The elevator dings all too soon to take him away. "See you later?"

I nod my head as the doors close, because I can't say yes. The truth is, I don't know what I'm going to do.

always remember me

My feet scurry down the hallway as I rush to the pediatric therapy clinic. There are twenty minutes left in Lily's OT session, and if I make a run for it, I'll have about eighteen of those minutes to fill Max in. I round the last corner of my sprint and nearly run head-on into a doctor.

"Excuse me, sorry," I say, and attempt to sidestep him. He steps in the same direction and then again when we try a second time. It's an awkward waltz until I stand still and let him move around me. It figures; even in the most urgent situations, for me, calamity rules. I'm muttering a quiet curse under my breath when I enter the waiting room.

Max sits with his ankle propped on his knee and his nose in the latest edition of *Fit Pregnancy* magazine. The other moms in the room are all pretending to be indifferent to his presence; it's comical. His head pops up, and he smiles broadly when he sees me approaching. This makes the other mamas seethe . . . indifferent, my ass.

"Sweet Caroline," he greets me and pats the seat next to him. "How'd it go with your stranger?" He closes the magazine and turns sideways to face me.

"You," I murmur low enough that the ears around us can't hear. "You and your 'it's coffee, not commitment,' but you know what? It's still a big 'I-like-you-let's-do-burgers-and-oh-by-the-way-my-mom's-dying' mess!"

"Whoa," he replies, "back up." He furrows his brow as he tries to find the sense in what I've said. I regale him with the story of Tate's mother's cancer, and how he broke down in the cafeteria. Max listens intently as I tell him about how I held Tate's hand and let him cry on my shoulder, how we talked about Lily and what happened to my hand, and finally how we were meeting for dinner at six.

"Can't you see?" I plead with him. "We're flirting with this affection we have for each other around these huge events in our lives. Am I nuts? I feel a little crazy." With a heavy sigh I slouch back in my seat, mentally exhausted. I don't know if I'm making sense to anyone else, but it makes sense to me. Later on, I don't want Tate to be reminded of the worst time in his life when he thinks about me. It makes me cringe to think about what he'd say when someone asked him how he met me. "Great story! I met her when I found out my mother was dying." Fail.

"I hear you," Max reassures me, "and I feel you. However, you can't predict what may or may not happen. You can only control how you react moving forward. If you feel like you need to draw a line, then draw it. If Tate's the man he sounds like, then he'll respect that. You have to decide what you're comfortable with, and go from there. Talk to him tonight. Tell him how you feel."

"What if I'm overreacting?" I lament. "What if I read him wrong and he doesn't feel the same way? I'll make an ass of myself." I mean, it is pretty presumptuous to waltz into Giff's and suggest that we tone down the attraction we have to each other, when neither of us has copped to it.

Max sighs in frustration. "You aren't getting it, girl. I spent five seconds with the dude and could see how much he's into you. You aren't assuming anything; you're setting the pace, and there's nothing wrong with that." He gives me a mischievous smile and starts to hum the song "Falling Slowly."

"You're such a girl," I tease. He responds by adding words and volume to his serenade. "Shh," I snicker, as the moms around us perk up and start staring. He leans his head back and belts out the chorus with gusto. I bury my face in my hands and start laughing. That's how Lily and her OT find us, laughing like a couple of lunatics with the rest of the waiting room watching curiously.

"Mama, Maxy, Mama, Maxy," Lily croons. The change in her chant surprises me. Her speech therapist smiles in surprise as well. I know she chants for the people who mean the most to her, and it makes my heart swell to hear Max included. Her therapist marvels at the consonant combination of short A and long E. It's not lost on Max either; I notice the way his face softens when she says his name. She's got him wound tight around her pinky finger.

"Lily Love," Max answers. Lily launches herself into his arms and peppers his cheek with kisses.

"My Maxy," she declares, and rests her head on his shoulder. I swear there is a collective sigh among the moms. Max is oblivious; he's all wrapped up in my girl.

"Your Maxy has to go to work, Lily Pad," I explain. "You and I are going to meet up with Daddy."

"You gonna be okay?" Max asks as he places Lily back on her feet.

"Oh yeah, I'm good," I say. "It's his night with her. She's getting used to his new place. No worries." When Peter first left, our Lily exchanges gutted me. It would take me the entire course of Lily's absence to recover. Now they're so routine, there is barely any discomfort. I suppose that has a lot to do with the fact that I'm beginning to fill my free time with things other than mourning the loss of what I thought would be my life. New friends, a renewed interest in writing; I'm learning to bend with the changes, not break, and it feels hopeful.

"Call me after dinner," Max calls out as we walk away. I look over my shoulder and stick my tongue out at him in defiance.

"Yeah, I wouldn't want that thing in my mouth either," he teases. In choreographed unison, every mouth in the waiting room drops. My face blushes scarlet.

"Wha . . . I . . . pshh . . . " I stammer through meaningless gibberish as Max walks past us, laughing hysterically.

"I crack myself up." He snickers on his way out. "Call me." He's gone before I can collect myself enough for a comeback.

"Who was that?" Lily's OT asks. I forgot she was standing there. I'm so scattered, I've been completely ignoring her.

"That's my friend Max," I reply. She lets out a slow whistle.

"Some friend you got there, Ms. Hunter." She stares at the door wistfully, perhaps willing him to return.

"Indeed." I smirk at her reaction to him; it's commonplace with the ladies. "The best kind of friend there is."

That is the God's honest truth. He is the best friend I've ever had.

• • •

Peter's car is parked in the driveway when we arrive at the house. I wait for the sting of nostalgia to rear its head, but time has proven effective in wearing down its sharp edges. To say I'm relieved sounds cold, but I am relieved for the progress marked by the absence of longing. It was not my intention for the future not to include Peter. But whether or not it's intended, all that is left of our connection is our daughter.

When I pull into the garage, Peter appears in the doorway. All the talk of where to draw lines has me inspired to go over some things with Peter. First order of business: this is not his home anymore. I think it would be best to assert some boundaries that include taking back the key to the house. I don't want it to be an argument, but it seems like there's been some wavering on where each of us stands lately. I don't want to invite any more confusion into my life. At the end of the day, we're still a family. It's best to be one on good speaking terms and not one fraught with angst and bitterness.

lily love

"Hey," he greets me as I step out of the car. "How'd it go?" He opens the back door to release Lily from her booster seat. She clings to him like a little monkey, covering his face with kisses. Seeing her with him is a good reminder why we will do well to be careful with each other: Lily.

"It went well; we're getting by. Learning to let our friends help out," I say. I leave Max out of the equation to prevent another argument about it. Peter knows that he stayed over to help with Lily. He wasn't thrilled about it, and he happily let me know exactly what he thought, but he understood why it couldn't be him.

Lily hops out of the car and looks back and forth between Peter and me. I wonder what's going on in that beautiful head of hers. Is she confused to see us together in some moments and apart in others? Does she understand?

"Maxy make pan-a-cakes," Lily proclaims proudly. Peter scowls. Ass.

"Yes, he did, Lily Pad," I affirm for her.

It would be nice if Peter could think of her and not his pettiness right now. It irritates me when Lily tries to engage him in her way and he's too self-involved to notice. It's funny how details like that don't make themselves known until you see things from another perspective. Max had no problem meeting Lily on her level and enjoying her. I didn't notice Peter's unwillingness to do that until now. It's always about her coming to him, and that's just not fair.

"You could at least acknowledge her, Peter. How is she going to understand reciprocal conversation if we don't teach her how to use it?"

Peter ignores my comment and escorts Lily into the house. It's not my job to smooth things over between him and Lily anymore. I give myself a mental reminder and resist the urge to intervene further. He's going to have to learn how to talk to his daughter without me there to facilitate. It's my fault as much as it is his. I was overbearing and controlling where Lily was concerned. He didn't do much because I didn't let him. He didn't argue, but clearly that didn't make either of us happy. Why is it that these things only become apparent in hindsight?

So we aren't destined to repeat our mistakes. I know this, but it irritates me how masochistic the whole thing is: you've got to screw up royally in order to learn how not to. I follow them into the house and freeze when I see Peter rummaging through the fridge.

"Don't you have a Coke or something?" he asks as he looks.

"No," I answer. "You were the Coke drinker. I don't buy pop for me or Lily." I fold my arms over my chest and wait while he closes the door.

"Well, that sucks," he states matter-of-factly. "Maybe you could keep a couple in here for when I come over."

Breathe, Caroline. 1 . . . 2 . . . 3 . . .

"Peter, you don't live here anymore. I'm not going to keep drinks here for you." I fight the urge to add, "You stupid ass." Hello? Is anyone home? We're in the process of divorcing here, not setting up camp in each other's space.

"No, I guess that wouldn't make sense." He sighs.

"Ah, ah, ah," Lily yells. She's making a play for our attention; I know this is derived from anxiety, and guilt punches me in the gut. She doesn't need to be an audience to our conversation. I take for granted that she doesn't understand as much as other children her age. However, she is keenly aware of people's feelings, and is very sensitive to them. She has to be picking up on the tension. Shame on me for forgetting that.

"It's okay, Lily Pad." I squat in front of her and take her hand. "Why don't you go get your bunny and a couple of books to take to Daddy's?"

Lily leans in and touches her nose to mine, gently sweeping back and forth. "Ugga-mugga," she murmurs.

"Ugga-mugga, baby," I reply, as she disappears upstairs to fetch her things.

"What does that mean?" Peter asks.

I'm not going to get irritated.
I'm not going to get irritated.

Okay, I'm flipping irritated!

"It's from *Daniel Tiger's Neighborhood*," I answer. Peter stares at me blankly. "Her favorite TV show? C'mon, Peter, you aren't that disconnected. It's how Daniel's parents say, 'I love you.'" I look at him in disbelief when he shows no sign of recognition at all. "You should watch with her and get caught up."

"I don't spend as much time with her as you do, Caro," he defends. "I can't know everything."

"Are you serious?" I snap. His audacity has me seeing red. "Knowing your kid's favorite TV show, that's too much for you?" I look over my shoulder to see if Lily is coming back. At this point, I just really want him gone. "Do yourself a solid and take some time to get to know your daughter, without using me as an excuse not to."

Peter flinches like I've slapped him. "I'm sorry. I didn't mean for it to sound like I blamed you," he says. "Everything is so different now; it's just a lot to get used to."

"I know it is," I agree. "It's a lot for us, but even more for Lily. She can't take a backseat to any of our problems; in fact we need to amp it up and make sure she feels as safe and secure as possible. A big part of that is helping her feel understood." I try not to sound condescending, but it's hard when I feel like I shouldn't have to be saying any of this in the first place.

"You're right." He nods. It's my turn to stare blankly. This is way out of character; it's never this easy. "I've been self-absorbed and insensitive to both of your needs."

Warning bells go off in my head, the moment "both of your needs" leaves Peter's lips. I eye him suspiciously.

Where in the world did that come from?

"You don't need to worry about me, Peter. It's Lily's needs that we both need to focus on." I hope that redirecting him back to Lily will inspire him to get back on track. Whatever he may perceive as my needs can't possibly measure up to what they actually are. We haven't been in tune with each other like that in more years than I can count.

"Don't be like that, Caroline," he insists. "I get it now. Lily's tantrum, you breaking your wrist—it was the wake-up call I needed. I was premature to leave; I should've stayed and fought harder."

His pleading catches me completely off guard. It's just like him to change his mind and expect me to jump right on board with whatever he has in mind. It makes me so mad I snap in my frustration.

"It's not like you left last week. You moved out months ago, Peter. Our divorce papers are drawn up, for chrissakes! It's a little too late for you to have a change of heart."

"It's not too late to go back, Caro," he argues, and steps toward me.

I step away. There isn't an argument he can present that would make me want to return to a relationship that made us both so unhappy. Realizing that has been one of the hardest things I've ever done. In the end, it came down to happiness, not love. The antithesis of what we're conditioned to believe—all you need is love. It was a rude and painful awakening to discover that fraud. There was never a loss of my love for Peter, just my ability to make him happy.

"I don't want to go back, Peter," I admit, and my heart aches as I watch his face fall. It's the first time I've been able to say that and mean it. It's painful, realizing that you're ready to leave someone you loved so much in the past. More than anything, I feel resigned. It's time for me to let go. "What we were before didn't work. I don't want to go through that again." Seeing him hurt is so hard, and I don't want to cause him more pain. I just want him to understand that we need to focus on the future, and moving forward.

"What happened to us?" he murmurs. I don't know if he means it to be rhetorical, but I offer up my insight anyway.

"Sometimes love just ends." My voice breaks. I've said the same to Max, but admitting it to Peter hurts so much deeper. "It's not always somebody's fault; it's just the way it is. I don't know why ours ended, but it did, and now we have to move on." It's the sad truth, and knowing that makes it hard to stake any faith in love. If it doesn't last, then what's the point?

Peter leaves the kitchen to go help Lily collect her things. He doesn't look at me, and he doesn't say anything else after that. I don't want to hurt him; I just don't want to be stuck in this holding pattern of grief anymore. When they're ready to leave, I kiss Lily's cheek and walk them to the front door.

"I will never forget what was good between us, and I don't ever want to." Peter's words stop me in my tracks.

"I don't want to either, Peter," I answer, "but it's gone."

"I know," he whispers, and turns his face from my view. "It doesn't mean that I'll ever stop missing it, though." When he looks at me again, his eyes shine with unshed tears. The resignation in them conveys the pain of letting go. "Bye, Caroline." He's spoken those words a million times over the least thirteen years, but this time there is a finality.

"Goodbye, Peter."

Acceptance is part of growth, but damn if it doesn't hurt like hell.

off we go

I watch Peter's taillights disappear around the corner, while his words churn through my head. I don't ever want to forget the good parts of our life together, and I don't want to wallow in the bad. Sometimes I get caught up in romanticizing a life that no longer worked for me, and doing so only serves to sabotage the future. I don't want to be destined to repeat the mistakes of my past. I want to learn from them and grow, so I can do better the next time around.

It makes me think of Tate, and all the chaos surrounding us. Despite all of it, something about us just clicks.

Mick Jagger's muffled voice flows from my pocket, interrupting my Tate-dream. I don't need to look at my phone to know who's calling.

"Paigey," I say cheerfully. "When are you coming home?" Ever since our adventure at the Ale House, I've been craving more time with my sister. The years of hiding inside Lily's issues damaged more than just my relationship with Peter; I pushed Paige away, too. I didn't realize just how much I missed her company until I spent some quality time in her presence. I'm so grateful she doesn't hold it against me.

"I'm home," she sings. "I know Peter's got our girl, so I'm coming over to take you out." My heart stutters with anticipation and fear. This was not the way I was planning on telling her about Tate, but I don't want to lie about why I can't go out with her.

"I can't do it tonight," I say.

"What do you mean? You're not in your sweats with a gallon of rocky road, are you?" She thinks I'm wallowing in self-pity. Ha!

"No, I'm not. I have plans tonight. That's all." Silence on the other end of the line. "Paige?"

"'That's all,' she says," Paige grumbles. "Are you going to tell me what's going on or do I need to beat it out of you?"

I smile at her frustration; I'd rather she be annoyed with me than hurt. The last thing I want is for her to think I'm blowing her off.

"I'm meeting a friend for dinner," I offer. It's a decent start, and it's certainly true enough.

"You have a date and you didn't tell me?" she yells. Way to jump right in there, Paige.

"No, it's not a date. It's dinner."

"Is he paying?"

"Technically he said, 'Let me buy you a burger at Giff's.'"

"It's a date."

"Paige!"

"Who's the lucky guy? Please tell me it's Max, so I can have vicarious sex with the Adonis."

"PAIGE!"

"So . . ." She waits impatiently.

"Buttons on your underwear," I retort. I need a minute to collect my thoughts; I'm still choking on her Max comment.

"That's it, I'm calling Mom."

"Don't you dare," I howl. All I need is another lecture on the sanctity of marriage and how no one in our family has ever been divorced. Worse yet, she'll offer to come over and babysit. The last time that happened, I ended up taking care of both of them.

"C'mon, Caroline," she whines, "don't make me beg."

"OK," I concede. *Just take a deep breath, girl.* "Do you remember the stranger from the cafeteria?"

"Mr. Dimples?" She sounds intrigued, which makes it easier to spill the rest of the details.

"Yes." I laugh. "His name is Tate." I tell her the very brief, slightly quirky, and remarkably sweet story of Tate and me. I make sure to take my time, sharing every detail as it comes to mind. When I'm through, she's quiet on the other end. It steals some of the wind from my sails. I know the doubts are coming.

"So, he's never been married?" she asks.

"I don't know," I admit. "I only know he isn't married now." Her question strikes a chord. I feel a little foolish for not knowing. I mean, his relationship status is an important factor in all of this.

"His mom's got cancer, huh?" I recognize her concerned-mama tone. Something has got her worried. I brace myself for the impact of whatever she may say. "Do you really think this is the best time to be starting something with this guy?"

She's right. I know she is, and yet I can't seem to stay away. How do I explain it without sounding like a pamphlet for codependency?

"I hear you, Paige, I do," I assure her. "I can't describe it. He just draws me in. He reminds me much of myself, and I want to be his friend during this time. I'm also attracted to him; I can't help it. He's adorable and funny and smart and he gets me . . ." I trail off at the end, feeling silly for carrying on. Afraid that I failed to make my point.

"I just don't want you to get hurt, Caroline." Paige's voice is thick with concern. "He sounds absolutely wonderful. I just want you to be careful with your heart."

"I love you for worrying about me, but I plan on taking it very slowly," I promise. "I don't want to invite any more heartache into my life. You can count on that."

"I know you don't, sweetie." She sighs. "Sometimes heartache finds us despite our intentions. I'm worried that this slightly damaged—albeit wonderful—guy is an invitation to hurt."

"You're right." I can't argue with her logic, and I know that she's only looking out for me. "But, Paige, I would rather risk a broken heart than a lifetime of wondering what would've happened if I'd gone and had that burger."

"Well, shit," she harrumphs, "how am I supposed to argue with that?"

"I love you, Paigey."

"I love you, too, Caroline. All I ever want for you is the best; I hope you know that."

"I do, Sis. I promise."

I don't know if it's like this with all sisters, but there's something innate and unspoken about the bond Paige and I share. I don't need her to justify anything she's said. Without her ever telling me, I know how she feels, and I know, above all else, that she wants to see me find happiness. She is more than just my sister; she's the cheese to my macaroni, the yin to my yang, my soul sister, and I couldn't imagine my life without her.

"You'd better call me the second you leave Giff's," she warns.

"Of course, I wouldn't dare leave you hanging."

entwined

No . . . *no . . . no . . .*
I'm tempted to call Paige back and beg for advice.
Forget it, girl. You can do this on your own.

I stare at the heap of clothes piled on my bed, and a wave of self-doubt crashes over me. There are sundresses, skirts, and countless tops with varying sleeve lengths. Nothing that I'm satisfied will be appropriate for dinner, nothing that feels right. I don't need to make a fashion statement; I just want to feel like me. My recent runway style has consisted of little other than yoga pants and hoodies. Don't get me wrong; I *love* yoga pants. They're a closet staple for every woman I know. They shouldn't, however, be the only type of pants you own. Given the sheer number decorating my bed, I need to heed my own advice. Guilty as charged. On a hefty groan of frustration, I fall face-first into Mount Mom Wear and consider letting it suffocate me.

Pipe down, drama queen. Less whine. More thinking.

This is all so new to me. I'm not used to considering myself in the equation, let alone mulling over my own personal style. Do I even have one? Not really. Just my generic mom-iform of cotton knit workout clothes. The irony is, I don't exercise in them. Chasing Lily and managing her schedule has successfully sucked my energy dry. Good Lord, I feel pathetic.

The clock mocks me: *5:15 and you're still in your panties.* Stupid clock. It's time to break up the pity party and get real. I just need to pick something that feels like me. It can't be that hard, but who am I exactly?

You are Caroline Hunter, snarky, sarcastic goofball.

Yes, I am. Not *just* that, but it's a fair summation of my personality. I know I've got something in this mess that can reflect that. I roll off the summit of loungewear and head back into the closet. Sometimes simplicity is the best, and what I have in mind is simple and very "me." I grab my best pair of jeans and my favorite graphic T-shirt. It reflects my love of music and my sense of humor. It has the cover artwork for AC/DC's *Highway to Hell* album but instead reads, "ADHD: Highway to Distraction." I feel the Cheshire Cat grin spread mischievously across my face. Feeling a lot like the person I used to be, I grab my Chuck Taylors for good measure. With a final spin in the mirror, I'm set to go.

Welcome back, Caroline.

• • •

I pull into Giff's with a few minutes to spare. I feel good about the choice I've made and find myself anxious to see what Tate thinks. Thinking of him brings on a reflexive sigh. Oh God. I'm like a swooning teenage girl.

You know what? Screw it. It feels good, so I'm going with it.

Stepping into the diner is like stepping into a time capsule. Dion and the Belmonts are playing on the jukebox, and a black-and-white checkered floor leads into a dining room filled with red vinyl booths and a long lunch counter. Wiping down the freckled laminate countertop is a waitress in a pink button-down retro uniform and an even more retro beehive hairdo. She lifts her head to smile, revealing *Francine* embroidered on her apron.

"Anywhere you want, doll," she says and sweeps her hand in a wide arc, encompassing all of the diner. It's just her and the short-order cook in the back, but they run this place with military precision. She snaps her gum and gives me a wink, continuing to shine the counter.

"Actually, I'm meeting a friend," I reply. My initial confidence wavers when a quick sweep of the dining room comes up Tate-less. My heartbeat drums loud in my ears as embarrassment replaces my excitement.

"Is this your fella?" Francine points over my shoulder; when I turn around Tate is jogging up the steps. It's impossible for me to prevent a smile from spreading across my face. He barely slows his momentum as he swings the door open and rushes inside.

"Hi," he pants. His smile gets me every single time. He's shaved, so his dimples have their full effect on me, making me smile in return. "I'm sorry I'm late. I had to make a pit stop." He hands me a bouquet of red carnations and Shasta daisies.

"You stopped for flowers?"

He dips his head and blushes. "I did my best with the gift-shop offerings," he says apologetically. It's so adorable I can't resist, so I lean in and kiss his cheek.

"They're perfect," I murmur. His blush deepens further, and so does my own. What we must look like. I peek over his shoulder to find Francine watching us with wistful reverence. Tate clears his throat, bringing my attention back to him.

"Shall we?" he asks, leading me to a booth tucked away in the back. I can't take my eyes off my flowers. I can't remember the last time someone bought them for me. Maybe when Lily was born? I don't know. There's no way for Tate to know this, but Shasta daisies are my favorite flower and red is my favorite color. Coincidence? I guess, if you believe in them. Divine intervention? Some things are too perfect to happen by accident. That's what is running through my head when I see the card tucked in among the blooms. I pull it free and let my eyes linger over his words.

YOU'RE ~~GET~~ SWELL

For Caroline: a completely unexpected, and perfectly timed, surprise.

Warmly, Tate

Perfectly timed? I'm afraid to ask what he was thinking when he wrote that. Timing is the thing that concerns me the most. I had planned on taking it slow and getting to know each other for a while—but then, he seems to already know me in many ways. Peter never brought me my favorite flowers. When he brought me flowers, he chose roses, because that's what he thought I should like. Tate isn't even aware of what he did, and he hit the nail on the head. It scares the crap out of me.

"You really think the timing is perfect?" I ask timidly. He arches an animated brow at me and opens his mouth to reply.

"What'll it be, Pinky Lee?" Like an apparition, Francine materializes at the table, whipping a pen out from behind her ear. I bite the inside of my lips to keep from laughing at the comedic timing.

Tate pauses to unleash his dazzling smile and holds up his index finger. "Hold that thought," he says to me, and turns his full attention to Francine. "We'll do two of the cheeseburger platters—one with fries and one with rings—and a vanilla milk shake. Two straws." He waits for me to nod my consent before he lets her go. "Thank you, Francine."

"Be right back, Jimmy Mack." She tucks her pen into her nest of hair and shimmies away, singing along to Martha and the Vandellas on the jukebox.

"She's a trip." Tate laughs. His eyes still sparkle with amusement when he returns his focus to me. "Timing?" He backtracks. "Yes, absolutely perfect timing, to answer your question. From the moment we met, you've been my bright spot in an otherwise dark time."

My breath hitches as his words hit me. I'm blown away by the confidence he has in his explanation. I don't know whether to be flattered or terrified. We've only known each other for a few days, after all. That should be setting off alarms in my brain, telling me to run screaming for the hills. Instead I find myself a bit envious of how sure he is. The only alarm I hear in my head is the one warning me not to be a coward.

"You should know, daisies are my favorite and red is my favorite color." I smile when his face lights up with pride. It feels like I'm stepping out on a high wire without a safety net. Adrenaline courses through my blood, flooding me with an insurmountable high, while the unforgiving ground beneath waits for me fall on my face.

"They just looked like you." He smirks, clearly pleased with himself. "I'm glad to know that I got it right." I don't know if it's possible to be both cocky and humble at the same time, but Tate is trying his best for both, and it makes me want to lean across the table and kiss the smug smile off his face.

"You have no idea," I say. My eyes home in on his mouth when he starts to chew his bottom lip thoughtfully. I squirm in my seat and swallow audibly.

"I don't want to scare you, Caroline." My eyes lift to his at the sound of my name. Pools of melted caramel beckon me with a sweetness I crave more than I can afford to admit. "I just can't stop thinking about you."

Oh, my sweet, forgotten libido, that is the most romantic thing anyone has ever said to me.

"Tate," I start to say, but I have no idea where to go with it. That's a lie. I want to say, "I can't stop thinking about you, either," but I have enough sense to know that diving in headfirst is a bad idea. That doesn't stop me from wanting to trace his dimples with my fingertips and taste his mouth . . .

"I'm not going to pervert our connection by misleading you about how you make me feel," he whispers, his eyes never leaving mine. Pervert? Nice choice of words. It doesn't matter how softly they're spoken; their impact is jarring. "I'm out of control, yet completely at ease with it when I'm around you. You make me feel alive, which blows my mind, because, Caroline . . ." He reaches across the table and lays his hand on top of mine. I tell myself to close my eyes, to break our connection, but I can't. "I didn't know I wasn't living, not until the day you left your latte at the coffee bar."

Gobsmacked. Stupefied. Astounded. Bewildered. Astonished . . .

I start to go through all the relevant adjectives I can think of to keep me from diving across the table into Tate's lap. I can't decide if he's brave or reckless. I'm overwhelmed with emotions and hormones, and that's not a good mix. Somebody's got to be the voice of reason here. I force myself to pull back my hand and turn away. I have the perfect opportunity when Francine returns with our food.

"Bottoms up, Buttercup." She winks at me, and then makes a point of pulling two straws out of her apron to stick in the milk shake. She smiles to herself as she retreats back to the kitchen, singing "Then He Kissed Me" by the Crystals. It's not even playing on the damn jukebox.

Not you, too. Betty Sue.

"Caroline, look at me, please," Tate pleads.

I'm not going to be a coward, but I'm not going to be an idiot, either. I unmask the myriad of feelings swimming in me and pray that when he looks at me he can see it all: fear, excitement, happiness, and terror. All of it battering my common sense, leaving me fragile and exposed. Our eyes meet again, and the rest disappears.

"You don't have to be afraid of me, because you hold all the power here," he says. "You call the shots; you decide on the pace. Whatever it takes to make you believe you're safe with me, because you are."

"Have you lost your mind?" I squeak, as all my bravery flees the scene and panic sets in. My skin feels tight, like I'm going to burst out of it at any moment. The pressure the sling is putting around my neck is unbearable. I jerk my arm over my head, relieving my neck from the constricting straps. Freeing my arm is another story, as the Velcro from the brace is hung up in the fabric. I want the damned thing off, and after one final yank, it sails across the table, hitting Tate in the chest. I feel caged, cornered by his feelings and mine. Their power is palpable between us; it makes my resolve crack with each moment that passes. Control is my only security, and I can feel it slipping through my fingers. It pisses me off. I blow a rogue hair out of my eyes and fight the urge to cry in frustration.

"Sanity is overrated," he answers. "You know, you're beautiful when you're flustered." So much for inspiring reason.

"Stop," I practically beg. "You can't just bulldoze me with all of your feelings and then expect me to know what to say. I can't think with you coming at me like this. It's not fair." A tear escapes down my cheek, and I watch shame cast itself over Tate's face.

"Don't cry, Caroline," he pleads. He moves swiftly, maneuvering out of his seat to slide in next to me. I tense at his close proximity and try to fight the overwhelming urge to lean into him. "I don't want to bulldoze you. I just need to know whether you feel this *thing* between us, too. I don't want to scare you away." He brushes his hand along my jawline, savoring my skin with his gentle touch. The hum of electricity that crackles between us sends a trail of goose bumps along my arms and legs.

"Why aren't you married?" I flatten myself against the far corner of the booth. The more space I can put between us, the more capable I'll be of asking my questions (or so I think). From this vantage point I see the hunger Tate is fighting against. His eyes dance back and forth between my lips and eyes. "Don't even think about kissing me until we clear some things up."

His lips turn up at the corners when he replies, "Then I guess there's no doubt about whether I get to, just when?" I flush a deep shade of crimson as my rebuttal is used against me.

"You . . . I . . . you, I mean . . ." I stutter and fail to defend myself. Tate's amusement only makes it harder for me to speak, so I'm grateful when he takes pity on me and moves on.

"I was in a relationship for eight years. We never married, but we were engaged for the last year. I ended it a few months before our wedding, because I realized that I was only doing what people expected me to do, after all the years we spent together. It wasn't what I wanted, though. She agreed with me, so we called off the wedding together.

That was four years ago." He leans in toward me, and I flatten my back against the wall. His smile widens as he asks, "What else do you want to know?"

"Why didn't you want to get married? Didn't you love her?" I settle into my seat, anticipating the story unfolding. My stomach calls out to the French fries in front of me; I pick at my plate while I wait for him to continue. Taking his cue from me, Tate pulls his plate across the table and grazes his food while he talks.

"Laura and I met while we were in college. We were friends for a few years first. We were both engineering students, we had the same hobbies, ran in the same circles. So, during our senior year, we decided the two of us made sense together and started dating. I loved her very much, but I think there are different kinds of love. I *wanted* to love her more than I did, and I guess that's why I proposed. After seven years, I thought taking the next step in our relationship would spawn something deeper between us." He sighs.

It makes sense. And it makes me feel better knowing that he was in a long relationship like that. I find that far more reassuring than if he'd been a serial dater, or commitment-phobic.

We sit in silence while we finish our burgers, giving me a chance to really think about what I want. Despite the overwhelming anxiety, I want Tate. It makes no sense. I don't know how to fit him into my life, or how I can fit into his, but it feels possible when we're together, which defies all logic. For all the mess we bring to the table, we click.

Every so often I catch him scooting closer to me in the booth. In turn, I find myself peeling away from the wall, drawn closer to him, too. Eventually we end up elbow-to-elbow, sharing our milk shake, soaking in everything that's transpired.

"So what ever happened to Laura?" I finally ask.

"She met someone else, got married, and ended up having a family of her own." He smiles at me, and I can see the genuine affection he has for her. He's happy for her, and that's part of what I've come to expect and like about him. "She had twins two years ago. A boy and a girl, just like me and Tarryn."

"So you guys are still close?" I hate sounding insecure, but I want to know what I'm getting into beforehand. I keep my eyes focused on my plate.

Please, please don't be carrying a torch for your married ex-girlfriend.

"You don't have anything to worry about, Caroline." He tucks my hair behind my ear, and I lean into his touch. "Laura and I were always better friends than anything else. I'm not in love with her."

His hand lingers on my neck, where my pulse is fluttering violently from his touch. How does he always know what I'm thinking? It makes me squirmy, which makes me want to crawl under the table.

"I don't have any right to be worried, Tate. You aren't mine." The last thing I want is for him to think that I'm the overzealous possessive type; I just want to understand their relationship.

He shakes his head and laughs softly at my statement. Fabulous, he thinks I'm a nutter.

"Oh, Caroline." He chuckles. "I was hooked the moment I walked into the courtyard and found you banging your head on the table. When we started talking, I felt this effortless connection to you. I can't explain it." I whip my head toward him to argue, but he places his finger on my lips. "I'd just gone a round with my mom's oncologist about her prognosis. I was looking for someplace to clear my head, when I saw you. You were my breath of fresh air. I forgot about cancer for the first time in weeks. I saw the beautiful woman I'd had coffee with, and I welcomed the distraction, but sitting with you that day breathed life back into me. So, before you argue with me, let me pontificate—I feel alive when I'm with you."

"Pontificate, huh?" I mumble from behind his finger. "That's some vocabulary you've got there, Michaels." You'd think he'd move his hand when I started speaking. Instead, he watches my mouth form words, and rubs his finger along my bottom lip. The way he's touching me is making me dizzy. I'm practically panting with wanting him.

"I learned from the best," he whispers. Tension coils tight in my belly when his breathing begins to parallel my own. I brush my hand along the path of his Adam's apple as he struggles to swallow. My fingertips vibrate against his skin when he speaks my name. "Caroline."

I press my lips against his finger, and I feel him tense with restraint. No longer capable of holding back, I move my hand around to the back of his neck and rub my nose along his jaw.

"Kiss me, Tate." His name barely escapes before his lips meet mine. My heart nearly explodes from the ferocity of emotion swirling between us; the heat alone will certainly set the table on fire. The silk of his hair threads through my fingertips as I close my eyes and let him kiss me. The warmth of his lips spreads like wildfire through my body. It makes me shiver, despite the heat radiating between us.

"Don't mind me." Tate and I leap apart at the intrusion. Francine hands Tate the check and arches an eyebrow at me. "You have fun, honey bun." This time she's singing Peggy Lee's "Fever" while Tate pulls out his wallet. I just got busted making out at Giff's; fun is not the word I'm thinking of. Mortified, maybe. Escape? Why, yes, thank you. That sounds *great*.

"Caroline," Tate calls as we walk into the parking lot. "Don't."

"Don't what?" I ask absently, searching my purse for my keys. He puts his hand on my shoulder to stop me and spins me around to face him.

"Don't run," he says.

I look at him and cringe. I see the fear in his expression and I feel terrible, because running is exactly what I want to do.

"Tate," I start, but lose track of what my point was going to be. "I don't know what to say."

"You were going to say that we shouldn't have kissed," he says. I won't contradict him with a lie.

"You scare me, Tate. I don't think rationally when I'm around you." I dip my head in defeat, but Tate cups my cheek, forcing me to look him in the eye.

"I feel the same way, Caroline, but I can't stay away." His eyes plead with me to understand, and I do, because neither can I.

I wrap my arms around his torso and nuzzle into his embrace.

"I don't want you to." I shock myself with the boldness of my response. I don't want him to stay away, and I don't want to either. I don't know what I'm doing, and I have no idea how it'll all play out. I just know that he's special, and he makes me feel things I didn't think I'd ever feel again. I can't explain it, I just feel it—he's worth the risk.

moondance

Tate and I stand in the parking lot holding each other for a long time. I don't know what the next step is, and I'm afraid of what letting go will mean. Do I go home? Does he go back to the hospital? It's not like we can pretend nothing happened, but I can't figure out where to go from here.

"Maybe we should find somewhere to talk," Tate suggests. "I'm not ready to let you go yet."

His admission goes a long way to relieve the anxiety churning in my gut. The last thing I want right now is to go home to an empty house and overanalyze our kiss to the point of madness. God, that kiss. I will never stop thinking about that kiss.

"Caroline?" Tate says. "Where did you drift off to?"

Recovering, I say, "Oh, I was just thinking about where we could go. I know a place, but it would be a short drive. Are you comfortable being away?" I ignore the stab of guilt I feel for trying to lure him away from the hospital. I tell myself it's not *too* selfish to want to milk every minute out of this evening. Who knows what tomorrow is going to be like? There is so much uncertainty ahead, it can't be wrong to want to savor this moment.

"I'm fine. Mom's in good hands with Tarryn." Tate punctuates his words by kissing the top of my head, making me feel cherished. It's not a feeling I'm accustomed to, and I like it. For the last five years I've been appreciated for the role I've played as a mother and a wife, but I haven't been cherished since before Lily was born. I don't even know if I can pinpoint the exact thing Tate's doing. I've been held in the arms of a man for thirteen years, but it's never felt like this.

Reluctantly, I let Tate go. The cool evening air fills the space between us, and I shiver. It's impossible to know if it's because of the chill or the overwhelming need to hold him again. He smiles down at me with an affinity that steals my breath. I don't know what I've done to inspire that kind of ardor, but I never want him to stop looking at me this way.

"Come on," I urge him, as I pull him toward my car. I laugh when he arches his eyebrow at me. "It'll be a surprise. Trust me." I unlock the doors. Tate pauses to scratch his head at my Prius. "What?" I challenge.

"I don't know." He shrugs. "I guess I was thinking you'd have a minivan or SUV."

"Do I strike you as a soccer mom?"

"Not even remotely," he answers as he climbs inside. I drop into the driver's seat, next to Tate. "You're so much more than that."

The words are simple, but the sincerity of them is what makes my heart flutter. He's known me for less than a week, and yet he sees me in a way that no one in my life ever has. It's the most unsettling feeling I've ever had. Still, I wouldn't trade it for anything.

To change the subject, I say, "One of my favorite places is just a few minutes up the road. You can't tease me, okay?"

All of a sudden, I feel self-conscious about my decision to share this spot with him. He's going to think I'm a sap, or a nerd. Both, probably. What's with all this impulsivity lately? It's not like me to make a knee-jerk reaction; I always think things through and plan carefully.

"I won't poke fun." He chuckles. "I promise."

lily love

The closer we get, the more nervous I become. Before I know it, we're turning into the gate of the Robert Waldron Jr. Botanical Garden. I find a place to park while I try to come up with an explanation of the garden at night without sounding like a nerd. I peek at Tate from my periphery and find him looking around with curiosity.

The smells of damp earth and fragrant blooms fill my senses as soon as I close the car door behind me. The familiar scent helps to ease my anxiety about making a fool of myself. It's only a big deal if I make it one, right? Right. So much easier said than done. Tate smiles at me from across the top of the car, waiting on a cue from me. Warmth emanates from his eyes, giving me the boost I need to meet him on the sidewalk and take hold of his hand.

"There is a moon garden in the center of the grounds. I come here when the weight of the world is too much and I need solace from the fray," I ramble nervously.

"Moon garden?" Tate asks as we walk along. I swear he can sense my nerves, because he starts to brush the back of my hand with his thumb. Back and forth. Ebb and flow. It stills the cacophony of my thoughts.

Cement gives way to mulch where the sidewalk ends and the garden's pathways begin. Fireflies light up the foliage with a whimsical glow as the path leads us through a canopy of weeping willows. Every step brings me closer to the peace of mind I always find here. The added tranquility of strolling hand in hand with Tate makes the anticipation even greater. He's either going to love this place or hate it. There's really no room for in-between.

"It's the only part of the gardens that blooms at night," I explain. "They bloom in response to the moonlight, so it's called a 'moon garden.' See?" I point ahead to a break in the trees, where the soft glow of the moon's luminescence casts down on a sea of moody white flowers and shimmering greenery. Tate's pace increases, and he grips my hand tighter. "I used to come here at night, after Lily's bedtime, and just think. It was the only time of day when there was actual silence. Being here has always helped me find peace."

I sigh, coming to a standstill where two dimly lit lanterns, hanging from shepherd's hooks, mark the entrance to the sacred space where I come to hide. I don't tell people about this place, because I don't want it polluted with the memories of others. It needed to be pure of the world I was hiding from. A space where the silence could swallow my cries, and where I could grieve in secret. Now I've brought Tate here, and I'm not even sure why.

"Beautiful," he whispers.

I turn my head and find him looking at me. I mean *really* watching me, like I'm something to behold. I feel drunk from his wonderment, completely incapable of turning away, as he pulls me deeper into his eyes. The moonlight and fireflies work their ethereal magic, blocking out each of the hindering doubts I've clung to, leaving nothing but Tate and me. Without a single concern for the consequences, I rise onto my tiptoes and kiss him softly.

"Caroline," he breathes against my mouth, sending electricity crackling down my spine. He returns my kiss with reverence, worshiping every part of my mouth with his. Warmth engulfs my body as I lean into his embrace. Tracing a path along my spine, his hand comes to rest in the small of my back. He holds me firmly against him, careful not to crush my arm between us. Every move, every touch is amplified by the enchanted dominion of the lunar blooms lit up by moonshine and fireflies.

I never gave much credit to those who talked about getting swept up in a kiss. It seemed irresponsible and dangerous to allow your baser urges take over without regard for the consequences. I've always thrived on being cautious and maintaining control—until now. Tate has complete power over me, stoking a yearning in me I never knew I had. Nothing matters to me in this moment except the way I feel in his arms. His mother's illness, Lily's diagnosis—all of it ceases to exist as I am consumed by his kiss.

When our lips finally part, he keeps me close by tucking my head under his chin. Just when I'm about to ask him what he's thinking, he utters the words that erase any doubt whether he feels the same way. "You make the rest of the world disappear."

I couldn't have said it better myself. The world is but a speck of light beneath us on this tightrope. Whether there's a net to catch me is no longer material. The fall is inevitable, and when it comes, I want to fall feeling just like this.

windmills

The hope taking root in my soul is dangerous. I know this, and yet here I am nuzzled up to Tate in the place most sacred to me. Somewhere deep in the coffers of my better judgment, my common sense is demanding an audience, and I couldn't care less. I've spent my entire adult life being responsible, fastidious, tame, and wholly monotonous.

You're about twenty years late for anarchy, sister. You're too old to start chasing windmills.

"'I know who I am, and who I may be, if I choose,'" I mutter to myself. Tate looks at me curiously, and it's only then I realize I've spoken out loud. The moon glows just bright enough to illuminate the recognition on Tate's face.

"Tilting at windmills?" he murmurs, cocking his head to the side. How does he do that? How does he always know what to say? It's the most unsettling thing I've ever felt.

I break free from Tate's arms and sit on the bench, burying my face in my hands. I feel too exposed, my heart too accessible for comfort. The seat bows with Tate's weight as he sits next to me. The soft chirping of crickets punctuates the silence building between us, but words just won't come. I feel foolish, but I find myself afraid to speak. Each time

lily love

I do, whether I intend to be heard or not, Tate burrows himself a little deeper under my skin. I thought *I* was the one who got to set the pace. It doesn't feel that way to me at all.

The bench creaks in protest when Tate shifts his weight toward me. "Where did you go?"

I know I'm not being fair, and Tate is patiently waiting for me to clue him in. My hesitation stems from this adverse fear of sharing too much, too soon. How can I explain without exposing more than I'm ready to?

"You surprised me," I finally offer. "I was not expecting you to know, let alone reference, *Don Quixote*." I stifle a giggle when he looks at me, shocked and slightly affronted. As quickly as anxiety had me by the throat, it slinks its way back to the shadows.

"I'll pretend not to be insulted by your flagrant lack of confidence in my notable quotables." He sniffs.

For just a brief moment I'm sickened to think I may have truly offended Tate. I steal a peek at him, and that's when I catch him smirking.

"You ass." I laugh, and playfully swat his arm.

"Gotcha." He chuckles, tilting his head toward the sky. He closes his eyes and draws in a deep breath. When he lets it out, he turns his face toward me and I'm struck by the vulnerability I see reflected back at me. His tone is filled with uncertainty when he speaks again. "I don't know what to do when you pull away like that. I'm scared, too, you know." He reaches for me.

"I'm sorry." I try to turn away, but Tate cups my face in his hand, gently turning me back toward his concerned gaze.

"I don't want you to be sorry," he says, shaking his head. "I want you to talk to me. If I do something wrong, if I say something that scares you, I just want the chance to fix it." His eyes pin me with their sincerity, and it sets my doubt free, flooding my thoughts and words in one big rush.

"You didn't do anything wrong, Tate," I promise him. "It's nothing that you can fix. I don't want you to be anything less than who you are.

153

It's just every time I show you a piece of myself, you show me your perfect mirror image of it. How can that be?" My voice soars up an octave as full-blown hysteria kicks in. "You can't possibly be real. There has to be something wrong with you. Good God, no one can be *that* perfect; it's unnatural. The only other man I've ever heard quote Miguel de Cervantes was my English professor my freshman year of college. He was older than dirt and had a face like Droopy Dog. He spoke, and drool would slide down the creases of his jowls and drip off the bottom of his chin. It was disgusting . . ." I'm aware that I'm rambling, but I can't seem to stop the stream of consciousness, now that it's exploded out of my brain.

"Hold on," Tate interjects. I freeze midsentence, with his hand still holding on to my face. I clamp my mouth shut and start to squirm in my seat, waiting for him to speak. "Did you just compare me to your ancient English prof who drooled and grossed you out?" When he says it like that, it really does sound terrible.

"I didn't mean that you were like him physically, just that you were similar in your literary references," I defend myself.

"So I don't physically remind you of Professor Spittleton, but my literary prowess brings him to mind? I fail to see how that's an improvement," he says, dropping his hands from my face.

I try so hard not to laugh, it ends up coming out as an undignified snort. The look on his face only makes me laugh harder; mixing with Tate's guffaws, we fill the garden with our merriment.

"I have the propensity to ramble," I say between snickers. "I didn't mean to sound like I was drawing a comparison. Honest."

"I love the way you ramble." Tate smiles. "It's adorable, and no one can make me laugh like you do."

"That's me," I say. "Calamity Caroline, comic relief."

"Captivating Caroline," Tate responds. "I don't see anything calamitous about you. A bewitching enigma, but never a calamity."

I stare at him, blank-faced for a moment, before the weight of what he's said settles in.

"A what?" I ask, amazed at his choice of words.

"An enigma." His lips pull up at one corner, giving him the look of a shy boy. "A mystery."

"I know what it means." I tilt my body, tucking my legs beneath me to face him. "I've always used that word to describe Lily."

He drapes his arm across the back of the bench, brushing my arm. "Do you think you're any less of a puzzle?"

"I don't know," I admit. "I haven't spent a lot of time thinking about myself at all, honestly."

His eyebrows pinch together in deep thought. It makes me crazy when he looks at me like that. It's impossible to know what he's thinking, only that he's churning out some interpretation of my craziness.

"The fact that you haven't is the biggest mystery of all." He tucks a strand of hair behind my ear and lets his fingertips brush my cheek.

"I'm not some puzzle you can solve, Tate." I look at him warily. Pedestals are for falling off of, and if he elevates me any higher I'm going to get a nosebleed.

"I don't want to," he responds without hesitation. "'Solving' implies there's a problem, and there isn't a thing I would change about you, Caroline."

I arch my brow slowly, pursing my lips in suspicion.

"Not one thing?" I challenge. My bullshit meter is measuring off the charts. I'm all for a genuine compliment, but I don't need sunshine blown up my ass just because it sounds good. No, thank you.

"Well, maybe one thing." He grins wide and mischievously. Jerk.

"Really?" My voice drips with sarcasm as I fold my arms.

Tate only smiles wider and closes the last of the gap between us. My breathing becomes erratic as our thighs brush against each other, but I fight to maintain my outward annoyance. He takes it all in stride as he leans closer.

"I would only change how much you doubt me," he whispers against my neck.

My eyes flutter closed at the feel of his breath across my skin. It soothes and stokes me at the same time, until I'm certain I'll combust from the tension. Just as I'm sure I can't take another second of his slow torture, he pulls back and levels me with the warm intensity of his eyes.

"Trust is something earned, Tate." I mean it to be a warning about his lofty expectations, but my voice is weak and uncertain. It comes off sounding like something I question more than I believe. His eyes hold me with the promise of their sincerity, and I want so badly to get lost in them, to trust that he's worthy of my faith. But I can't. Not yet.

"I will earn it, you can count on it." He smiles, completely unshaken by my caution. Dimples winking, eyes shining, he's irresistible.

Oh, man. I'm in so much trouble.

somewhere only we know

Somewhere between stolen moonlight kisses and secret garden promises, I find myself growing less guarded. My boundaries are becoming more pliant to the possibility that Tate is an exception to the rules by which I live and breathe. In particular, the one where I promised myself to take my time and not rush into anything. The more time I spend in his space, the more enthralled I become with the man he's showing me he is. I don't want our evening to end—but I know that the time is drawing near for me to take him back to the hospital.

There's no way to predict what tomorrow will bring with it; I only know that what's growing between us cannot take precedence over the realities we're facing. I have a daughter who needs me to advocate for her, and a divorce agreement that needs finalizing. Tate's mother has only a few months left to live. These are not circumstances that any kind of relationship flourishes under. The logical part of my brain knows this. Still, my heart yearns for Tate with a ferocity I can't ignore or deny. Nor do I want to.

"The next time we come out here, I need to bring my camera." Tate's voice pulls me back from my wandering thoughts. Leaning forward, with his elbows on his knees, he's studying one of my favorite flowers.

"I'm glad you like it here; I wasn't sure what you'd think." I smile as pleasure stains my cheeks. "Do you like photography?" I ask curiously.

"It's my passion," he murmurs as he studies the landscape of blooms. I can picture him here, squatting with his camera, adjusting the lens, framing his shot.

"Are you any good?" I tease, but somehow I already know he is.

"I hope so." He shrugs. "It would be a shame for the people who hired me if I sucked." A professional photographer, too. Mother of pearl, this man just keeps getting hotter. What else don't I know? He reaches out to test the texture of the flower petals, smoothing them between his fingers.

"It's a Casablanca Lily," I say. "It's gorgeous, isn't it?"

"Breathtaking," he replies, clearing his throat when his gaze returns to me. "Sorry, I get carried away when I find portrait ideas for my portfolio."

"No apologies." I shake my head. "You're passionate about your craft, and you just zeroed in on my favorite moon bloomer. Nothing to be sorry for at all."

His face lights up at my praise. "I don't do portrait shoots," he explains. "I sell limited copyrights to most of my catalog for stock-photo use, so I can make a living and then shoot what I really want to in my free time."

"Wait, didn't you say you studied engineering?" I distinctly remember him saying that he and Laura had been in the same engineering program together.

"I did," he confirms. "I have a bachelor's degree in mechanical engineering. I worked in the field for a few years, but it just wasn't for me. I've always been passionate about photography; I just didn't think I could make a career out of it. After a while, I realized I could be safe and bored as an engineer, or I could take a leap of faith and see what happened. Best thing I ever did."

Leap of faith. Yes, I'm learning a thing or two about those.

"That's very inspiring. We should all be so brave where our dreams are concerned. Maybe you could show me some of your stuff sometime," I suggest. I frown at my watch, suddenly wishing I hadn't checked. "Wow, it's already ten fifteen."

He winces. "I really should get back to the hospital. I'm surprised Tarryn hasn't started lighting up my phone."

With a heavy sigh, I take in a final scan of what is now my shared sanctuary. All the wanting in the world couldn't keep the evening from coming to a close, but I cling just a little longer, holding on to Tate's hand as we stroll back to my car.

The drive back to the hospital is quiet, making me more anxious with every mile closer we get. For all the talking we did, we haven't discussed where things go from here. Was this just a nice distraction for a night? Are we friends? Are we more? Are we crazy? Well, of course we are. Duh.

The stoplight ahead flashes yellow, and I mentally flip the mocking "yield" warning the bird. If I had any restraint I *would* be yielding, thank you very much. Although some would argue that I'm an adult and should have more self-control than a hormonal teenager, I'm clearly just a slave to my traitorous heart. At least I haven't slept with him . . . yet.

Oh, Lord. If that is the last shred of dignity I can cling to, I'm in really bad shape. I let out an audible sigh, and Tate reaches out and puts his hand on my knee. It makes my skin flush with heat, and I find myself gripping the steering wheel tighter.

"Penny for your thoughts?" He starts encircling my knee with his fingertips. It's my kneecap, for chrissakes, and you'd think he was encircling my nipples, the way they're pushing through my shirt right now.

"Are you cold?" he asks, showing his concern by rubbing my knee up to my midthigh. He's warming me up, all right. "You've got goose bumps." Yeah, thanks for noticing.

"Yeah," I lie. "I guess I'm a little chilly. Night air and all." I should be telling myself that I want him to stop, but what I really want is for his hand to drift a little higher . . .

Tart.

Oh hush. Who asked you, anyway?

"I was just thinking that we talked about so many things, but we didn't talk about if we wanted to see each other again." I feel so lame. Is this what I've really relegated myself to, a blatant fishing expedition? *Do you like me? If yes, check here.__ If you think I'm a pathetic loser, check here.__*

"I mean, I know I want to see you again, and I know you'd like to see me," I quickly correct. "It's just that we've got a lot going on, and I don't want you to feel obligated to call me. I get it."

I really don't want him to feel like he's got to take time away from being with his mother. If anything, I'd like to know how I can ease his burden, not amplify it. After all the time I've spent submersed in just my own problems, it's shocking to find myself willing and wanting to be involved with someone else's. I don't want to blow this, but every time I open my mouth I'm sticking my foot in.

"Caroline." One word, and by the tone I can tell that I'm not going to like what's coming. "I don't know what the next few months are going to look like for me."

Isn't that what I've been saying all along? Then why does it hurt so much to hear it coming out of his mouth? I knew this was the reality. I knew it, and I chose to get swept up in it anyway.

"Tate," I interrupt him before he can continue and break my heart. A heart that I'd been adamantly trying to protect. So much for that. "You don't have to explain. Really. I understand." I completely understand, but it doesn't make my heart ache less. I've got clarity, dammit. Shouldn't I get a free pass on the pain? Sheesh.

"What can you possibly understand? You just cut me off."

It's the first time I've heard Tate irritated, and that hurts worse than his blowoff. We pull up in front of the hospital and I throw the car into park. I stare at my lap, afraid of what I'll find if I cave and look at Tate.

"I don't know what the next few months are going to look like. I'm not going to have a lot of time for much of a life, but the time I *do* have I'd like to spend with the one person who's actually made me forget about the fact that mine is falling apart." He throws his hands into the air, exasperated. "Please."

I'm not sure if he's pleading with me, God, Buddha, or some other kind of higher power. Why do I keep presuming to know what he's thinking? Do I think so little of myself that I can't fathom anyone wanting to make time for me? No wonder the poor guy's frustrated; I can't shut up long enough to get out of my own way.

"I'm s-sorry, Tate," I stammer. "I just . . . I . . . uh . . ." I have no idea what to say. What is the protocol for a situation like this? *Hooray, I'm so glad your dying mother isn't going to put a damper on things?* Or *Let me see how long I can pawn off my kid, so we can spend some more time making out?*

"You still don't get it." Tate's soothing voice breaks through my self-damning thoughts. My breath comes in short, shallow puffs. I struggle to no avail to maintain my composure, embarrassed to find myself fighting back tears. "I'm going to make it my mission to show you how wonderful you are, if you'll let me."

I take a deep breath and pour out my heart, before I can talk myself out of it. "I want you to be a part my life. Any way I can have you, I'll take you." I pause for a moment, wanting to get the next part exactly right. I have no idea how to tactfully broach my concern about Lily, about how he might react to her specifically, without making it sound like I have no faith in him. I'm just scared he'll be intimidated by her needs. Hell, *I* feel that way most of the time.

Movement in my peripheral vision distracts me. A tall, willowy brunette is pacing outside the hospital doors. Tate turns to see what I'm looking at. At the same moment, the brunette looks toward us and smiles. If the resemblance wasn't obvious before, her dimples are a dead giveaway. Tate signals for her to head our way and gets out of the car to greet her. I step out too and tentatively head around the hood to meet his sister.

"Tarryn, I'd like you to meet Caroline." Tate drapes his arm around my shoulders as I reach out to shake Tarryn's hand. One eyebrow arches high above the other as she takes me in. She looks so much like Tate it's uncanny.

"It's lovely to meet you, Tarryn," I manage to say without stammering. She's elegantly beautiful with long wavy hair and a big glowing smile. Everything about her is a reflection of Tate, except her eyes. They're a lighter shade, I think. Not quite hazel, not quite brown, they're unique, and sharp as a tack as they take me in.

"Likewise, Caroline." She smirks at her brother. I start to squirm, but Tate's arm holds me steadily against him. Some sort of silent twin language is passed in the looks the two exchange. The more firmly Tate squeezes my shoulder, the higher Tarryn's eyebrow goes. "I was just coming outside for some fresh air. Mom fell asleep about an hour ago," she says, looking back and forth between us with interest. I feel like a trespasser as she fills Tate in on the details of their mother's evening.

"I was just going," I say, slinking out from under Tate's arm. He catches my hand before I can escape back into the safety of my Prius.

"Caroline, wait," Tate pleads. A subtle smile plays at Tarryn's lips as she watches the scene unfold between us.

"Please don't mind me." She grins. "I was just headed back upstairs, anyway. Tom is waiting for me. Good night, Caroline." She leans in to kiss her brother's cheek and whispers something in his ear. With a quick wave of her fingers she's gone, vanishing back into the hospital, leaving a wake of awkward silence behind her.

"That was bizarre," I say. "I'm sorry. I hope you don't feel ambushed." Poor Tate. I doubt he wants the added stress of explaining to his sister why he was sneaking off to have dinner with some strange woman.

"No, *I'm* sorry," he says. "I didn't realize she'd be stalking the lobby waiting for us to return." He shakes his head, watching where his sister disappeared through the front doors.

"What do you mean?" I furrow my brow in confusion. "She knew you were going out to dinner?"

"I told Tarryn all about you," he admits as he absently reaches up and smoothes the space between my eyebrows. "She's known about you from the start." He lets his hand drop and tips his face toward his shoes, smiling sheepishly.

"You told her about me?" I ask incredulously.

"I haven't shut up about you." He laughs nervously. "I guess I shouldn't be surprised she came down to check you out. We're lucky she didn't drag Tom down with her."

"Tom," I repeat in confusion. "Who's Tom?" I'm completely dumbfounded. My brain can't seem to catch up to the fact that Tate's been chatting me up to his family. I don't know why it should be a surprise, though. It's not like I haven't bent the ears of Max and Paige, soliciting their advice.

"Tom is my brother-in-law," he answers. "He's upstairs, I'm assuming, or back at my house. They're staying with me for the time being. They live in Wilmington, where Tom is from. His parents are staying with my niece and nephew while they're here with Mom."

I'm grateful to know that I'm not the only one who rambles when they're nervous.

"Who did you say I was?" I don't want to interrogate him, but I'm instantly curious about how my presence is being explained to the people in his life.

"At first, I told her I met a beautiful and fascinating woman in the cafeteria." A hint of color tints his cheeks, making my heart melt. "Each time I ran into you, I'd go back and fill her in on how incredible I think you are. That's all."

"Oh 'that's all,'" I tease. "I hope I live up to the hype." A fresh wave of nerves threatens to sweep me away at the thought of our anticlimactic introduction. I cringe, remembering my lack of finesse. I barely said a word.

"You already do." He gives me a knowing grin. "She whispered her approval before she bailed." He laughs at my shocked expression. "I believe she said, 'Nice choice, T. Don't mess it up.'"

"She doesn't think it's inappropriate?" The words leave my mouth before I can think better of it.

Verbal diarrhea. I think there's medication for that.

"Hey." Tate brings his eyes level to mine. "She doesn't think anything of it. She knows we can't always plan when good things come into our lives. She feels the same way I do—grateful that I've met someone wonderful during a time I thought I'd be alone."

My breath catches in my throat, thinking of Tate enduring his mother's death on his own. Tarryn has Tom to lean on, but where was Tate going to lean?

"You're not alone, Tate," I say. I want to promise him, but I can't. My good intentions toward Tate are second to being a mother to Lily. Wanting to be there for Tate seems so possible, until you add in the needs of my developmentally disabled child.

"I'm not now." He gives me a sad smile, and it breaks my heart. "Why do you think I'm so grateful for our timing?" God, I hope he really means that.

He kisses my forehead and walks me around to my car door. I'm blown away by his willingness to just accept me during such a deeply personal time in his life. He and his sister are open, warm, and every single thing I wasn't during my own hardships with Lily. Funny how I thought I was the one who'd be imparting the wisdom of experience to him. I have the distinct feeling that he's going to be teaching me more than I anticipated.

"I had a wonderful time tonight, Caroline. I really needed it, too." He leans his arms against the car on either side of me, shutting out the noise around us. "Once my mom gets transferred and settled in, I want to see you."

He kisses the top of my head before he tucks me under his chin. I wonder if he expects me to say no. He probably does, considering how apt I've been to push him away.

"Day after tomorrow." I tilt my head up and kiss the tip of his nose. "It's Peter's weekend with Lily, so he'll pick her up Thursday afternoon and have her through Sunday afternoon."

He lifts his head, bringing our lips just a breath apart. "Thursday it is." He brushes his lips against mine in a gesture so sweet, it makes my knees weak. "In the meantime, is it okay if I call you?" he asks me bashfully.

"Anytime you want to talk, call me. Okay?" He nods his agreement.

Pushing off the car, he opens my door. The vacancy left between us is accentuated by the loss of his warmth. It makes me miss him immediately.

"Call me or shoot me a text when you get home, so I know you made it," he shouts as I shut the door. I nod and wave awkwardly as I drive away. It was a beautiful evening, so why do I suddenly feel like I'm floundering? I check my rearview mirror and find Tate standing by the curb, watching me drive away.

i'm not who i was

Driving back home from the hospital is simply an array of reflexive right and left turns. My brain no longer registers the landmarks between there and home; it's the exact invariable route it was the first time I drove it with Lily. When I arrive at the house, my key fits in the dead bolt the same as it did before. The house appears as it has from the day we bought it seven years ago. Everything is exactly the same as it was before I left this evening, but everything *feels* different.

When Peter moved out, a void opened up inside this space. A hole where I believed his presence had made up part of the ambience of our home. After he left, the empty space became a living entity lurking in the hallways. It felt like a menacing presence, a cold spot in the corner of the room that made the hair on your arms stand at attention. I knew it was there; I just tried to pretend it wasn't and hoped to God it wouldn't suck me into my television set in the middle of the night.

Now here I am standing in my foyer, and I don't feel it. I don't feel anything at all, actually. No phantom shadows, flickering lights, or moving furniture. The ghost is gone. This doesn't exactly serve up much of an epiphany, when you consider the events of the last few months. The true marvel is realizing the haunting wasn't Peter's ghost, nor mine. It was the misery the two of us grew so accustomed to setting our standard of living to.

At first I excused it as proof of my survival. If I felt miserable, then surely it was evidence that I was still alive and breathing. A dead soul can feel nothing, wholly numb. Then the misery spread like a pervasive virus throughout every aspect of my life until nothing was left but the bar to which I measured how *alive* I was by how desolate I'd become. I told myself that trying to absorb our collective pain over Lily's disability was a tribute to how much I loved Peter, that learning to endure the burden would make me a better wife, somehow.

I can count on one hand the number of times in my life where a series of events triumphantly clicked into place. This is definitely one of those moments, when clarity you didn't know you were seeking kicks you right in the ass. The despondency I allowed myself to wallow in was *not* a testament to living. Feeling that kind of anguish on a daily basis was proof of nothing more than how skilled I was at punishing myself for Lily's condition. Tragic as it sounds, I'm grateful that Peter walked away when he did. If he hadn't, I'd still be gauging how much life I had left in me by how much despair I felt. I'd still be clueless to my own demoralization if I hadn't met Tate.

He is unapologetically grateful I stumbled into his life. He doesn't worry about the fact that it's the same week he's putting his mother into hospice. Albeit subconsciously, I expected him to walk away, because it just seemed like too much. How could he possibly reconcile starting a relationship when his mother is dying? How could he want to start a relationship with a single mother of a special-needs child? This has "disaster" written all over it. So why can't I stay away?

It's not like we were looking for each other. In fact, it was quite the opposite. For whatever reason—serendipity, kismet, whatever you want to call it—we just kind of happened. Naturally, I panicked and made every effort to discount what was happening. Who wouldn't? The last thing either one of us needs is a relationship steeped in codependency. My greatest fear is that this connection is born from the desperation we feel about our lives. That once he finally meets Lily, our relationship will fall apart. I'm terrified to go through something like that again. Still, my heart has eclipsed the valiant efforts of my logic, and I'm okay with that now.

Tate's different; what's acceptable to him is to hang on to whatever joy he can, despite his mother's illness. He comes at it from the idea that life is chaotic enough; our feelings don't need to be. He likes me, and praise cheeses, I like him. That could be enough for right now, if I let it be.

So let it be. Let. It. Be.

I pull my phone from my purse and stare at the screen, wishing for something witty and charming to say. Tate has me seeing a whole myriad of things in a different light, but the one thing that stands out the most: me. He makes me see myself in a way I haven't been able to before, and I like the woman I'm becoming. I want to throttle her a lot of the time, but I see her value in a way that has been completely lost on me until now. I'm not entirely sure how I got to this point in my life without having a clue who I am, but I'm really glad that Tate has been able to give me a glimpse of myself from his perspective. I would love to tell him that, but trying to fit that into a text message would be difficult. Still, I'd like to convey how much I enjoyed spending time with him.

Me: Made it home . . . Thank you for a lovely evening.

Tate replies immediately.

Tate: Glad you're home safe. It was rather lovely, wasn't it?

Me: Spectacular :) Looking forward to another one soon.

Tate: Me, too . . . good dream material for tonight ;)

Me: *swoon* Sweet dreams, then. I'll talk to you soon.

Tate: Sounds perfect. Sweet dreams to you, too #dreamgirl

Dream girl? My cheeks flood with the heat of my pleasure. I've never been anyone's "dream girl" before. If I have, then I've been too daft to know it. The possibility of being Tate's is almost too good to be true. I really want to be. The desire of wanting to be his dream girl strikes me with such force, it takes my breath away. It scares the living daylights out of me, because I know I don't have the willpower to walk away if he rejects Lily.

Paige is going to kill me.

secret garden

Air bursts from my lungs in shallow puffs, leaving me dizzy. Tate's arms secure me against the length of his body; his lips fervently move against mine. A moan escapes from my lips as his knee nudges its way between my legs. His tongue strokes mine, igniting a passion that threatens to burn me alive.

"Caroline," he groans into my mouth. "I want you so much." His hands are everywhere, making me ache with heady awareness. I want so badly to feel him move inside me, I swear I'll die with wanting. His fingertips skim my rib cage as I undulate against his thigh. I can feel myself climbing to the peak of our combined desire.

"Tate, please," I beg, pulling his shirt above his head. "I need you."

"Dance, little sister," he whispers in my ear. Confused, I pull back and look at him. He levels his melted caramel eyes on me and repeats, "Dance, little sister, dance."

I come awake with a violent start, nearly pitching myself off the couch. My cell phone is glowing on the coffee table, the Stones singing persistently, waiting for me to answer Paige's call. Frantically, I grab for the phone and cringe when I see the time: 12:05 a.m.

"Hello?" I croak into the phone. Maybe if she realizes she woke me up, she'll take mercy on me. Yeah, right. She'll be even more irritated that I was able to fall asleep before calling in the highlights of the evening.

"Don't you 'hello' me," she shouts. "Do you know what time it is?" I was right; her voice is laced with annoyance.

"Paige, I'm so sorry. I must've conked out on the couch." *And was having a rather delicious sex dream that you woke me up from before the big finish. Thanks a lot.*

"Save it, sister," she grouses. "I've been sitting here all night waiting for you to call. How did it go?"

That's a loaded question. If I tell her how well things went, she's going to think I'm insane.

"Um, well . . . uh . . ." I stammer. "Oh, hell, Paige. I don't know what to say," I whine. It's the truth; I don't know what to say that won't green-light an effort to have me committed.

"Did he kiss you?" she asks tentatively.

"Yes."

"Did you like it?"

"Yes, Paige." I roll my eyes at her line of questioning. Did I like it? Does a bear shit in the woods? "I liked it a lot."

"Hmm," is the only response. What the heck is that supposed to mean?

"That's it?" I complain. "You ring me up to read me the riot act, guilting me about forgetting to call, and all I get is 'hmm'?"

"I'm thinking, you cow," she sasses. "Did you at least talk before making out with him? How come he's single? Is he divorced? What does he do for a living?"

"Whoa, whoa," I interrupt. "He's never been married, but was in a relationship for eight years. He's a photographer—" I start to explain, but it's Paige's turn to interrupt.

"A photographer?" she asks. "He didn't ask you to pose nude, did he?"

"Paige Christine Hunter," I threaten, "if you make fun, I won't think twice about hanging up on you."

"Sorry, no more interrupting, I promise. I will just listen from here on out," she says.

With a deep breath, I begin with Giff's, telling her about the flowers, the conversation, and the kiss. That first perfect kiss. True to her word, she listens to me pore over the details. It's nice to be able to savor the finer points of the evening with her. I catch her sighing wistfully when I tell her how he told me I make him feel alive and out of control.

"Jesus, Caroline," she breathes into her phone. "He sounds like a dream. How did you guys leave things at Giff's?"

I hesitate for a moment, wondering how I'm going to explain the next part of the night, or if I even should. Paige doesn't know that I've been sneaking off to the moon garden to think for the last few years. No one does, except Tate. It is my refuge, a place where I didn't want anyone to come looking for me, let alone find me, until now. It wasn't a place that I thought I'd ever share with anyone, and now I've shared it with Tate. I don't want to hurt Paige's feelings, and I don't want to breed any unnecessary comparisons. I want her to accept and like Tate, not feel a sense of competition.

"Well, we didn't part ways at Giff's," I start. "I took him to my thoughtful spot. A place where I go to get my head on straight, when I'm dealing with life stuff." I wait anxiously for Paige to say something, to give me a clue where to steer the conversation from here.

"You took him to the moon garden?" she asks in a meek voice.

I'm glad my butt is planted firmly on the couch, because I'm certain that you could knock me over with a feather right now.

"What?" My voice comes out as a startled whisper. "How do you know about that?"

"Caroline, I knew you were disappearing somewhere at night." I listen, shocked, as Paige continues to tell me how she came to find out about my secret hiding place. "When Lily first started showing signs of delay, I came over a couple of different times at night when I knew she would be down for the evening. I thought if I surprised you, you wouldn't have time to throw up the walls you'd been building to keep us all out. Peter never had an answer for where you were, just that you'd gone out for a drive to think. Around the second or third time I came by, I started to get worried. Peter didn't seem to know what to do, and I think a big part of him didn't want to help me figure it out. I think he felt that if you wouldn't talk to him, he couldn't handle you talking to me. So, one night, I came a little earlier than usual and waited for you to pull out of the garage. I followed you into the botanical park. In fact, I trailed you for a whole week, just to make sure your visits there weren't a fluke. I felt like a creeper at first, but I had to make sure you were okay. I sat where you couldn't see me and watched over you, because it was all I could do."

"Paigey," I sniffle between tears. "Why didn't you tell me?"

"How could I?" she sobs into the phone. "It was so clear that the garden was where you let everything to the surface to feel. You never showed any emotion to any of us during that time, yet in that garden I watched you set all of that angst free. I didn't want to stop you from feeling it; I knew you needed to in order to deal with it. I just always figured you'd tell me about it when you were ready." I hear the hurt in her voice, and I wish she were here for me to hold on to.

"I never meant to exclude you," I swear. "I just didn't know how to let anyone see how broken I was back then."

"I know that, Caro," she says. "I'm not mad at you. If anything, it shows me how much you trust and care about Tate already. I know you wouldn't bring anyone to the garden lightly."

"No, I wouldn't," I agree. "At first, I thought I was bringing him there to share a place where he could go to think. After we got there, I realized that a part of me needed him to know what that space means to me. He gets it, without my having to explain at all."

"Then I'm really glad you brought him there," Paige says. "Hopefully, he can get the same peace of mind out of being there that you have."

"I hope so too, Paigey." I sigh.

I make sure to tell Paige about the more rational bits of conversation we had, too. The parts where we acknowledged where our priorities lay, and how neither of us can afford to indulge in getting carried away, given the responsibilities of our lives at present. He has his mother to consider above all else, and I have Lily.

Paige makes comments of support and understanding, but I hear what she doesn't say, too. In her subtle hesitations and the way she holds her breath in certain places, I know she's holding back her "be carefuls" and "make sure he's worth your trusts." The fact that she doesn't indulge her urge to say it and rain on my parade just makes me love my sister even more.

The love I feel pulsing through my veins for her, for Lily, and for my new life—*that* is my proof of life.

writing to reach you

After I make plans to see her the next day, Paige and I say our good nights and hang up. For as easily as I'd drifted off into sensual slumber before, sleep is evading me now. Thousands of thoughts scatter themselves in a multitude of directions in my mind. I lie in my bed staring at the ceiling, trying to follow where the light from my window and the light from the bathroom begin and end: the silver-blue radiance from the moon on one side, and the soothing yellow glow from the bathroom vanity on the other. The cool and warm tones would clash on an artist's palette, but fusing on the ceiling, they create a striking balance. Silver brings a shimmering depth to an otherwise dim glow. Yellow adds a softness to the sharp edges of blue, creating an aquamarine river running down the middle of the two beams. It's an odd amalgamation of texture and light, but it generates a beauty like nothing I've ever seen.

So does life, I suppose. Naturally, we try to choose colors that complement one another. Otherwise we end up with a palette riot that makes little sense and causes chaos instead of Zen. But if we're too careful, we just end up picking the same color over and over, and end up with no picture at all. We can try to outsmart life and meticulously choose varying tints of the same color and end up with an eerie portrait of just shadows. Whether it's one solid color or a hundred different shades of it, it's like painting your whole house beige and calling one room "Nomadic Desert" and another "Latte."

I turn my head and let my eyesight adjust to the wall on the far side of my room. Peter and I spent countless hours poring over color swatches, trying to decide on the perfect shade to complement our home. I didn't want to paint each room a different color, not even the bathrooms. I wanted the floor plan to "flow," with a similar color scheme throughout. I can't help but laugh out loud at myself when the name of the shade pops into my head: Timeless Taupe. My entire house is a sea of beige.

I put aside my effort to resume my dream of Tate and turn on the bedside lamp. It effectively washes away all evidence of my midnight epiphany, bathing the room with light.

You need to buy a couple of gallons of paint.

What I need to do is hire a painter, but before I do that, I need to determine how I want to color my life. I'm no good with a paintbrush; art is not my forte. However, I am pretty decent with words—I just haven't tried in a very long time.

Before I can talk myself out of trying, I jump out of bed and pad down the hallway to the den. I bypass the light switch and stumble through the dark until I reach the desk lamp. I don't want to taint the ideas swimming in my head with any uninspired neutrality, biscuit, buff . . . whatever you want to call it. It's boring.

I sit down at my computer and tap the keyboard, bringing the desktop to life. I push away the memory of the last ineffective time I tried to use the voice-activated software. Paige bought it for me after my stroke, so I could continue to write via dictation. I wanted to chronicle my recovery and Lily's developmental milestones. When that story didn't want to get written the way I was trying, I banished the software to the corners of my computer's hard drive. If I couldn't tell the story the way I wanted to, then I wasn't going to tell it at all.

After a few unsuccessful searches, I find the program I need. My heart vibrates with excitement as the blank page and blinking Record button stare back at me. I think of all of the things I'm learning about myself, life, friendship, and love. All the things I want to do and experience. I outline in my mind and then hit Record.

I'm not sure how long into the early morning I sat talking to my computer before I fell asleep. When I wake up, I peel my cheek off of the desk and try to knead out the kink in my neck. Rubbing the sleep from my eyes, I squint at the word counter on the bottom of the screen: 3,602 words. I don't think I've ever written so much in one sitting. I read back through the beginning of my story and smile to myself. It's not crap. I kind of like it. I just might have something worth pursuing here.

My attention is drawn to the file name I've chosen, and an involuntary rush of goose bumps covers me head to toe. *Lily Love.* The story is mine, but it's a fictionalized version. Anyone who knows me will know it's me. This story likely won't get told the way I want it to, either, so what makes it different from the last? I think it's knowing that it's still a work in progress. There is no definitive outcome; I've just got to wait and see how things play out.

I stretch my arms above my head and wince as I arch my back. The clock blinks 5:45 a.m. I'm too old to fall asleep at my desk. I save my work from the evening and shut down the computer. Peter won't be here with Lily until 8:30, so I shuffle back down the hallway and climb into bed. Sleep takes me hostage before my head makes contact with the pillow.

Tate follows me into my dreams, waiting for me in the moon garden with Shasta daisies and red carnations.

the luckiest

It's Thursday morning before I know it. Between Lily's therapy appointments, a follow-up for me with an orthopedist, and dinner with Paige, my plate has been too full for me to stress over when I might see Tate again. We haven't talked on the phone since yesterday morning, when he called to say he'd woken up thinking of me. Thank God he couldn't see my face, because I turned bright red when I thought of the way he'd starred in my dreams.

They were able to ambulance his mother to St. Joseph's without incident, and so far he and Tarryn are pleased with the care she's receiving. Forty-eight hours doesn't seem like a lot of time, but in hospice care it's a matter of life and death. Their mother's condition has continued to deteriorate. Tate has kept me updated by text, but clearly he wants to give his attention where it's needed.

When my phone rings, I expect it to be Tate with an update. It just seems like things are changing faster than he anticipated with his mother. I don't think anyone is ever prepared to lose someone they love, and I don't think Tate was expecting his mom to worsen so fast.

I smile, hoping it will lend some buoyancy to my tone. "Hi, there."

"Good morning, Sunshine," Tate replies. His voice is thick and raspy, reflecting the lack of sleep he's had during the night.

"How are you doing?" I know he's not doing well. Still, I want to make sure he knows he's got the floor to talk about whatever he wants.

"I'm hanging in there, I guess." He sighs. "The nurses here have been a godsend. They explain everything as it's happening and why they are doing or not doing certain things for my mom."

I can't imagine what he must be going through. "Is there anything I can do?" I ask. "Can I bring you or Tarryn anything?" I cross my fingers and pray that he says yes so I can be of some use.

"Well, that's why I was calling," he says sheepishly. "I was hoping you would bring by something I'm missing."

"Anything, Tate." I don't even flinch at the desperation in my voice. "Peter's taken the day off to spend with Lily; he'll be by at eleven to pick her up, and then I'm yours."

"Mine, huh?" He chuckles, leaving me blushing at my choice of words.

"You know what I mean," I mumble.

"I hope so," he says, "because I could really use seeing your smile."

He sounds so tired, and part of me wants to insist that he use any free time he has to rest, but it's not about me. It's about what he needs, and if he wants me, I'm going to be there for him.

"I can certainly arrange that." I grin. "Why don't I bring you guys something for lunch?"

"Nah," he replies. "I'm not hungry at all. I just really want to see you."

My heart doesn't know what to do. I remind myself that he wants comfort from me, not pity. Support without charity. I can do this.

"What time works best for you?" I ask, looking at the clock. It's nine in the morning. I have two hours before Peter gets here.

"As soon as you can." He tries hard to keep it light and funny, but the sadness seeps through.

"I'll come right after Peter leaves," I promise.

"Are you sure you don't mind?" he asks softly.

"I will never mind time I spend with you, no matter where it is. You can always count on that."

"It's just, a guy doesn't strive to have a second date with his girl at the hospice center."

"Oh, am I your girl?" I tease lightly. "If that's the case, then do I get to wear your class ring?" I'm rewarded with Tate's rich, reverberating laughter. The sound is like a soothing balm on my frayed nerves.

"You're my dream girl, remember?" he teases back.

"How could I forget?" I sigh dramatically. "It's not every day a boy tells you that you're the one he's dreamed of." I choke on the last of my words, unable to prevent them from spilling from my mouth.

You were supposed to keep it light, you moron, not put words in his mouth.

"Oh, Caroline," he whispers softly. "You have no idea."

My breath catches in my throat and tears pool in my eyes. How do I deserve this man who regards me like I'm a prize that he's won? His life is in shambles and he still has the ability to tell me how much I mean to him. Even when I accidentally put him on the spot. Is he for real? Will he still feel this way with Lily's needs as part of the package?

"Oh, I might have some idea." I smile to myself.

"You remind me that there is still beauty in this world." His voice is thick with emotion, and it sends my heart into a tailspin. I cannot be falling for this boy, not yet. Not now. Not until he meets Lily.

"Tate." I stop to garner what little courage I can find and pour it out into my words. "You make me want to taste life the way you do. You live with your heart wide-open, and give of yourself, even when no one would blame you if you didn't. You inspire me to be better. You're a wonderful man."

The line is silent, and I fear that I have finally frightened him off.

I hear him suck in a breath and it's my only clue that he's still there. It's driving me crazy that I can't see the expression on his face. It terrifies me, not knowing what he's thinking.

"You," he says softly, bringing my heart to stillness in my chest. "I'm none of those things apart from who I am when I'm with you."

Tears stream silently down my face as I listen to him continue to give pieces of himself to me, even in his grief. "Then I am the luckiest girl in the world," I whisper.

"Hurry, beautiful girl," he pleads, unabashed in his appeal for me. I desperately try to reason with my heart as it demands to belong to Tate.

Traitor!

"I'll be there before you know it."

I'll be there for him any way he'll let me. I just pray that I don't lose my heart to my madness in the process.

pitter pat

Thump-THUMP. Thump-THUMP.
     When I close my eyes, I focus on my heart beating. I know it's still there, drumming a steady rhythm in my chest, but it feels like it's no longer mine.
     What did you do? How could you let this happen?
     I told myself over and over to be careful, not to allow myself to be swept up in those damned dimples! If I'm honest, the dimples may have highlighted my attraction to him, but his heart is what makes it increasingly hard not to fall ass-over-teacups in love with my stranger . . . who's no longer a stranger, really.
     I pace around the kitchen island, trying to rein in my rising anxiety. On my third lap, I steal a quick look into the living room to make sure that Lily is still engrossed in her dollhouse. She's playing, happily unaffected by her mother's nervous breakdown. Thank God for small favors, and all that crap. I steal a look at the clock on the stove—it's 9:15. Only fifteen minutes have passed since the phone call that set this crazy train in motion.
     You can't be falling in love with him, Caroline. You're not impulsive, or careless, or fanciful . . .

I know I'm not, and that is precisely why I'm scared to death. This is *not* me. I don't behave this way. What the hell is wrong with me? I look at the clock on the oven again—9:16. I need something to do, or I'm going to lose what's left of my mind in the next hour and forty-four minutes.

In times like this, it can only take a moment for anxiety to trample my calm. It must be the control freak in me. I need something to help keep me grounded. I make a beeline to the pantry, where a quick scan of the shelves tells me that I have just enough pasta and crushed tomatoes to make a manageable one-hand pasta dish. I grab garlic, spices, cheese, everything and set a pot of water to boil. Perhaps there will be comfort in following a recipe to a predictable result. I won't be too creative. After all, the whole point of the exercise is to create the illusion that I'm in control. Any kind of culinary disaster would debunk that fantasy, and I need to believe it. Just a little while longer.

When Lily first started to have severe problems, my anxiety was barely manageable. After putting her down for her afternoon nap, I'd spend those two hours baking. Come to think of it, that was the only thing I found calming at the time. I guess that hasn't changed much.

An hour and a half later, I have a steaming casserole dish full of baked ziti. The house smells like an Italian restaurant. I feel purged of my escalating panic, until I realize I've just created another problem.

What the hell are you going to do with all this food, Caro?

Crap. I hadn't really thought that far. At least back in my baking days, I could send the treats to the office with Peter. I don't exactly have that kind of liberty now. Tate said he wasn't hungry, but maybe the hospice center has a kitchen where visiting families can store food. I grab my phone and look up the main number. As the phone is ringing, I start to lose my nerve and wonder if I should just hang up and send the food next door to my neighbors.

"St. Joseph's Hospice Center, Roxy speaking."

"Uh, hi. I was just wondering if there's kitchen space available for the families of your patients."

"Sure," Roxy replies. "There's a stove, oven, and refrigerator for everyone to share. However, you should know there's really no need for any patient families to cook. We get a lot of food donations from the community and local churches."

"Oh," I say, as the lightbulb in my head goes on. "So if I wanted to bring in a covered dish, any visitors could enjoy it. Not just a specific family?" This could be a really good thing. I can indulge my need to stress-cook and St. Joseph's can reap the benefits.

"Absolutely," Roxy answers. "It's a really great way to show some love. Most people who have family members here forget to eat at the regular times. It's nice to have things available for them whenever they think to stop for a bite."

A plan forms in my mind. "When I bring by my dish, do I have to sign in or something?"

"Just let the receptionist at the front desk know why you're there, and she will make sure it gets to the kitchen," she chirps.

"Great, will do," I reply. "Thanks, Roxy."

I barely have time to end my phone call when the doorbell rings, sending Lily into a spastic sprint for the front door. She opens it and jumps into her father's arms, covering his face with wet kisses.

"Daddy here, Mama!" she sings.

It makes my heart swell with joy to see her so happy to see her dad. It's easy to get caught up in the things that are difficult about raising a child like Lily. The rare and precious things are harder to hold on to when you feel like you're jumping from one crisis to the next. Watching Lily dote on her father is a beautiful reminder of how deeply she feels things. She loves without limits, pouring her little heart into everyone she comes into contact with. She may not be hitting cognitive goals, but she excels in the areas of empathy and compassion. I relish the moments like this, when I'm reminded of what a gift she is. I can't imagine my life without her.

lily love

Peter approaches me cautiously, still carrying Lily in his arms. "It smells incredible in here, Caroline." He stops, leaving ample space between us.

"Thanks," I mumble, suddenly feeling uncomfortable. I don't want to make Peter a part of anything I'm doing for Tate, but I need help. "Would you help me carry this out to the car?" I point at the Pyrex dish cooling on the counter.

"Sure." He sets Lily on her feet and grabs the oven mitts. "Ziti? Who're you taking this to?" His question is innocent; I don't sense any animosity in his tone. Still, I don't want to get into it with him.

"St. Joseph's Hospice Center," I say. "I heard that the community can bring food for the families of patients. I thought it would be nice." I'm not lying, but I'm not being completely honest, either.

"That is really nice," he agrees as he carries the ziti out to my car. The awkwardness between us is so thick I could slice it into pieces and serve it up on crackers. Peter and I shuffle around each other, unsure of what to say or do. I take refuge on the far side of my car and sigh in relief when he takes Lily's hand and leads her to his car.

"Here," I offer, "I'll grab her bag from the foyer." I dash into the house, grateful for the momentary diversion. I check and double-check her bag, making sure she has all her meds, clothes, Bun the Bunny. I rush back outside and hand Lily's things to Peter. "Everything is here, Peter. If she's missing something for some reason, just call me."

"If I need something, I'll figure it out." He shrugs. "It's about time I did, right?"

I can't help but smile. I'm proud of him.

"You'll be fine." I nod, and I know he will be. I don't have any special insight that he doesn't. I'm good with Lily because I didn't have the choice not to be. When there isn't someone there to tell you how you're supposed to navigate this stuff, you figure it out on your own. That's the thing about being a parent to a child with special needs: there's no way to gauge what you're capable of. You never know how much you can handle until you don't have a choice. Those are lessons we have to learn on our own, and Peter's mettle will be tested just like mine was, and that's the way it should be.

"You're a great dad, Peter."

And I know in my heart he will be.

something to say

My palms begin to sweat against the steering wheel as I make the left turn into the parking lot at St. Joseph's. I find a close spot to park in and start the process of meditative breathing to calm my frazzled nerves. Om . . . positivity in . . . om . . . negativity out . . .

Namaste, you crazy bitch.

I tap my forehead on the steering wheel, trying to figure out how to silence the ornery voice in my head. She's getting awfully snarky, and I'm starting to bristle at her rolling commentary.

A soft knock on the window elicits a bloodcurdling yell from me. Tate opens my door and peers in sheepishly.

"We've got to stop meeting like this." He chuckles.

All of a sudden the whole scene is so absurd to me, I double over with laughter. Tate attempts to look concerned, but is fighting back the urge to join me. He looks constipated, which only makes me laugh harder, watery eyes and all.

"You scared the crap out of me," I manage when I can breathe again.

"I saw you pull in," he explains. "I didn't mean to scare you."

"It's all good." I smile up at him as he holds out his hand. Warm bliss envelops me as he pulls me from the car, into his arms. Then he kisses me senseless, right in the middle of the parking lot.

"*Now* it's all good," he whispers into my ear. I lean against the doorframe so I don't dissolve into the asphalt. Sweet baby carrots, that boy can *kiss*. "What's that wonderful smell?" He sticks his head in the car and breathes deeply.

"I know you said you weren't hungry, but I made something you and Tarryn can have later when you are. It's okay if you don't want it; the nurse at the front desk said that stuff like this can be shared with everyone. So, no pressure . . ." I ramble.

"You made this for me?" Tate picks up the dish and smiles warmly at me. I feel bashful and self-conscious, so I give a noncommittal shrug.

"Well, you know, I don't want you to starve or anything." He closes the car door and turns to face me, pinning me with an intense stare.

"You're taking care of me." There is no question about it. It's very much a statement. "This means more than you could possibly know."

"I bet I can guess." I run my hand along the stubble on his cheek and let his caramel eyes consume me. "You have a mother and sister you need to be strong for, but you thought there was no one to be strong for you."

He clears his throat.

I wrap my arm around his waist, and he wraps his around my shoulders. Even when we're side by side, there's a fierceness with which he holds on to me, and yet he's gentle in his mindfulness of my arm. That's exactly how I'd explain his affection for me. He never holds back from showing me how impassioned his feelings are, but he's always delicate with the way he handles mine. I never knew anyone could regard me that way.

Pulling me in closely, he kisses the top of my head. I place my hand on his chest to keep from falling over. I let him hold me this way until the frantic racing of his heart slows beneath my hand.

"Let's get this food inside, and then you can fill me in on how things are going," I say.

The first thing I notice when we step inside is how quiet it is. It's peaceful, and absolutely heartbreaking. A petite nurse with a bouncy blond ponytail waves as we step into the reception area.

"Hey, I'm Roxy. I think I spoke to you on the phone." She smiles widely at Tate and me.

"How could you tell?" I ask, surprised.

"Most of the goodies we get are sweets or deli platters. When I talked to you earlier, you said you were bringing in a 'dish.'" She gestures toward the casserole Tate's holding.

Tate leans in and mock-whispers in my ear, "You offered up my ziti to everyone?"

Roxy laughs. "There're also labels in the kitchen for people to mark what they don't want to share."

I blush a deep red and elbow Tate in the ribs. "I didn't know if my cooking would be received well, and I didn't want it to go to waste."

"Anything you make for me won't only be received well, but will be held in the highest regard." He kisses my hand, and my face flames even more.

"Oh, he's smooth, girl. You'd better keep your eye on him or he'll run away with your heart," Roxy teases. I force a smile on the outside as my own heart bounces in my chest. Roxy's innocent comment strikes so close to the truth.

"Only if she agreed to run away with me," Tate returns with his heart-stopping smile. Roxy cocks her head to the side and looks me in the eye.

"Is he for real?" she asks, and all I can do is nod my head. What I really want to do is correct him and say, "You mean me *and* Lily, right?" But he can't have an opinion on something I'm unwilling to discuss. I really need to stop being such a chicken.

"Wow." She sighs wistfully. "You're in trouble."

I know I am.

We make our way to the kitchen, where Tate grabs a couple of plates to fill and label for himself and Tarryn. A quick look around the kitchen area makes me feel even better about my new project. There are pans of cookie bars, containers full of muffins and pastries. In the fridge there're fresh fruit and vegetable platters, but nothing to really make a meal out of.

"Whatcha thinking about?" Tate asks, just before he takes a bite from the plate he's made. I smile to myself at the sight of him devouring my cooking.

"Just that I'm glad I brought something to eat," I answer. "There doesn't seem to be much more than snack food here. It makes me feel good. That's all." I don't tell him that I want to continue to bring in cooked meals. I'm going to do it because I want to, not for his recognition or praise.

"This is wonderful, really superb," he mutters between bites.

"Thank goodness, because it would've been really awkward if it'd sucked." I laugh.

We sit in comfortable silence while Tate eats and I watch. It gives me time to think, which can be a good or bad thing, depending on how you look at it. I'm going to take it as a good thing for the moment.

What I feel for Tate and what I hope he feels for me is real. That's not really the issue, though. How we move forward from here—now, *that* is an issue. Tate is good at making me feel like I'm the most amazing woman in the world, and God help me, I don't ever want him to stop. I'd like to think that I've done my fair share of making him feel like the incredible man he is. What I want is for us to be able to talk about what's going on, outside of swooning, with the same candor we've shared so far. I hope more than anything that when Tate's had his fill of pasta, he'll fill me in on what happened to make him so forlorn earlier. Perhaps sensing my weary thoughts, he lifts his eyes to mine and heaves a heavy sigh.

"I'm so glad you're here," he says. I hold my breath and wait to see what he'll say next. "This place is such a blessing, but it's all so overwhelming. I don't know what I'm going to feel from one minute to the next—grateful that there is a place like this to help me take care of my mom, guilty for not being able to take care of her on my own, or angry we're here at all. It's exhausting." He leans back in his chair, tipping his head toward the ceiling.

Empathy can be such a contradiction. It allows me to identify with Tate's pain, but it can't help me resolve it.

Be careful what you wish for.

Wish, the most foul four-letter word there is. No one ever seems to get what they wish for. Life is just one fable after another, stories threaded together to teach us lessons about what we think we want and what we really need. I can't recall a single one in which a character wished for something, got it, and lived happily ever after. I want my happily ever after, dammit.

I drag a chair up and sit next to Tate. His head still tilted back, he rakes his fingers through his hair. I'm not even sure if he realizes I've moved.

There have been so many times when the weight of what was happening around me was too much. I just shut down, blocking out everything and everyone. Self-preservation doesn't always work, no matter what some might say. It preserved absolutely nothing for me to shut the world out. Peter and my family watched, unsure of what they should do. Until there was nothing left to do but pacify one another with, "Just give her some space; she'll come around." I never did, and eventually they all grew tired of waiting for me to snap out of it.

I place my hand on Tate's knee; I don't have words to lessen his pain. More often than not, there isn't a solution, and that's where I could really fail again. It took too long for me to accept that there was no way to cure Lily's disability. I wasted so much time searching for a resolution when the only one that could be made was acceptance. I hope more than anything that Tate can find that acceptance of Lily, too.

I know better now than to try to solve the unsolvable; I can't cure his mother's cancer. I'm not going to fall into the trap of telling him that she's going to be in a better place, or that her suffering will end soon. That isn't what he needs to hear from me. Honestly, he doesn't need me to say anything. I want him to know he's being heard, and that his pain isn't going to scare me off just because I can't fix it. I've learned the hard way that sometimes it's not about what we can fix, but what we have to learn to accept.

"You're not alone," I promise him, my throat constricting around the words.

Emotion courses through me as Tate turns his red-rimmed eyes to mine. In their infinite sadness I can see a glimmer of relief. He places his hand over mine and lets his lips curve slightly. We fall back into silence, but at least now he knows that I'll be right here when he finds something more to say.

in your hands

Eventually I put the ziti in the fridge and clean up Tate's plate. He hasn't said much, and that's perfectly okay.

"Let's go for a walk," he finally says. "You can fill me in on what you've been up to." He pushes in his chair and walks over to where I'm attempting to dry his plate at the sink. "You're going to get your cast wet," he murmurs, taking the dish from me. He dries it far quicker than I could've one-handed, and gives me a quick kiss on the cheek.

"Where do you want to walk?" I ask. I haven't seen the rest of the center, but from the parking lot I could see that it's backed up to the idyllic setting of the woods. I can only imagine how beautiful it must be back there.

"There're a few places to sit out back, and a trail we can walk," he says. Wrapping his arm around me, he leads me from the kitchen toward a common area resembling a living room. There are couches and armchairs facing a fireplace on one side, and another set that stare out a wall of windows on the other. Tate leads me to the windows, looking into the thick green of the trees. He points below us at the scarcely marked trailhead.

"It looks pretty," I say softly. "Let's start there."

"It's no moon garden, but it's still peaceful," he replies. "I've walked it twice in the last day and a half."

I love that he thinks of the moon garden. Well, I know he thinks about what happened in the moon garden. I'm glad that he thinks of it as a peaceful place, and not just where we made out. The memory of that makes me flush with heat. Being this close to Tate, I know that he can tell. That only makes me hotter than I already am.

Tate leads me outside and down a spiral staircase. Looking back up at the center, I get my first real glimpse at its architecture. From behind, the center is held up high on stilts. The entire back side of the building is a series of windows that face the woods. It's breathtakingly beautiful.

"All of the patient rooms face the back," Tate explains. "From my mom's room, because we're so high up, it feels like we're on a cloud, looking down at Earth. Mom loves it. When she's awake, she likes me to roll her over to the window."

"It's gorgeous," I tell him. "Someone put a lot of thought into finding this spot and building the center in just this way. It's amazing." We walk down a set of steps built into the hillside, to the trailhead. Tate looks over his shoulder at me and reaches back for my hand. Silently I take it, and we walk hand in hand into the brush.

"How's Lily doing?" Tate asks after a while.

I find myself hesitant, not wanting to talk about the things Lily is coping with. Sometimes it's just easier not to. It's hard to consider that moment when Lily becomes real and not just a concept. I'm terrified that everything developing between Tate and me will disappear.

"She's good," I offer, and nothing else. My eyes are fixed on the bumpy trail beneath my feet, so I don't see Tate until I run into him. He grabs my shoulders to keep me from stumbling and holds me there so he can look me in the eye.

"Tell me more about her," Tate probes. He's persistent, I'll give him that, and there's something in the way he's looking at me that makes me feel like I'm being tested.

"What do you want to know?" I try hard to sound casual, but I sound defensive. Shoot, I *feel* defensive.

"Please don't do this, Caroline," Tate pleads.

I narrow my eyes at him suspiciously. "Don't do what, Tate?"

"Don't hide inside my problems to avoid dealing with yours." His words are a punch to my gut. They're harsh, blunt, and totally true. He takes a step closer to me, and I take a step back. His eyes flash auburn with frustration when I step out of his reach. "That sounds harder than I wanted it to, but, Caroline . . ."

"Don't, okay? Just don't." My voice breaks as stubborn tears spill from my eyes. I turn my face away, cursing under my breath. Just once, I'd like *not* to dissolve into tears. Any show of strength at this point would be greatly appreciated. Shit. "You don't know how hard this is for me."

Tate looks at me, incredulously. "I don't know, and I never will unless you tell me. I asked about Lily because she's a part of who you are, and I want to know every part of you, Caroline. Not just the parts you want me to see. All of them." His chest heaves as he breathes, like he's been running to catch up to me. I guess in some ways he has. I want to believe him, but there's still the Lily factor. Until I know with certainty that he's open to all that is Lily, he can't possibly mean what he's saying. After all, *she* is the biggest part of me.

"I don't know what you want me to say," I whisper. He wants to know all of me, but I'm petrified of what will happen when he gets to something he doesn't like. That's why I'm not ready to share everything about Lily yet.

"I want you say that you have enough faith in me to believe I can be there for you, the way you've been here for me." He takes a hesitant step toward me, reaching for my hand when I don't back away. He holds his hand out between us, waiting to see what I'll do. I reach for it, meeting him in the middle, and lace my fingers with his.

"There's a lot going on with Lily right now, so it's hard to know where to start," I confess. Between her tantrum in the EMU and her impending registration for kindergarten, there is plenty to overwhelm him with.

"Why were you banging your head on the table in the courtyard the other day?" So much has happened between now and then, I'd almost forgotten about Cameron James, the parent liaison for the school district. "Tell you what, there's a bench up ahead, why don't we go sit?"

"Sounds good."

I'm grateful to have a moment to collect my thoughts. I haven't given much thought to Mr. James or what role he'll play in my life in the near future. There are so many questions I've been too scared to ask about what school will look like for Lily. I'm the worst kind of coward. I never thought I'd be the kind of mother who would allow her fear to hold her child back.

We walk for a few more minutes before the narrow trail meets up with a creek bed. Beside the trickling water is a bench with a brass statue behind it. The statue is of a man in robes, leaning over the bench like he's praying.

"Saint Joseph, I'm assuming." Tate gestures toward the figure.

"The patron saint of the dying," I murmur to myself.

The sculpted face is agonizingly beautiful. The artist didn't give him a peaceful expression. His face is twisted in pain, like he understands the hurt that death leaves in its wake. I wonder if there's a saint for the vacillating. I want Tate to be a part of my life; I'm just wary about whether he'll accept Lily's place in it. We're a package deal; non-negotiable. It's a tremendous responsibility to take on, for a child who's not your own.

We sit down on the bench, shielded by the hovering saint. If I was planning on curtailing some of the grittier points, or skimming the details, I can't do it now. Not with Saint Joseph's pained face staring down at me. What the hell am I being such a chicken about, anyway? Tate has all but begged me to unburden myself. He looks at me expectantly, waiting for me to resolve my anxiety and explain.

"Earlier that day, a social worker came to speak with me about Lily." It's just one sentence, but the first is always the hardest. "She wanted to go over the options we have available for her when she starts school next month. It was a really hard visit." I hesitate, unsure of how much of myself to reveal. "It still hurts to think about how limited our options really are. It breaks my heart that *my* little girl won't have the same first-day-of-school experience that other little girls her age will have." I dip my head and sniffle back a fresh wave of tears. Wrapped up in what to tell Tate, I forgot how much the telling hurts. I feel better that I told him, though. Not because the pain is somehow less than it was before, just because it's shared.

"Kind of like you've been robbed, huh?" He doesn't mince words or try to tell me it'll be okay. He hits right at the heart of my guilt.

"I shouldn't feel that way, though," I say. "I should accept Lily for who she is, not who she could've been."

"Hey." Tate dips his head, so his eyes are level with mine. "Grieving a lost dream isn't betraying Lily. It doesn't mean you love her less; it just means that you wish her life could've been different."

"It's not that simple," I whisper. I don't know why I bother; whispering won't soften the harsh truth I'm sharing. "I don't just wish things were different so Lily's life could be easier; I wish it were different so *my* life could be easier."

I'm a horrible person, and now Tate knows it, too. I try to hide my face in shame, but Tate tips my face toward his, holding me captive in his stare.

"You're human, Caroline." His eyes are intense, his tone adamant. "I don't know a single person who set out to be a lifelong caregiver to anyone, let alone their child." He lets me lean against his shoulder and cry my eyes out.

When I feel like I can speak again, I lay the rest of my guilt at his feet, suddenly desperate to have it all out in the open.

"You're right; I don't know anyone who would choose that for themselves or their children," I sniffle. "I can't get past this guilt in my heart. If I'd known that Lily would be born with this kind of disability, I would've stopped trying to get pregnant. What kind of person does that make me?"

I watch Tate's eyes as he takes in my words, looking for a hint of disgust in his expression. It never comes.

"That's an awfully big cross you're carrying there." He sighs.

I don't know whether to feel insulted or redeemed. It's not like I'm not aware that I crucify myself at every opportunity, but I never expected anyone to understand why.

"As for what kind of person you are? You're the kind of person who isn't afraid to own up to her own feelings, no matter how dark or ugly some may perceive them."

I want the ground to open up and suck me in; I knew I'd never be able to hide the dark and twisty piece of me.

Tate rests his hand on my shoulder and continues. "However, I think they're the most honest words I've ever heard anyone say."

I pull back so I can see his face more clearly. "You don't think less of me?" I ask, shocked.

"I think more of you, actually," he says matter-of-factly. "You could honestly be the bravest person I know."

An undignified snort erupts from me. He can't be serious. Me, brave? I'm the biggest chickenshit out there.

"Don't tease," I say.

"I'm serious," he insists. "No one I know would ever admit to feeling that way, but I promise you they'd be feeling it. It takes a lot of courage to put it all out there. I feel pretty special that you told me." He smiles at me, and my heart melts.

I'm in love with my stranger. I swore that I would slow the pace and take a step back. Instead, I let myself fall in love.

But there's no way I'm saying a thing. Despite his perfect words, I still can't believe he can accept me, Lily and all. How's that for brave?

take a chance

The walk back to the hospice center feels much shorter than our walk out to the creek. It makes sense that it wouldn't be a lengthy trek; it's just far enough from the building for it to feel like an escape. That seems to be a recurring theme in our budding relationship: we find ways to get far enough away from reality that we feel like we're escaping. I wish there were a way to prolong those moments, to stay in the refuge of our own world for just a little while longer. I want just a few more minutes of holding Tate's hand and pretending that I haven't gone completely mad by falling in love with him.

"What are your plans for the rest of the day?" Tate asks me, saving me from the cacophony in my head. He pauses at the foot of the spiral staircase and glances over his shoulder. He seems nervous, and it makes me smile. I can't help it; I'm thrilled to know I'm not the only one who gets a little jittery.

"Outside of spending time with you, I was going to do a little writing." I try to act like it's no big deal. I haven't told anyone that I've started writing again, but after spilling my guts earlier, I know I'm safe telling Tate.

"Writing, eh?" he shoots over his shoulder. When we reach the top of the stairs, he turns and smiles broadly at me. "Dabbling?"

"Ha ha." I smile back at him. "Yes, I'm dabbling with a story. If you're lucky, I'll let you read it sometime."

He leans in and whispers, "Oh, I'm already lucky."

Did someone say something about getting lucky?

He chuckles and I shiver when his breath skitters across my shoulder. Ignoring the warmth spreading through my body, I take a deep breath and try to act unaffected. "Why do you ask?"

"Well, I have something for you, but it's not here." He looks at me sheepishly. I can't help but wonder where his train of thought is going. I cock my head and wait for him to continue. "It's at my place." He crinkles his nose and bites his bottom lip. I think it's supposed to be Tate cringing, but it's the sexiest thing I've ever seen.

"Oh . . . uh . . . okay," I stammer. He smiles his relief, and his dimples just about buckle my knees.

"Tarryn and Tom are going to stay for a while so I can have a break," he explains.

"Of course," I reply. "Whatever you want to do, I'm free for the rest of the day." Suddenly I'm anxious to make a break for it with Tate and run away. We walk through the lobby of the hospice and pause at the front desk.

"Wait right here, okay?" he says. "I'm just going to let my sister know I'm leaving."

He's off down the hallway before I have a chance to reply. I'm thoroughly intrigued; my mind is running wild wondering what Tate has for me. Part of me—let's face it, a big part of me—is hoping it's a ploy to get me alone at his place. It's been a long time since I've had the desire to be alone with a man that way. I've thought about sex plenty; I just haven't missed it until now. My life with Peter was so broken, sex hadn't been a part of our relationship for a long time. In fact, we hadn't had sex in over a year when he left. The last time we did, it was after a particularly hateful fight that had left us both emotionally spent and raw. Not the best foundation to build a healthy sexual relationship on, but by that point, we were already experts on sabotaging ourselves.

lily love

Hey, knock it off! This is not a threesome.

I shake my head; I don't need to be thinking about Peter right now. What I should be thinking about is whether I can emotionally handle a physical relationship with Tate. I need to figure that out before I find myself in an awkward position, like pinned beneath his hard, naked body. I close my eyes as images of Tate's nude form assault my imagination. He's hovering over me, with his hips pressed against mine. His lips brush my neck as his hand cups my breast—

"Caroline."

My eyes fly open at the sound of my name. I find Tate's eyes burning into me. My face flushes with heat as I look away. I am so busted, and from the look on his face, Tate knows *exactly* where my thoughts were. He stays silent as he guides us out of the building into the parking lot. When we get to my car, I muster the courage to look at him again. Big mistake. His soulful eyes bore into me, and I swear they can see every thought I've ever had.

"Follow me," he says, and all I can do is nod in agreement.

He reaches around me to open my door, making sure not to touch me. I can't tell if it's because he's thinking the same naked thoughts that I am, or if he's afraid of mine. Either way, it's unnerving. I want to wrap my arms around his neck and kiss him senseless, just like he's done to me, but we're in the parking lot of a hospice. Talk about inappropriate.

I slide into the driver's seat and force myself to smile casually at Tate. "See you there?" is all I can think to say. Some wordsmith I am. I wait for him to step out of the way so I can close the door, but he doesn't move. Instead he rests his forearms on the doorframe and leans into my space. He surrounds me, his presence consuming me. "Tate," I whisper. I want to tell him that I need to go home, that I'll see him some other time, because I'm all out of self-restraint.

"Follow me," he repeats, like he knows I'm wavering. "You're killing me, Caroline." He squeezes his eyes closed, like the sight of me is too much. I want to die; he must have whiplash with all my back-and-forth. "If you don't stop looking at me that way, we're not going to make it out of the parking lot." He smirks at my expression, which I can only imagine must reflect something between "mortified" and "horror-stricken." A quick flick of my neck and I'm facing my lap. The curtain of my hair shields me from Tate's penetrating stare.

"Well, if you don't let me close my door, we won't be making it out of the parking lot, either." I lift my eyes back to his and grin. A little humor to cut through this tension. I really hope it works, because I might burst into flames if he keeps looking at me like he wants to climb on top of me right here.

Taking a step back, he chuckles under his breath as he closes my door. He taps my window and gestures for me to roll it down.

"Your smart-ass sense of humor doesn't make you any less sexy." He arches his eyebrow and winks his dimples at me. Damn. "Just sayin'."

In my rearview mirror I watch him cross the parking lot. I can't believe I'm following him back to his house, knowing what might happen. Better yet, hoping that it does. While this newfound boldness is shocking, I find it far more startling that I'm okay with it.

desire

I watch in fascination as Tate disappears into a black Toyota Highlander. I think he really enjoys knocking me off my game. Can't a girl just lighten things up a bit? Oh, no, the tenderness of our connection is heating and fostering a whole different set of feelings in me. Tate just stokes the flame until I feel like I want to climb out of my skin. I roll my head in circles on my shoulders, but it does nothing to help me relax.

I follow Tate for about ten minutes, to the edge of town. The tiny rectangular land-lots of urban living give way to open acreage. We pass the horse farm where Lily has equine therapy and turn left on one of those little dirt roads you'd fly past unless you knew what you were looking for. Eventually we pull up to a small Craftsman-style cottage, set against what looks to be tobacco crops on the right and open land on the left. I follow Tate around the side of the house and pull up between him and a second building. My curiosity is piqued when I step out of the car and look around.

"Mechanical engineer, photographer, and tobacco farmer?" I tease. "Is there anything you can't do, Mr. Michaels?"

He comes to a stop at the back bumper of my car, leaving just enough space for me to think I'm safe.

"Come here." His voice is as rich and warm as his caramel eyes. I stand completely still, terrified to take a step toward him and terrified not to. "Caroline."

His tone commands me to focus on him as he walks toward me. I hold my breath when he reaches around me, waiting for his body to come into contact with mine in some delicious way. Only when his hand closes over mine do I realize that my arm is folded behind me, white-knuckling the door handle. He peels my fingers away from the car, and begins rubbing them until the circulation comes back. "Are you okay?"

"Of course. Why do you ask?" I try to smile, but my lips quiver to betray my nerves.

"Because you're looking at me like you're scared to death of me." He brushes my cheek with the side of his hand. "I just want to spend time with you. The last thing I want is for you to be scared of me."

"I'm only scared of how badly I want you." I cover my mouth with my hand, shocked that I spoke out loud. Tate's lips part, and his eyes burn into me with so much intensity, I'm sure I'll burst into flames. He tugs my hand away from my mouth, letting his thumb drag across my bottom lip.

"Jesus," he whispers. "You're killing me, Caroline. I've never wanted someone as much as I want you."

Knowing that the desire is mutual leaves me feeling dizzy and drunk. Inhibitions long forgotten, my tongue darts out to graze the pad of his thumb. His breath hitches as he watches me taste him. Suddenly his thumb is gone, and his mouth is hot on mine. He nips at my lip at the same time he reaches around and grabs hold of my bottom. I moan at the sensation, giving his tongue room to explore my mouth. He pulls us around the front of my car and lifts me onto the hood. I gasp as the heat from the engine seeps through my shorts, but it's nothing compared to the fire Tate's generating in them. Nudging my knees apart, he steps between them and grabs my face in his hands.

Passion ignites his kiss, making me tremble at his touch. When he pulls back, I whimper at the loss of him.

My eyes drift open to Tate unfastening the Velcro straps of my sling, sliding it carefully from around my neck. When his eyes lift to mine again, I'm struck by the reverence I find there. Not just lust from wanting me, but something more, something deeper that gives me hope that maybe he could be falling, too.

"Wrap your arms around my neck," he pleads.

He doesn't need to ask twice; I drape my arms around him, and at the same time he pulls me flush against him. His erection is hard and hot between us; it makes me feel wanton and desperate for more. He lifts me with ease, and I wrap my legs around his waist. His lips are back on mine as he crosses the yard. Once he clears the front steps of his house, he lets me slide down the front of his body so he can pick his pockets for his keys. He mutters a curse as he fumbles with the lock, until the door finally swings wide.

He hesitates at the threshold and looks back at me. "I swear I have something for you. This isn't why I brought you home with me. We can wait; I don't want to rush you."

I didn't know I could be more turned on than I was already, but I am. I couldn't stop myself from having him if I wanted to—and God knows I don't want to. I want in his bed. Now.

I lean in close to his ear, so the touch of my lips and my breath can punctuate my words. "Where's your room?" I run my nose along his neck and kiss his pulse point, where the frantic thrum of his heartbeat vibrates against my lips. Tate lets out a growl and then the world goes completely upside down. I squeal as Tate tosses me over his shoulder and makes a break for the hallway. I can hardly breathe, I'm laughing so hard.

I smack his ass. "Whatever happened to 'I'm not really a Neanderthal'?" Then, as quickly as I was upended, I'm flat on my back in the middle of Tate's bed.

"I do seem to go a little Cro-Magnon around you." He smiles devilishly. The bed dips as he climbs his way toward me, nudging my feet apart as he goes. Any hope I had of stopping vanishes as he leans his body into mine. I gasp when Tate's hand brushes my bare skin where my tank has ridden up. He stares down at me with piercing eyes, asking permission to continue. I feel beautiful and sensual under his scrutiny. Without any nervousness, I lift my arms and arch my back in invitation.

He takes his time, kissing every inch of skin he exposes as he lifts my shirt higher. It's driving me crazy. He's unwrapping me like I'm a gift. Savoring my skin, murmuring words of gratitude and awe as he goes. My breasts strain against the lace of my bra, begging for Tate's touch. Sensing my need, he frees me from the rest of my tank and pulls down the cup of my bra. When he takes my nipple into his mouth, my hips buck into his. I'm too lost in the way his tongue is licking fire across my skin to care that I've grabbed fistfuls of his hair to bring him closer.

Soon we're nothing more than a tangle of limbs and clothing we're desperate to shed. The need to feel Tate's skin against mine is as keen as my next breath. Somewhere between my head and my heart, wanting him has morphed into a need so powerful, I don't know how I've lived without him so far. My hormones are waging a war of their own, ready to stake their claim where Tate is concerned.

"You are so beautiful," Tate groans, shaking me from my reverie.

I could say the same for him; his tall, lean frame is mapped with dips and valleys of toned muscle. A dusting of hair spans his wide chest and gradually narrows over his stomach. The faint trail that's left leads to the unabashed evidence of his desire for me. It makes me heady with power, knowing I made him feel that way. He brushes his lips along my collarbone and up my neck. I undulate my hips, so his erection slides deliciously between us.

"I want to be inside you so badly," he growls. He *growls*, and it's the sexiest thing I've ever heard.

"Please, Tate," I beg, not caring how shameless I sound. He rolls away to root through his nightstand, producing a foil packet. Softly panting, I shift my hips in silent invitation as he rolls the condom down his length.

"Look at me," Tate demands, and I'm helpless to resist. The intensity of his stare holds me captive as he pushes into me. My eyes flutter shut at the divine sensation of my body opening up for him. "Open your eyes, Caroline." Tate's tongue sweeps the seam of my mouth. "I want to see your eyes when I'm buried in you."

Up until this point in my life, I didn't think I was one of those girls who liked bedroom talk. That was until Tate started talking about being buried inside of me, and now I can't wait to hear more declarations just like that from him. I open my eyes to his lust-filled gaze, and I know that Tate feels every bit of what I'm feeling. He wants me just as much as I want him. He lifts his hips to ease out of me, his eyes burning into mine when he thrusts forward again.

"Oh, God, Tate," I moan, as pressure begins building deep in my belly. I lift my hips to allow him deeper, savoring the way he fills and stretches me in a way I've never felt before.

"You feel so good . . . Jesus . . . so good," he pants, finding a rhythm that drives us both wild.

Just when I feel like I can't take any more of his sweet torture, my body clenches down on him as an orgasm explodes through me. Our eyes still fixed on each other, Tate watches as I come apart underneath him.

Never in my life have I felt so wholly enraptured by anyone.

"You're. So. Sexy," he grunts between thrusts, as his own need reaches a fevered pitch. Gripping his pumping hips, I pull him even harder against me. "Ah, Caroline!" My name comes out on a strangled cry as his body shudders and empties inside me.

into the mystic

I have no idea how long we lie sweat-slick and panting. I'm in a haze of postorgasmic bliss and don't really care anyway. I grumble my dissent when Tate rolls off of me.

"Did I hurt you?" He shifts his weight onto his side so he can take my broken wrist in his hand.

"The last thing you did was hurt me." I smirk.

"Hmm," he murmurs, kissing the tips of my fingers. "Still, I should be gentler with you." He hovers at my ring finger, which trembles worse than the rest of my hand. It's easy to forget that the hemiparesis still affects me when my hand is immobilized in a brace. Instinctively I curl my fingers into a fist, wanting to hide it from Tate. He kisses my knuckles before he asks, "Why does your hand shake, Caroline?"

Instant mood killer.

"You don't really want to talk about it now," I insist.

"Tell me; it doesn't change anything," he swears, "I just want to know." His eyes are so sincere; it makes me want to believe him.

"When I was in labor with Lily, I had a stroke." It felt so nice to be desirable and sexy, but that changed the second I said "stroke." Now the only thing I feel is like an invalid.

"Preeclampsia?" he asks. I can only nod. "Tarryn had that with my niece; she went on bed rest for her last trimester." He reaches for my arm, encouraging me to lie back down with him. He tucks me against his chest and waits for me to continue the story.

"I didn't present with it until late in my pregnancy. The day we found out, my labor was induced, and then everything went crazy." I gasp in surprise when Tate's hand slides across my stomach. My instinct is to shy away further, but I force myself not to pull away.

"It amazes me what a woman's body is capable of," he murmurs reverently as he flattens his palm between my belly button and my pubic bone. With great tenderness, he traces a heart where Lily grew inside my body, kissing its center in adoration. The need to tell him that I love him overwhelms me, but I can't. Not yet.

"Do you want to have children someday?" I inwardly curse myself for bringing it up. It's questions like these that can quickly remind me how little promise there is for a future with Tate. He isn't going to want to take on the care of a special-needs child or share the spotlight with one. And what if he *does* want children? That's definitely a deal breaker, considering my body wasn't very good at being pregnant. Understatement of the year.

"I love children, but I've never had an overwhelming desire to have my own." He continues to stroke my stomach with his fingertips. "I love my niece and nephew more than anything in the world. I can't imagine loving my own child more than that, or loving Jay and Jennifer any less. Love is love, regardless of biology. It's our own willingness to share it that matters most." He lifts his eyes to mine, and I see his love reflected back at me. It steals my breath and makes me wonder if I'm just as transparent.

"That's beautiful, Tate." His eyes still have me entranced by their flagrant emotion. They soften further as a smile splits his face. I want him to love Lily like that, and I'm scared that he won't.

"Wait right here." He rolls over and grabs his jeans off the floor. He moves with more energy than he should have, after the amount we just expended.

"Where are you going?" I ask sleepily, snuggling further into the bedsheets that smell just like him. Yum.

"It's a surprise." He flashes his dimples, and all other coherent thoughts are gone.

He disappears down the hallway, leaving me alone and deliciously naked in his bed. I prop myself up on my elbows and take in his bedroom. I didn't get much of a chance to see it before (not that I minded). The furniture is dark and masculine, but what stands out the most are the photographs. They hang on the wall in all shapes and sizes. No particular pattern or theme, but they're fascinating in their chaos. There are photos of the fields outside his house, in different stages of seasons. Some are unrecognizable landscapes, and others are candid shots of people I don't recognize. There's palpable emotion in each frame that blows me away. I can't believe he ever considered doing anything other than this.

I lean over the edge of the bed and grab the first article of clothing my hand comes into contact with; it's Tate's shirt. Pulling it over my head, I drink in his unique scent and smile. I pad over to the wall of photographs to get a closer look. That's where Tate finds me upon his return, studying his art.

"Hey, there." I follow the sound of his voice to the doorway. He's holding something behind his back, watching me intently.

"Tate, these are stunning. You've got a gift for capturing a feeling, not just a subject."

He saunters over to where I'm standing, lips twitching, trying not to smile.

"Nice shirt." He smirks as he leans in to kiss my cheek.

My face flames and I laugh at the irony. He's kissed every inch of my naked body, and I'm being bashful about wearing his shirt.

"I'm glad you think I'm talented," he says matter-of-factly. He takes his hand from behind his back and holds out a large cardboard envelope for me to take. "I really did ask you back here to give you something." Opening it, I gasp when I pull out a gorgeous black-and-white photo of the Casablanca Lily from the moon garden. Its texture and shading make it look almost like it's mourning. It's the most beautiful thing I've ever seen.

"When did you have time to do this?" My voice shakes with emotion as I run my fingers over the outline of the petals.

"I went back with my camera last night." He shrugs like it's no big thing, but his eyes dance with his excitement. "I got some great shots, but I wanted this one for you." He flips the photo over in my hands and points to where he's marked the back.

Tate Michaels Photography 2013

"Lily Love"

"That's the name of the song I've sung to Lily since she was a baby," I whisper. How could he know that?

"It's a song? Really?" He sounds truly surprised. "I just thought that title fit. It's your favorite flower from the moon garden; it's your daughter's name . . . there's a lot of love surrounding that word."

I love you! Come on, you want to say it.

"It's an Irish folk song by the Chieftains," I start to say, but can't continue. Tears flood my eyes and spill down my face. He doesn't need to tell me that he loves me; he just showed me in a most undeniable way. He cups my face in his hands and looks at me with worried eyes.

"I didn't want to make you cry," he says, gently sweeping away my tears. "I wanted it to make you happy."

"H-happy tears," I stammer between hiccupping breaths. He takes the picture from me and places it on his dresser. On a heavy sigh he wraps me in his arms, holding me tightly to his chest and tucking me under his chin. My very favorite place in the world.

"You scared me," he breathes into my hair. "I thought I really screwed up."

"You didn't screw up. You paid attention to what was important to me, took in the things that I shared, and then showed me that I was on your mind." I turn my head up to make sure he understands what I say next. "You make me feel known and cherished, and I've never felt that way." I have to practically bite through my tongue to keep from blurting out, ". . . cherished and loved," but I'm not going to tempt fate tonight. We have no business talking of love. We hardly know each other, and Lily is only a series of stories I've shared with him, not a tangible little girl with profound needs that need to be met daily. Yet here we are staring into each other's eyes with more love than I could've ever hoped for.

"I'm so glad you like it," he whispers against my lips. "By the way, you are more than cherished." His lips are soft and firm against mine, eliciting a blissful sigh from me. His tongue slips between my parted lips, stroking and licking mine, leaving me breathless and weak-kneed.

He guides me back to the bed, where he strips off his jeans and his shirt from me. He pulls me in close, and I shiver when our bodies press together. His deft hands electrify my senses, just as they did before, but now everything feels different. We replace the frantic rush of our desperation for each other with reverent explorations. I show him with my body what my words can't. We make love until the orange glow of dusk shines through the window. I don't even know what time it is, and I don't care. I want to push the rest of the world away and disappear with Tate.

I can't do that, though. Reality is on the other side of the threshold, waiting to remind us that life doesn't stand still for anything.

the world as i see it

"Now, let's throw some clothes on; I have something I want to show you," he says and starts gathering our clothes off the floor. I pull on my panties and am rooting through the pile he's assembled when I feel his eyes on me. I turn around and find him fastening the top button of his jeans, leveling me with a look of pure intensity. I fold my arms over my chest, suddenly feeling very exposed.

"What?" I start to squirm when he doesn't look away. He shakes his head and chuckles to himself, which only makes me feel more foolish. "*What?*" I insist. I spot my bra peeking out from under his bed and dive for it, suddenly grateful for something to do. When I fasten the last hook around my rib cage, I turn back toward Tate. He's still in the same spot he was in before, looking at me in much the same way.

"You're beautiful," he says.

"Thanks." I blush scarlet red. "Bathroom?" That's the third one-word reply I've made in five minutes. I need a moment to get myself together.

"At the end of the hall," he answers, and then pauses like he has something to add.

I brush past him and pretend I don't see his hesitation. I wish he'd just say whatever it is he has on his mind. Since starting to write again, my imagination is a vast playground for assumptions. His eyes bore holes in my back as I walk down the hall, but still he stays silent.

"Are you okay?" I ask. He nods, but doesn't say anything. Maybe he just needs a minute, too.

"Caroline." I look over my shoulder to where he's watching me from the doorway. "It's nothing bad; I just can't believe you're here." That's it? That's what Mr. Heart-On-Sleeve was struggling with? Sensing my apparent doubt, he pushes off the doorframe and strides up to me. He tucks a strand of hair behind my ear, letting his hand linger on my face. "What I feel for you is a lot to process. I may not always have an immediate answer for what's buzzing in my brain, but I'll never lie about it."

"Okay," is all I can manage to say.

My head is swimming with so many emotions it feels like I'm drowning. I'm relieved that he isn't secretly harboring feelings of regret for sleeping with me, I'm pissed at myself for even thinking that for a minute, and I'm all swoony inside from the honesty of his confession. I reach up on my tiptoes and kiss him softly, to reassure him and myself.

"I'll be out in just a minute," I promise as I close the bathroom door behind me. When I hear Tate's footsteps retreating back up the hallway, I close my eyes and lean against the door. When I open them again, it takes all of my effort not to shriek at the beast staring back in the mirror. My hair is a nest of tangles, sticking out every which way. The new hairdo is rivaled only by the smudged mascara under my eyes. I look just like the disaster I am. I open and close some of the drawers beneath the sink until I find a wide-toothed comb. I run it through my hair until every knot and snarl are smooth again, and splash cool water on my face to rinse away the makeup. Just a few minutes after my retreat, I emerge from the bathroom feeling a hundred times better and ready to face Tate. I find him in the kitchen, pouring two glasses of white wine. He glances up when I walk in.

"I thought you might like to have some wine," he offers. I take the glass from him and savor the crisp tang of the wine. "Feel better?" he asks tentatively.

"Much, thank you." I sigh. "Now, what were you going to show me?"

Tate's face lights up, and I can't help but get a little swept up by his enthusiasm. "House tour first; then I want to show you my studio." He claps his hands together and pauses for a moment.

"This is the kitchen." He motions with a sweep of his hand. It's charming, with its white country cabinets and butcher-block countertops. A row of bar stools are tucked under the bar top. I can picture Tate and Tarryn's family eating here. This room just feels like the heart of the house, a space where they would migrate to.

Tate grabs my hand and leads me into a large open area off the kitchen. "This is supposed to be the living-slash-dining combo, but I always eat at the kitchen bar, so room for living it is." I knew it. He walks me past the overstuffed couches and armchairs to a set of French doors that lead outside.

"This is my favorite part of the house," he says, leading us onto a deck that spans the entire back side. It faces the open land I saw when we pulled up, and the view is absolutely breathtaking.

"This is gorgeous, Tate."

"I thought you might like it." He wraps his arm around my shoulders and kisses the top of my head. We stand there for a while, just soaking it all in, and I feel the dull ache of regret for having to move on.

"This concludes the tour of Chateau Michaels. The only thing we didn't get to was the guest room, but you don't need to worry about that. When you're here, I want you in bed with me." He smirks. He drops his arm from my shoulder and takes my hand. "Now, let me show you my studio."

He guides us down the steps of the deck and around the side of the house where our cars are parked. As we approach the secondary building, he pulls a key from his pocket and unlocks the door. Tate steps through the door before me, flipping the switch, bathing the studio in light.

"W-wow," I stutter. "This isn't what I was expecting at all."

The space before me goes against every stereotype I have of a photography studio. There's no darkroom, no pungent odor of developing fluid. It's a world away from the brooding and moody image I have stuck in my head. The walls are a sage green, and each photo displayed on them is encased in a unique frame. Some are ornate wood, some are scrolling iron, but no two are alike. His chestnut desk faces a window that looks out over the tobacco fields; it is paired with the most hideous chair I've ever seen. It's a worn-out brown velour armchair on wheels. That's being kind. It looks like something Goodwill wouldn't even accept. Outside of the brown monstrosity, his studio is warm and open, nothing like the monochromatic, utilitarian studio I'd imagined.

"Since I deal in stock-photo catalogs, the majority of my prints are digital." He walks over to his desk and taps the keyboard belonging to a big-screen iMac. It brings to life a scrolling slide show of Tate's work. "I don't deal with a darkroom anymore. If I need film developed, I can rent darkroom space in town by the hour." He plops down in his fantastically ugly chair and props his feet on the desk. "So, what do you think?" He holds his arms wide, clearly very proud of his studio, as he should be. It is as unique and eclectic as its artist.

"It's amazing, Tate." I chuckle without meaning to. I can't help it; the sight of him in that terrible chair is ridiculous. I can't believe he would mar his creative space with something so grossly misplaced. The more I fight against laughing, the more urgent the need becomes. "I'm sorry." I snort. "That chair is awful." He looks completely affronted, which only makes me double over in laughter.

"Do not dis my lucky chair," he warns. "Every major copyright I've sold, I did sitting in this chair." He pats the armrest, and a faint cloud of dust floats into the air.

I nod my head as I take in his reasoning, thinking carefully before I respond. "Okay," I acquiesce. "Have you ever sat anywhere else while vying for one of those contracts?"

"No, I haven't." He rocks back in his chair as he thinks, bringing a cacophony of shrieking springs to life. I don't know how he can stand it; my ears are practically bleeding.

"How do you know if it's lucky if you haven't tested your theory against another chair?" He looks out the window, and for a minute I assume he's taking it under consideration. Then it dawns on me that he's concentrating on not laughing.

I smell a rat.

He makes the mistake of glancing in my direction, and loses what little control he had left. He throws his head back, howling in laughter. I still don't know the punch line, but his laughter is so infectious I can't help but laugh along with him. Once he's calmed to hearty chuckles, he offers up an explanation.

"My chair broke last week, and I haven't had time to buy a new one. I needed something in the meantime, so my neighbor let me raid his old storage shed. Isn't this great?" He laughs.

"Did you bomb it for fleas before you brought it in here?" I tease . . . kind of.

He stands, grinning devilishly as he pulls me toward him. "Are you afraid you'll get cooties, now that I've been contaminated?" He rubs his cheek into my neck, tickling me with his scruff.

"It's a little late to be worried about that." I giggle. I glance over his shoulder at the computer screen, catching the time and wishing I hadn't.

"It's almost ten o'clock," I say. I dreaded this moment all day; still, I knew it would catch up with me sooner than I wanted. "I should get going soon."

Tate halts his tickle attack and sighs against my shoulder. When he leans back, his face looks just as disappointed as I feel.

"I suppose I can't hold you hostage here forever," he laments. "I don't want you to go."

His confession pulls at my heart, and I want so badly to stay. Still, I know that staying over is something I'm not ready for yet, not until he knows Lily.

"I wish I didn't have to." I smile weakly. "We'll see each other soon, right?" I try my best to sound encouraging.

"Absolutely," he answers, "and we'll talk on the phone when we can't."

My heart sinks when I realize just how little opportunity there is for us to be alone like this. I'm going to miss it terribly.

"Sounds like a plan," I agree. Before melancholy has the chance to sweep me under, Tate pulls me tight against his body.

"This sucks," he says.

I chuckle against his chest. "Yes, it does, but we'll figure it out." He looks down at me with a dimpled smile, and I melt.

"Call me when you get home," he demands. "I want to know my girl is safe."

Safety is such a relative term. Until I know whether or not he can accept Lily, my heart isn't safe at all.

change

The drive home from Tate's was a myriad of wildly swinging emotions. Giddy highs when I allowed myself to indulge in the memory of his touch and how wonderfully loved he made me feel. Plummeting lows when the fear of losing my heart in the process became overwhelming. *Kismet*, I repeat on a loop in my mind, until my nerves begin to calm. Now here I am, sitting at my kitchen table, chamomile tea in hand, waiting for divine wisdom to take over and help me figure out what to say when I call Tate. Before I have that chance, my phone lights up next to me.

"Would you think I was crazy if I told you I missed you already?" Tate's rich voice soothes me.

"Nah. Rumor has it that the feeling's entirely mutual."

His deep laughter fills me with warmth, chasing my anxiety farther away. "I thought you were going to call me so I knew you made it back."

"I'm sorry I worried you." I dip my pinky finger into my tea to test the temperature. Smiling as I lick it, I marvel at how much influence Tate already has in my life.

"Don't apologize; I'm glad I get to hear your voice one more time tonight." He chuckles softly.

"It is pretty nice to hear your voice, too." Seeing his name light up the screen filled me with more happiness than I've felt in long time. It's amazing how little I missed feeling this way, until I could feel it again. With Peter, I fell in love while I was still learning about myself. We discovered life and grew together, before Lily. Ironically, it took losing Peter to really figure out who I was. Even though it took pain to bring me here, I'm so very grateful that I'm here.

"I'll let you go get settled in; I know you've got a big day tomorrow." His thoughtfulness amazes me. I don't think I'll ever get used to it, and I don't want to. "Let me know how it goes with the school district?"

"You bet. And you let me know how things are with your mom, and if you or Tarryn need anything, okay?"

"I will," he replies. "Good night, beautiful girl."

"Good night, Tate."

• • •

"You *what*?!" Paige shrieks so loudly I have to pull the phone away from my ear.

"Paige, I don't have time for this. My meeting is in ten minutes." It's the second time this morning that I've had to remind her that she'll have to wait until tonight for more of the story. The first time was this morning, when I dropped off Lily so I could meet with Cameron James alone. I had to blow off her questions completely. She was annoyed but had no choice but to back off, considering Lily's impressionable ears. Apparently, giving her minor details to tide her over until tonight isn't helping.

"You can't just lay that on me and then bail," she complains. "You spent the day at his house doing what? Playing pinochle?"

"If you don't like my answers, then you shouldn't press me for the story when you know I don't have time to tell it," I snap. I love Paige, but this isn't about her. "I'll see you tonight and you can pick my carcass like the vulture you're acting like." I swing open the heavy door leading to the lobby of the school district's building. I scan the list of departments until I find Exceptional Children on the third floor.

"I'm sorry," she grumbles. "I just want to know you're all right."

"I'm fine, Paige," I promise. "In fact, I'm great, so stop worrying. I'll see you tonight." I spin around until I find the elevator and press the Up button.

"Okay."

"I love you," I tell her as I get on the elevator. "I've got to go." I hit End before she can say goodbye. I just want a few uninterrupted minutes before my meeting. This morning has already been a whirlwind. I woke up early to give myself a few hours of writing time. When I called Cameron James's office, he encouraged me to come meet with him sooner rather than later.

"There are several appointments we'll need to make for Lily, and the sooner we can meet and get those scheduled, the better," he had said. When he asked if we could meet this morning, I didn't hesitate. Peter couldn't make it out of his meetings, so we agreed I'd go alone. We both want Lily to have as much time as possible to be evaluated and considered for placement. This morning that meant getting showered, dressed, and downtown in under thirty minutes. Combined with Paige's prying, it's been one heck of a morning. The bell chimes for the third floor, and my moment of peace is over.

"Caroline Hunter for Cameron James," I tell the receptionist behind the glass. She signs me in and then motions for me to sit in the adjoining waiting room. Pamphlets for every kind of disability line the wall. Down syndrome, autism, PDD-NOS, ADHD, the list goes on and on—but none of them are for unspecified developmental disabilities. I guess that spectrum is too broad for one pamphlet. Still, it frustrates me. How can anyone help her if they don't understand what's wrong?

"Ms. Hunter?" An older man with salt-and-pepper hair waves me back. I follow him to a small office and wait to hear how our world will change once Lily starts school.

"Cameron James." He holds out his hand. "Pleased to finally meet you."

We shake and sit across the desk from each other. Having forgone my sling, I pick at the frayed edges of Velcro on my cast. I'm hoping he doesn't ask about my wrist, because I have a terrible feeling it will influence his opinion of Lily.

"So, we have your daughter, Lily, as entering kindergarten this fall?" He opens a file folder on his desk.

"Yes," I answer. Well, that was easy enough. It would be great if all of the questions could be answered with a simple yes or no.

"Can you confirm her birthdate for me?" He smiles at me over his readers and looks back over Lily's file.

"January twenty-four oh-eight," I reply. I sincerely hope he isn't trying to lull me into a false sense of security before blindsiding me with the tough stuff.

"And she has an unspecified developmental disability with global developmental delays, and epilepsy. Is that also correct?"

"Yes," I say. "She's a trouper, though."

"I see," he mutters as he studies the file. "She scored extremely low on the Wechsler Preschool and Primary Scale of Intelligence at sixty-eight," he reads. Before he can repeat back the scores from the Developmental Assessment of Young Children and the Vineland Adaptive Behavior Scales, I interrupt.

"Mr. James, you don't need to go over the results again. I know what they mean," I say softly. "I just really want to know what they mean for Lily's placement. I want to prepare my family for what to expect. I hope you understand."

"Of course," he says. "The district will run their own assessments, though. We can't use the data provided from private testing."

"Actually," I reply, "those tests were run by a school district–appointed psychologist when Lily was three years old. I thought they were valid through second grade."

"Oh . . . You're right." He nods. "It looks like I misfiled Lily's records with those of some incoming students who haven't been processed by the district yet. I assumed, because she wasn't enrolled in the pre-K program for children with disabilities, that she hadn't been tested by our district. My apologies."

"It's all right. We opted out of the pre-K program so Lily would have more time for private therapies. I kept thinking if I got her more help, she'd catch up," I admit. "Will that affect registering her for school?"

Mr. Cameron gives me a sympathetic smile. "Not at all, Ms. Hunter. We can use these scores to determine services and then test her alongside the rest of her class for placement once school begins."

I'm sure he thinks this news will make me feel better, but it only makes me more nervous about how he'll answer my next question.

"What kind of class will she be placed in?" It's the one thing I know will change everything, but I can't avoid asking it any longer.

"Oh." Mr. James's voice raises in surprise. "Mainstream, of course. We don't use a self-contained classroom model. Instead we use the coteach method, which brings the special-education instructor into a classroom as a full partner to the general-education teacher. We'll pull Lily out for speech and occupational therapies, according to her IEP, but she'll be mainstreamed otherwise."

I blink back tears I really don't want to share with Mr. Cameron James. Taking concerted deep breaths, I make sure I'm hearing him correctly.

"You mean Lily will attend our neighborhood school, not a special-education center?" I'm too afraid to hope that I'm right, because it will crush me if I'm wrong.

"Yes, ma'am."

Two words confirming that my baby will indeed have her first day of school like every other child. That Peter and I will stand with a hundred other parents sending their children to school on the first day, just like everyone else. I want to weep with joy, I want to shout from the rooftops, I want to call Tate and tell him my good news. It's an automatic reaction, I tell myself. Good news—call Tate. My heart vibrates against my ribs as another thought pops into my head: I want to call him because I want him to know Lily.

"Tell me what school you're districted to, Ms. Hunter."

"Gadero Park Elementary," I reply.

"I will give them a call this morning and set a time next week for an IEP meeting. That way we can figure out how we can best support Lily in the classroom before the school year begins." He stands and shakes my hand across the desk. "I hope this makes you feel better about the school year."

"Absolutely, Mr. James. Thank you so much for your time."

"My pleasure." A smile lights his face, and I know that he's sincere. He walks with me down the hallway and opens the door to the waiting room for me. "I'll give you a call with a meeting time at Gadero Park, okay?"

"Okay, Mr. James. Thank you."

I feel a little like Dorothy waking up in Oz after being whisked away by a cyclone. The colorless, two-dimensional world I thought would be school for Lily was just swept up by a cyclone named Cameron James, and spit out into a Technicolor wonderland called Gadero Park Elementary School. Tears of joy sting my eyes, but I wait for the safety of my car before I let them flow out of me. I clung for dear life onto a fear that did nothing but hinder progress, all the while convinced that I was steering us in the right direction.

It amazes me, this beauty I found when I finally let it all go.

ungodly hour

"Tell me why we're doing this again?" Paige whines as we pull into the hospice center. "We could be back at your house eating this." She lifts the edge of the aluminum foil and sniffs the dish of chicken and noodles she's holding in her lap.

"We're doing it so Tate, his family, and other families with loved ones here can have a nice meal tonight," I scold. I swear, sometimes I wonder who's the big sister here.

She folds her arms over her chest and sticks her tongue out like a cranky three-year-old. "Well, you could've put a little aside for your sister." She sniffs indignantly.

"Oh shu'up, you brat." I smack her on the arm playfully. "I'll buy you dinner; quit whining."

"Ouch." She laughs. "You know I'm kidding, right?"

"I know you're a pain in the ass," I tease. "Now get out of my car, and carry that in for me." I take a quick scan of the parking lot while we unload the car. I don't see Tate's Highlander. Part of me is disappointed that I won't run into him, and the other is happy he found some time to get away for a little bit.

"Seriously, I think you're doing a really great thing," she says as we walk through the front doors. "I'm really proud of you."

Paige's words fill me with pride. She's right; I am doing a good thing, and it feels really nice to be able to do it for someone else.

The receptionist grips the telephone to one ear and hands me the kitchen sign-in sheet with the other. Once I have that filled out, she waves us through toward the kitchen area. I'm showing Paige the drawer where the labels are when she blindsides me.

"I'm not going to ask you if you slept with him, because I can already tell you did. And I'm not going to ask you if you care for him, because I know you wouldn't have slept with him if you didn't," she says matter-of-factly.

I grip the edge of the countertop while my head spins wildly, leaving me dizzy and breathless. "Jesus, Paige," I huff, exasperated. "Don't hold anything back."

"I'm just going to ask one thing," she warns. She levels her navy-blue eyes on me, and I brace for whatever she may say next. "Does he know?"

I busy myself with filling out a label, trying to act like this conversation is not a big deal. Paige reminds me so much of Tate in the way that she can home right in on what I'm thinking and lay it all out for inspection. It's seriously uncanny, and I'm slightly bummed that Tate isn't here to meet her. I know that once she meets him, she'll love him, too.

"Know what?" I stall. It's weak, I know; I just don't want to have to defend how I feel or how he makes me feel.

"Does Tate know that you're in love with him, Caroline?" She lays it all out there.

"I haven't told him, if that's what you mean," I answer. It's the most honest I can be. I haven't told him that I love him, but I sense it's something he already knows. Paige doesn't need to know that, though. She's freaked out enough, from what I can tell by the way she's pacing the floor.

"What else could I mean?" she shouts, throwing her arms in the air.

"Pipe down, drama queen," I hiss. "This isn't the place for your theatrics." I'm an adult, for chrissakes, not some foolish child.

"Caroline," she says softly, "I'm worried about you. You've given your heart to this guy and you hardly know him. Is this a casual thing? Are you dating?"

"No, Paige," I insist. "These aren't casual feelings for Tate. We want to see where this goes; we don't want to see other people. Everything is fine." I don't know if I'm trying harder to convince her or myself. I just want to go back to yesterday, when I was with Tate and everything felt possible.

"Does he feel the same way about you?" she asks incredulously.

"Yes." Paige and I spin toward the voice at the same time. Standing in the doorway with puffy, red-rimmed eyes is Tarryn.

"My brother is crazy about Caroline, whoever you are." She dismisses Paige with a wave of her hand before facing me. "Can I talk to you for a minute?"

My heart sinks to the pit of my stomach when I see Tarryn's expression head-on. This is not going to be good news. At. All.

"Of course," I reply. "Paige, why don't you wait for me in the lobby. By the way, this is Tarryn, Tate's twin sister. Tarryn, this is my sister, Paige." They nod at each other, neither sure of what to say. "I'll be out in a minute," I call after Paige as she walks out of the kitchen.

"Have you spoken with Tate?" Tarryn's voice shakes and her eyes fill with tears.

"Not since this morning. What's going on, Tarryn?" I wrap my arm around her shoulders as she sobs softly.

"She's gone," is all Tarryn can spit out as she fights to catch her breath.

Oh, no—Tate! Every angry thought I had toward Paige is lost, replaced with panic to find Tate.

"When, Tarryn? I spoke to him around eleven o'clock, but not since then. Does he know?" I cry with her, unable to stop the flow of tears for the loss of my stranger's family.

"We were both here with her. Around one o'clock she had another seizure and stopped breathing." She pauses to catch her breath. "She stopped breathing like last time, except they don't resuscitate. She was alert one moment and gone the next."

"I'm sorry; I'm so sorry," I whisper as we cry together.

"Tate took off before the funeral home came for her body," she sniffles. "I thought he was going to you; when I saw your car in the parking lot, I thought he'd come back."

"What do you mean, he took off?"

"I haven't seen him since they pronounced Mom. It's been almost six hours. Are you sure he hasn't tried to call you?" she asks desperately.

I pull my phone from my purse to double-check, and then dial his number to see if he'll pick up.

"You've reached Tate Michaels. Please leave . . ."

I tune out his generic greeting, trying to think of where he may have headed.

"Tate, it's Caroline. Please call me; I'm so worried about you." I look up at Tarryn and shake my head. I can tell from the look on her face that she's frantic with worry and devastated by her loss.

"Jay and Jennifer never even got to say goodbye," she whimpers, lost in her grief.

"Don't worry about Tate; I'll find him," I promise, and I have a feeling I know where he might be.

I leave Tarryn to finish tying up the loose ends at St. Joseph's, and take Paige back to her car. Once I'm alone again, I gun it across town to the one place I'm almost certain he'll be.

where you'll find me

The parking lot is so dark when I pull in that I almost miss Tate's truck parked in the far corner. Relief washes over me when I get closer and realize that it *is* really his car. I've found him, just as I promised Tarryn I would. Now I've got to go figure out what condition he's in.

I close the door gently, unsure of whether he may run if he knows I'm here. I swallow the rising guilt for being here at all; it seems almost like a betrayal to be here encroaching on his grief. I chose this very spot for my own pain because of its secrecy and seclusion. Who am I to deny him the same privacy?

I am the person who won't let him go through this alone. I will be the person I always wished had come looking for me, refusing to let me push them away from my pain.

I walk through the canopy of willow trees, but no calm greets me tonight. Up ahead I see the soft glow from the lamps marking the entrance to our garden, but I don't see Tate. Anxious to find him, I find myself sprinting down the path, calling out to him. The longer my calls go unanswered, the more worried I become. I brush past the Casablanca Lilies, the white lavender and moonflowers, anywhere I can think of until I come to the foot of a bordering tree. There, seated on the damp earth, Tate watches me silently.

"Tate," I cry, and take a step toward him. His eyes stay fixed on my movements, but he makes none of his own. Slowly I kneel next to him and try to gauge his reaction. When he doesn't flinch or back away from me, I take his face in my hands. "I've been so worried about you. I'm so sorry, baby." His eyes squeeze shut as his breath hitches in his chest. I pull him against me and pray for all of his hurt to bleed into my body. His agony is so palpable, I can feel the fingers of it reaching in and ripping my heart from my chest. When he wraps his arms around me, I'm helpless to do anything but hold on while he silently weeps.

It takes tremendous strength not to say, "It's okay," or "Everything will be all right," because it isn't, and it won't be, and suggesting it will is an insult to the magnitude of his loss. When Lily was first diagnosed with a delay, every time someone said, "She'll be okay," it dismissed everything I was feeling as her mother. I would've preferred to be slapped in the face than told one more time that everything would be all right. I'm never going to do that to Tate.

"Tate," I whisper as I run my fingers through his hair. "You don't need to say anything, but I need you to listen to me, okay?" He nods his head against my chest. "I'm going to give Tarryn a quick call to let her know I found you, and I'm bringing you home with me." His body stills, and I fear that he's going to argue with me. "You don't have to be alone, Tate. Let me be there for you."

He pulls himself out of my embrace, and I steel myself for him to tell me to go home, go away, get out of his space. What I know of pain is how it hardened me, how it pushed me to isolate myself and lash out at those who loved me. It was never something I considered inviting anyone else to be a part of, and I still struggle with not wanting to divulge the depth of my own sorrow to others—even knowing how much better my life would be if I did. It's a nefarious poison that can steal your life from you if you're cocky enough to think you can handle it alone.

lily love

"She would have loved you."

"I would've loved her, too." I know I would have. How could I not love the woman who gave me Tate? I wish I could've known her, if for no other reason than to tell her how very much I love her son. Wherever she is, I hope she knows he's not alone.

"Let me take you home."

I hold my hand out to him, and he takes it. Together we leave the moon garden behind—for now.

i may not let go

Just before I pull out of the Robert Waldron Jr. Botanical Park, I send a quick text message to Tarryn to let her know that Tate is with me and that I'll have him call her soon. I'm grateful when she texts back to let me know that she and Tom are on their way to meet her in-laws and pick up her children. Selfishly, I want this time alone with Tate. I know the next few days are going to be a bombardment of family and friends that I don't quite fit into yet. The last thing I want to do is make things harder than they already are.

It's late when we pull up to the house, and exhaustion weighs heavy in the dark circles under Tate's eyes. I can only imagine how physically and mentally spent he must be. I want to get him inside so he can clean up, have something to eat, and get some much-needed sleep.

A sudden rush of nerves ripples through me when we walk through the door. I feel silly. It's the last thing that Tate is going to be thinking about, but I hope he feels at home here. Better yet, I want this to feel like home to him.

"Are you hungry?" I ask timidly.

"A little." He sighs wearily.

"Let me get you a towel, and you can take a hot shower while I fix you something, okay?" I lead him down the hall to my bedroom, where he hesitates. "What's wrong?"

He shifts uncomfortably from one foot to the other. "Will this be weird to you, me being in the bedroom you shared with Peter? I don't want you to feel uncomfortable . . ." He trails off.

"Yes, it used to be Peter's room," I confirm. "However, when Peter served me with divorce papers a month ago, I had all of our old furniture hauled out and redecorated just for me. So technically, this is *my* bedroom."

"Oh, thank God," he says. "I don't want to sleep without you in my arms tonight."

I pull him into my room to show him the adjoining bathroom and where to find the things that he needs. A warm sense of satisfaction washes over me as I watch him strip out of his clothes and step into my shower. It's not all sexual, either. Don't get me wrong, the sight of Tate's gorgeous body makes me want to get naked and join him, but having him here in my space feels right, feels whole.

"I'll be back," I call out as I walk away.

It feels so domestic and normal, if you remove the hardship from the equation—but you can't. This love story is never going to be "normal," but I think that's exactly why it's got potential. We both know how cruel life can be, and we're both learning that you can't let the hard stuff keep you from living.

• • •

I brought back a tray with some soup and a sandwich for Tate, only to find him sprawled sideways across the bed, asleep in his towel. I tucked a blanket around him, wrapped up the food, and padded down the hall to my office, where I sit now, trying to find a way to start this new paragraph. So many emotions are battering my brain you'd think the words would fly off the page. Instead, I find myself plagued by a blinking cursor and nothing to say. I'm restless. I don't want to go to sleep, because I'm afraid I'll wake up and this all will have been a dream.

Tiptoeing into my bedroom, I ready myself for bed and climb in next to Tate. His face is turned toward mine, and I'm so relieved to see that it's peaceful in his sleep. Very gently, I lean forward and kiss his forehead. When I'm confident that I haven't woken him, I can finally tell him what I've wanted to for days.

"I love you, Tate."

be still my heart

Morning brings a heightened state of confusion along with it. As my brain lifts from the fog of sleep, I vaguely remember telling Tate I love him. I blink against the bright sunlight filtering into my room and fight to string together the details.

I brought Tate home from the moon garden.
I tucked him into bed after he fell asleep in his towel.
I kissed him and told him I love him while he was sleeping.
There's no panic, no fear, just peace in knowing what's in my heart and accepting it.

The next thing I notice is that I'm in bed alone. I prop myself up on my elbows and take a look around my room. The clothes I folded for Tate are missing from the chair, making me wish I'd woken up sooner. I swing my legs over the side of the bed and find a note on my nightstand.

    Caroline,
    Thank you for everything you did for me yesterday. I'm sorry I won't be here when you wake up; there are arrangements I need to take care of with Tarryn. I will call you as soon as I can.
    Love,
    Tate.

"Love, Tate." *I really like the way that sounds.*

I get up, brew some coffee, and start my computer. Already my mind is churning out the next chapter of *Lily Love*. I'm eager to sit down and get it outlined, before I forget what I want to say. There's been no shortage of inspiration, either. Between the highs of burgeoning love, the lows of Tate's tremendous loss, and the fear of how he'll handle Lily—I've got a lot of raw emotion to draw from. Writing has given me space to process the drastic changes of late. It just so happens that I've been able to weave it all into a story I'm no longer afraid to tell: mine. I don't know what I want to do with it yet; I just want to see if I can finish it. Maybe I'll query it; maybe I'll self-publish, who knows. We'll see.

My phone startles me out of my thoughts, and my heart speeds up a little when I see it's Peter.

"Is everything okay?" I don't even say hello.

"Good morning to you, too." Peter laughs easily. I release the breath I was holding in and relax. "I was calling to see if I could stop by to pick up our membership card to the Science Center. I thought it'd be nice to take Lily there today."

"Of course," I reply, distracted. "Stop by on your way."

"Hey, are you okay?" he asks.

"I'm sorry, Peter . . ." I hesitate for a minute, trying to decide how or if I should bring up Tate. "A friend of mine lost his mother yesterday. I've been preoccupied with that."

"That's terrible. Do I know them?" he asks with concern. I know he must think it's someone we know together.

"No, you don't know him," I say cautiously. "It's someone I met at the hospital, when Lily was in the EMU."

There's an awkward silence on the other end as Peter considers what I'm saying.

"Oh." The hurt is evident in his voice, and I wish there were a way to avoid causing it.

"Peter—" I start to say, when he cuts me off.

"Are you, like . . . are you seeing someone?"

"Yes," I say. "It's still very new."

"Were you going to tell me?" he asks.

"Of course, but I was going to wait until I decided it was time for him to meet Lily. I would never bring anyone into her life without talking to you first," I assure him.

"Wow," he says softly.

"Peter, I'm sorry," I say. "I don't want to hurt you."

"I gotta go check on Lily. We'll be by later." Before I can say goodbye, he hangs up.

I don't blame him; what is there to say? Eventually he will fall in love again, and I know it will sting. We loved each other too much for it not to matter.

I place my phone down on the desk and stare at the computer screen where I stopped to pick up the phone. I outline another chapter chronicling all the details of how Peter and I fell in love and then lost each other. I write it to remind myself that, moving forward, I can never repeat the mistakes of the past.

The doorbell rings just as I'm shutting down the computer. I open the door to find Peter standing on the front step.

"Hi." I smile at him, "Where's Lily Pad?"

"She's in the car," he replies.

We stand in silence for a beat, wondering what to say next. I don't want our relationship to be strained with awkwardness. I want us to be able to talk and be friendly for Lily. It hurts to think that we couldn't.

"Listen, I'm not going to pretend I'm not surprised or hurt that you're dating someone else." Peter pinches the bridge of his nose, a familiar sign of stress.

"Peter, I'm—" I start to say.

"Caroline, don't," he interrupts. "I don't want your apology. I just want you to know that all I ever wanted was for you to be happy."

"I know," I reply. "I want you to be happy, too."

"I know." He gives me a sad smile. Life has a strange way of coming full circle. Peter and I weren't able to make each other happy in the long run. You'd think it would bring some relief knowing that we've cleared the way for it. I think it's fair to say we're at peace with our decision, but it will always be bittersweet.

"Lily's waiting," he says. "Can I get our . . . the membership card?"

I grab the card from my wallet and walk with Peter out to the car. I can see Lily start to bounce in her booster seat when she sees me. She looks so happy, and I hope more than anything that she always will be. I stick my head into the backseat of the car to give her a hug and a kiss. She hugs me back with enthusiasm, and plants a wet kiss on my cheek. She's unbridled joy, and in that moment, I'm confident that Tate will love her. Who could help themselves?

I hope.

...

It's late in the afternoon when I get a text from Tate asking if he can come by. When he shows up at my door, it's with Shasta daisies and red carnations.

"Thank you for taking care of me." He smiles sheepishly, but it doesn't hide his sorrow.

"You don't have to thank me for that," I say.

"Tarryn and I spent the morning at the funeral home trying to figure out what to do. Mom didn't want a memorial service, but it feels wrong not to remember her in some way. Tarryn wants to bring her ashes home with her to Wilmington, which is fine, I guess." He pauses and hangs his head. "It's so surreal. I don't know what to do. I just feel so lost." I take his hand and lead him to the living room, where we can sit back and talk about the day.

I squeeze his hand and scoot closer to him on the couch. "I don't know what it feels like to lose a parent the way you did, but I know a little about the emptiness of feeling lost." I pause for a moment, hoping

I'm not overstepping by sharing. He may not be in a place where he wants his mourning compared to anything else, and I want to be respectful of that.

When he looks at me with curiosity, I take it as a sign to continue. "The day I found out that Lily had a developmental disability, I was completely blindsided. I'd taken her in for a speech evaluation, never expecting it would turn out the way it did. I felt like my whole future had been ripped away from me and replaced with someone else's life. I felt completely lost in my sadness, and I was certain no one could possibly understand how that felt. I shut down and pushed everyone out of my life. I guess my point is, I know how easy it is to disappear inside your grief."

"I'm sorry you went through that alone," he replies.

"I didn't have to," I say. "And neither do you." I lean my head on his shoulder and close my eyes. Redemption comes in the most unlikely places. I spent years telling myself that it would be too hard to let Peter see inside my anguish, so I pushed him away. It's humbling to see that just holding Tate's hand can connect me to his loss. It's beautiful in its simplicity.

"I love you, Caroline." The words come out in a whisper, making me doubt that I've heard them correctly. I lift my head to find Tate watching me through tear-filled eyes. "You remind me there's still beauty in this world. During the most painful time in my life, you've shown me more love than I knew possible."

My heart pounds frantically against my ribs at Tate's confession.

"I love you, too," I reply. The smile that spreads across his face makes me want to weep for what I have to say next. "But we have to take a step back, Tate."

"W-what?" he stammers. "I don't understand."

"There are so many things all happening at the same time, and I don't want to screw this up," I explain. "You need to be there for Tarryn right now, and I need to focus on working on this new transition with Lily. I'm not saying we shouldn't see each other; I'm just saying we should slow down, and make room for all of these changes instead of steamrolling our way through them."

His brows pinch together as he thinks about what I'm saying. He looks so conflicted I almost backpedal. "I don't like the thought of stepping back, but you're right," he says.

"You need this time with your sister to grieve," I say.

"Kindergarten is going to be a huge leap, for you and Lily," he replies.

"That's not the only transition I need to prepare her for," I say. "I want her to be ready to meet you." I smile when I say it, because I'm not afraid anymore.

If I needed confirmation, the dimples would've done it. They wink at me through his beaming smile. "I'm looking forward to spending a lot of time with both of you," he says.

"I want that, too." I squeeze his hand and lock my eyes with his. "Stepping back doesn't mean pulling away."

"I know." He smiles at me. "We're kismet, right?"

"Exactly." I grin back at him. No matter what happens, I know it will be okay.

head full of doubt

The next few weeks go by much faster than I expected them to, and before I know it my baby is about to begin kindergarten. Peter and I have met with Lily's team and have written an IEP—an Individualized Education Plan—supporting her inside a mainstream classroom. Twice a week for the last few, we've spent time in the classroom, getting her used to a new environment.

Everything is ready to go, but my nerves are keeping me from getting any sleep. Ignoring the time on the clock, I roll over and reach for my phone on the nightstand.

"Hello?" A very groggy Paige answers on the third ring.

"What if other children make fun of her, Paige?"

"Caroline," she yawns. "The teachers have already made plans to talk to the class about Lily. No one is going to allow her to be left out in any way."

"I'm sorry I woke you up."

"What's the matter, sis? Can't sleep?"

"No, I can't. My mind won't quiet down long enough for me to fall asleep." I sigh.

"Well, I know you're worried about Lily, but is there something else you need to talk about? Have you spoken to Tate lately?" she asks carefully.

Of course I've talked to Tate. I talk to him every day.

"Yes, I've talked to him," I say. "I just miss him." I've seen him a handful of times over the last few weeks. With Tate settling his mother's estate, and me getting Lily ready for kindergarten, it feels like forever. Despite that, we're doing well. We haven't been able to see each other as much, so we've relied heavily on talking on the phone. It's a mixed blessing, because while I miss him, we've gotten very good at communicating. Just one more week and I'll be introducing them. I can't wait to move forward. This step back has been good for us all, but I'm ready to get on with life.

"Well, you get to see him tomorrow, right?" she asks.

That's the real reason for my insomnia. Tomorrow I go to the hospital to get my cast off, finally. While I'm there, Peter is going to drop off Lily at speech therapy and meet me and Tate in the cafeteria. My stomach pitches nervously at the thought. A year ago, I would've never imagined I'd be introducing Peter to a man who could become such a big part of Lily's life. Still, it's only right that he meets Tate first and gets comfortable with him before Lily does.

"Yep, tomorrow's the big day. I get my cast off and I'm introducing my ex-husband to my boyfriend," I reply.

"Just another day for you, then?" She laughs softly.

"Oh, yeah. A day in the life for me." I sigh. "I'm not afraid as much as I'm nervous. I want to get it over with, ya know?"

"Kiddo, I can only imagine," she responds. "I'm proud of you. You've grown so much, and I'm so glad that you found someone who appreciates what you've been through."

"Tate is pretty magnificent," I say, "but I'm lucky, too."

"Yes, you both are. Now, don't sweat tomorrow. It'll be over before you know it."

Paige is right; it'll be fine. I just needed to hear someone else say it. Peter wants me to be happy, and we both want Lily to thrive. Tate is going to be a part of the picture, so we've got to be able to get along. We're all in complete agreement on that.

"It means the world to me to have your support, Paige," I tell her. "I don't know what I'd do without you."

"I know; who would you call at one a.m.?" she teases. "Seriously, I'm here for you and I'm on your side. Always."

"I love you, Paige."

"I love you, too," she replies. "You gonna be okay?"

"I'm going to use some of this mental energy and go write for a little while. Maybe getting it out of my head and on paper will help."

"Wow, Caro, you've been writing nonstop. How far in are you?"

"I'm about twenty-five thousand words into the story; maybe a third of the way done."

Hearing myself say it out loud suddenly makes my little writing project very big and very real. I never intended to write a book; I just wanted to write my story. After the first ten thousand words, I realized what a great novel it would make. At first, words and emotions flew out of my head and into the computer quicker than I could keep up with them. Once I hit my stride, watching it all unfold on paper made me realize just how far I'd come. I'm proud of myself for seeing this through, and I hope I find the courage to let someone read it.

"Have you decided on a name?" Paige asks. I pause for a moment, both scared and excited to tell her what I've come up with. The title was as important as the body of the story.

"*Lily Love*," I reply.

In a year, the title has come to mean several different things to me. In the beginning, it illustrated the journey of learning to separate Lily from her disability and love her just as she is. When Tate gave me his landscape portrait named *Lily Love*, it began to symbolize hope and second chances. Now it's the embodiment of my greatest desire and worst fear: whether Tate can accept the breadth of her needs, and fall for my little Lily Love.

"It's perfect," Paige responds.

"I think so, too," I say. "Good night, Paigey."

"Night, Caro."

our story

The need to purge my thoughts into my manuscript was bigger than I'd realized. I sat for hours shaping all of the emotions clogging my head into more chapters, and somewhere just before dawn, I finally fell into a peaceful, dreamless sleep. While the writing part was cathartic, the abbreviated sleep not so much. I nodded off for a few minutes in the exam room waiting for Dr. Haren, but it wasn't enough to shake my fatigue.

Now I'm tired and nervous, a combination that's allowed my fears to reach new heights. After all, life with Lily is impossible to capture with words. It's something you have to experience firsthand in order to really understand. I know that's the biggest concern that Peter has about anyone I date, as well. There's no way that either of us could truly prepare Tate beforehand. What if he gets a taste and decides he can't handle it? I'd move on, but I'd never get over it. That's what scares me the most. If Tate can't accept Lily, my heart will be irrevocably broken.

The aroma of roasted espresso beans greets me like a long-lost friend as I step inside the cafeteria. There's no sign of Peter or Tate, so I head straight for the coffee cart and order my skinny vanilla with a double shot.

"Make that two," Tate's voice calls from behind me. I spin around and am met with my favorite dimpled smile.

"Hey, stranger." I wrap my arms around his neck and give him a quick hug. What I'd really like to do is nuzzle my face into his neck and ask him to promise me that everything will be okay. He would, without hesitation, but I can't let him give his word when he doesn't know what he's committing to.

"I've missed you." He kisses the top of my head before letting me go to pay the barista. He shoots me a quizzical look as we make our way to a table. "You okay?"

"I'm fine." I cringe as the words come out of my mouth. "No, I'm not. I'm sorry. I'm so scared," I confess. "What if you and Peter don't get along? Worse yet, what if today goes smoothly, only for you to decide that Lily is too much for you to handle?" Tears well behind my eyes, sending me into a blinking fit to hold them back.

He leans across the table and wipes a rogue tear from my cheek. "You own my heart, and because Lily is a part of you, so will she." Attempting not to cry is pointless. What started as one becomes a deluge spilling down my face. "I know you're scared that I'm getting in over my head. What I need you to understand is, whatever lies ahead with Lily, you are worth every bump in the road."

"I love you so much." I sniffle.

"Then have faith in me," he pleads. "Let me show you how much I can love both of you."

I barely have time to blot my face and take a deep breath before I catch sight of Peter walking into the cafeteria. Tate follows the line of my vision and stands to greet Peter as he approaches.

"Tate Michaels," he says, extending his hand to Peter.

"Peter Williams," he says, shaking it. When Peter turns to me, his eyes reflect the weariness he must be feeling. "Caroline," he says, as he sits down.

"Listen," I say. "I know this is uncomfortable—"

"Caroline," Peter interrupts. "If it's okay, I just want to talk to Tate for a minute."

I force myself to swallow past the knot forming in my throat. "You want me to leave?" I ask.

"No, no," Peter answers. "I just thought it would be easier if I could say what I have to say."

I look over at Tate, who's taking it all in with a calmness I'm grateful for.

"Okay," Tate replies. "I'm all ears."

I shift in my seat to face Peter, wondering where his head is.

"First of all, I trust Caroline," Peter starts. "I know she would never bring someone into Lily's life who wasn't good for her. I'm not worried about that. I know you care about Caroline; I want to know how you feel about Lily."

"Peter," I say. "Tate hasn't met her yet. He can't honestly tell you how he feels about her."

"I know that, Caroline," Peter says, "but he is going to be in Lily's life. I want to know that he'll be good to her when you're all together. Her needs are a lot to handle; I need to know that he's up to the task."

"Caroline's been very explicit about Lily's needs," Tate says, "but I know that reality is not as neat as her explanations."

Peter shakes his head on a heavy sigh. "I don't want Lily to feel like you're only there for Caroline."

I can only sit back and watch as the man I used to love and the man I'm in love with now hash out the best way to love my daughter.

Tate leans in toward Peter, resting his forearms on the table. "I know I'm going to love Lily. Part of me does already, because she's Caroline's daughter, and I want to get to know her and discover the little girl she is."

"That's what I needed to hear," Peter replies. "I know you've got plans to meet her next week, and I needed to know where you stood before that. I hope you understand."

I know it's not easy for Peter to hear how Tate feels, but I'm so proud of him for putting his own feelings aside to make sure Lily's needs are met. He's grown so much as a man and a father.

"I get it," Tate says. "I hope you feel a little better about it now. It would be nice for Lily if you and I got along."

"That's the goal." Peter reaches his hand out, and they shake on it.

"Do I get to say something?" I ask. Two sets of kind, warm eyes fall on me, and I'm momentarily blown away by where my life has come. It took one to love me enough to leave so the other could come into my life. Life is a wonder, if complicated in its beauty. "Thank you both for putting Lily's needs first."

I would've never guessed I'd be here, but I'm so grateful I am.

• • •

One week later, Lily's holding my hand as we walk into the frozen-yogurt shop near our house. One wall is lined with several flavors of self-serve frozen yogurt, while the other houses a long buffet of toppings. It's Lily's favorite place to come for a treat. I'm not above a little bribery to smooth everything along. I'm hoping that putting her at ease with a familiar environment will help lessen some of my own apprehension. It feels like I've been waiting for this meeting my whole life, not just the last couple of weeks.

"Lily, do you remember who I said we're meeting?" I ask. Lily's focus is on the pictures above each flavor. She loves that she can choose by picture, and I love the confidence she gains by choosing on her own.

"Mama friend Tater. Wanda choco-wut, pwease," she says without missing a beat.

"Thank you for using your good manners—and yes, we're meeting my friend Tate," I reply. "Can you say 'Tate'?"

She furrows her delicate brow at me and repeats, "Tater." *Duh, Mom.*

"Caroline?" I look up from Lily's quizzical face, straight into Tate's dimpled smile. It still turns my insides to mush every time he unleashes it on me.

"Hi." I can't help the smile spreading across my own face. My heart pounds a frantic rhythm as the reality of what's happening sets in. "Lily, this is the friend I was telling you about."

She looks up at Tate and gives him a bashful smile.

"Your mama has told me so many wonderful things about you, Lily. I'm Tate." He takes her tiny hand in his and shakes it. The way he treats her, like any other child, brings tears to my eyes.

"Hi, Tater," she replies, and starts to flap her hands. "I like chocowut." Her face is lit up with excitement and expectation.

It takes everything in me not to jump in and try to settle her little arms down. Her flapping is a fundamental part of who Lily is and how she expresses herself. Tate needs to be okay with who she is, quirks and all.

"That's code for, 'I want you to put some in a cup for me.' She's a bit passive-aggressive when she's trying to tell me what she wants." I chuckle and hand Tate a cup from the dispenser. *She likes him.* The thought fills my heart, and I can only hope that Tate will feel the same.

"I like chocolate, too. It's my favorite," Tate says. "You'd better help me work this thing, sweetheart. I've never done this before."

Lily's eyes dart back and forth between Tate and me.

Not wanting her to feel conflicted, I take the cup from Tate. "I'll show you."

Lily smiles broadly and bounds toward the chocolate yogurt machine with Tate and me in tow. Lily's a little cautious, but for the most part, she seems quite taken with Tate. If he's intimidated, he isn't showing it at all, and it makes my heart sing to watch them together. She pulls at his hand impatiently as we make our way to the topping bar. Whatever she points to, she lets Tate add to her cup.

"Mama like wocky woad," Lily declares when they get to the cashier. Once again she looks at Tate expectantly, but this time he chuckles under his breath.

"I'll get it myself, Lily Love," I say.

"Why, Mama? Tater good helper!" she replies.

I try hard not to laugh, but she's so adorable, I can't help myself. My heart can hardly take the picture the two of them paint as they inspect their masterpiece.

"Can I make you one?" I ask Tate. Clearly it's going to be a while before Lily relinquishes the hold she has on her new friend.

He scrunches up his nose. "They have rocky road–flavored yogurt?"

"No." I laugh. "I get chocolate and add almonds and marshmallows at the bar."

"Ooooh," he says. "Well, then, I'll definitely take one of those."

"Will you be okay for a minute?" I ask Tate.

"I think so. What do you think, Lily?"

"Yup," Lily manages around a mouthful of treat. Her answer may be short, but it goes a long way to reassuring me that we're on the right track.

"Well, then, I'll be right back with two rocky roads," I say.

But I freeze in my tracks when Lily asks, "What your mama favowit flavor?"

Tate answers without hesitation. "It was cookies and cream."

"She not here?" Lily asks innocently.

"No, sweet girl, she's not," Tate answers.

"S'okay, Tater." She shrugs and continues. "I share mine."

From the mouth of my baby girl came the most beautiful sentence I'd ever heard. She can't recite her ABCs or count past ten, but she accepted a near stranger—*my* stranger—with an openheartedness she may not always receive herself. I'm so incredibly blessed that she is mine; that they both are.

epilogue:
the end where i begin

Tears blur my vision as the last words of *Lily Love* appear on my computer screen: "The End." I pause for a moment, wondering if that is truly accurate. The end of one part doesn't necessarily signify the resolution of the whole story. If anything, the last year of my life has taught me not to take the future for granted. With a verbal command, the cursor backs up so I can add another word in the last sentence: "Not The End."

I click Save and compile my story into a Word document. Maybe the fatigue of writing into the wee hours of the morning has shortened my memory, but I can't seem to remember why I was ever so afraid to tell this story the way it was supposed to be told. This may not be the life I imagined I'd have, but I'm exactly where I want to be. It took losing my marriage and myself to realize how mysteriously beautiful life is.

Once the conversion is complete, I open the file to make sure I did it right. My heart skips with excitement as my eyes skim over the first perfect line.

"For Lily: Every day you teach me, and everyone you meet, that different does not mean less. I love you more than life. Ugga Mugga, always, Mama."

chapter titles

"A Sorta Fairytale," Tori Amos
"Building a Mystery," Sarah McLachlan
"We Never Change," Coldplay
"What Do I Do Now?," Sam and Ruby
"When a Heart Breaks," Ben Rector
"Comes and Goes in Waves," Greg Laswell
"And So It Goes," Billy Joel
"Caroline I See You," James Taylor
"Fall Apart Today," Schuyler Fisk
"Gotta Figure This Out," Erin McCarley
"Talk," Coldplay
"Comfort of Strangers," Beth Orton
"My Little Girl," Jack Johnson
"Reason Why," Rachael Yamagata
"Fault Line," Black Rebel Motorcycle Club
"Bend and Break," Keane
"Mercy," OneRepublic
"Friend Like You," Joshua Radin
"Distance," Christina Perri and Jason Mraz
"A Beautiful Mess," Jason Mraz

"Always Remember Me," Ry Cuming
"Off We Go," Erin McCarley
"Entwined," Jason Reeves
"Moondance," Van Morrison
"Windmills," Toad the Wet Sprocket
"Somewhere Only We Know," Keane
"I'm Not Who I Was," Brandon Heath
"Secret Garden," Bruce Springsteen
"Writing to Reach You," Travis
"The Luckiest," Ben Folds
"Pitter Pat," Erin McCarley
"Something to Say," Toad the Wet Sprocket
"In Your Hands," Jason Mraz
"Take a Chance," Landon Pigg
"Desire," Ryan Adams
"Into the Mystic," Van Morrison
"The World as I See It," Jason Mraz
"Change," Jack Johnson
"Ungodly Hour," The Fray
"Where You'll Find Me," Audrye Sessions
"I May Not Let Go," Peter Bradley Adams
"Be Still My Heart," Peter Bradley Adams
"Head Full of Doubt," The Avett Brothers
"Our Story," Graham Colton
"The End Where I Begin," The Script

acknowledgments

Charles Sheehan-Miles: You made me consider the big "what if?" and then write about it. Thank you.

Steve: This was a tough one, and you stuck by me even when I wanted to give up. I love you so very much. Always.

Mom, Dad, Jamie, and Cynthia: You guys are biologically obligated to love me, but I appreciate it anyway. I love you with all my heart and soul.

My muses: Happy, David, Melissa, Kathy, Kelley, Jenn, and Andrea: I hope when you read this, you see pieces of yourselves amongst the characters. Your friendship is a precious gift, which I'm grateful for each day. I love you.

Melissa Brown: You're the cheese to my macaroni. You love me when I feel the most unlovable and chased me down when I went into hiding. I'm so grateful for your friendship and your guidance. I love you.

My Pretty Pieces: Pam Carrion, Cara Gadero, Jenn Haren, Francine Petro, and Janéah Rosecrans. Thank you for everything you've done for me. Your friendship is a gift I treasure, and I'm so blessed to have you in my corner. A special thank-you to Dr. Ivan Rusilko for bringing these girls into my life!

Maggi's Hanyaks: Thank you for all of your love and support! My life would be so different without you. Thank you for your faith in me.

Three Chicks, The Book Avenue, Brandee's Book Endings, Tough Critic Reviews, Maryse's Book Blog, and every book blogger who took a chance on reviewing *The Final Piece*: I would be nothing without you. Thank you for all of your passion and commitment. I'm eternally indebted to you.

JoVon Sotak: The most patient, wonderful editor ever. "Thank you" is not enough. Next time, maybe I can borrow your time turner.

Tiffany Yates Martin: Quite possibly the most fabulous critique partner / developmental editor I've ever had. Thank you for loving Caroline, Peter, Tate, Max, and Lily as I do. I can't thank you enough for the way you took my story and helped me make it everything I wanted it to be. Someday, I will collect on that kiss!

My team at Lake Union / Amazon Publishing: Thank you so much for all the hard work you put into making *Lily Love* a reality.

ICM and Gelfman Schneider Literary Agency.

Victoria Marini: My agent rock star. Thank you for taking a chance on me.

about the author

Maggi was born in West Des Moines, Iowa, and raised in Miami, Florida. She has deep love for the Heartland and really good Cuban food. When she's not writing, you can find her reading or singing into the end of her hairbrush. She's a steel magnolia and mischief maker, wrapped up and tied with a sarcasm bow.

Currently she resides in Greensboro, North Carolina, with her incredible husband and sons. For more about Maggi and future projects, you can follow her on Facebook (www.facebook.com/author.maggi.myers) and Twitter (@Magnolia_B_My).